SEVEN BODIES

V.J. RANDLE

BLOODHOUND BOOKS

For my lovely Dad, who I'm certain is always looking over my shoulder as I write.

'Don't you see? We're the Zoo... Last night, we were hardly human any more. We're the Zoo...'

VERA CLAYTHORNE, *AND THEN THERE WERE NONE*, AGATHA CHRISTIE

HOW IT ENDS

The bodies were inside.

A lone figure watched over them and waited, their breathing shallow and excitable. It took on a rhythmic quality against the churn and spit of the radiators springing to life.

The Tornivan Hotel loomed over the loch as if everything was as it should be. The snow on the driveway had already begun to turn grey and sludgy as the temperatures warmed, but the winds still howled through the hills before circling around the building's dark turrets. The sound of sirens called from nearby, as well as the churn of a helicopter.

Tyres rolled over the wet gravel. The main door swung open; it was unlocked. The first wave of officers entered. Shouts echoed up the stairs against the backdrop of fuzzy radios and under-the-breath swear words.

Eventually, the footsteps made it to the top floor. Hands grabbed the figure, dragging them roughly and efficiently out of the place. Commands were issued, orders were shouted.

Then, the rush of cold morning air, the aggressive push of the shoulder, the slamming of vehicle doors. Wheels skidded as

they reversed in haste. Driving away, the hotel looked idyllic –
the backdrop for the perfect weekend.

And it had been perfect. In the end.

48 HOURS EARLIER

JULES

Jules told herself to pull it together. Her face was blotchy and bloated. Mascara was smeared beneath her eyes. She had fifteen minutes before she had to be at reception, based on the first arrival time. She couldn't greet guests in this state. They'd take one look at her and jump straight back into their cars. And who would blame them? Who on earth would want to spend their weekend hosted by a blubbering mess like her?

The trouble was, the more she told herself to stop crying, the more the tears flowed. It was the same as yesterday morning, and the morning before, and, if she was honest, most mornings this year. Nothing seemed to help. Every day, her alarm drilled through the side of her skull, chasing away the remaining drag of sedatives, and she opened her eyes to that great, daunting yawn of a black hole.

She could not see what the point was anymore. The prospect of carrying out even the simplest of tasks overwhelmed her. She often imagined herself wrapped up tightly in her duvet, the door to her small attic flat closed, as the rest of the hotel crumbled and disintegrated around her.

But things could turn around today. She mouthed the words as an affirmation: *make this weekend count. Make it count, Jules.*

She shuffled out of the bathroom to answer the buzzing of her phone. Swearing softly, she rejected the video call. She'd forgotten that her therapy session had been rearranged. There wouldn't be enough time to do it now. And, anyway, she preferred to talk when she was calmer. She began typing what she hoped would be a good enough excuse to avoid paying for the cancellation – *apologies, last-minute hotel emergency! Chef's off sick, so I need to step in* – and perched herself on the love seat below the window that looked over the driveway.

This view was half of the problem. It was magnificent. The mountains reached purple and jagged into the heavy skies, piercing low-lying clouds, so their peaks seemed to float in space. The loch stretching alongside the driveway mirrored the landscape with such clear precision that it was as if the hotel was perched on the edge of a prism, where the boundaries of reality and reflection were blurred.

Jules placed a finger on the windowpane and traced the outline of the upside-down mountains on the loch. Her life was like them, she thought. A reflection of what she used to be, how she used to act. A half-reality. She looked the same, give or take a few comfort-eating pounds, but underneath her skin, she was a cold and watery mess of pills, alcohol, and caffeine.

She remembered the first time she had seen these mountains four years ago. Rob had been so excited to go the long way on their hike back to the campervan. She knew that he'd been keeping some sort of a secret, but she went along with it, pretending to complain her boots were rubbing to wind him up. When they turned the corner at the foot of the loch, she hadn't known what she was looking at. Rob had held her face in his hands. His fingers had been icy against her cheeks, but she hadn't cared.

'What do you think then?'

'Of the castle...?'

'It's not a castle. But, yes... do you like it?'

She'd laughed. She used to laugh all the time with Rob. His boundless sense of possibility, an almost childlike excitement at the world had been the thing that first attracted her to him. The place was run-down, obviously, but it was stunning, so lonely and beautiful nestled amongst the landscape.

'What do you mean?'

'It's for sale... needs work, but...'

'Rob—'

'Neither of us needs to be in London for work, do we? We could sell the flat and have money left over! Look, just hear me out... this is what we've always wanted, isn't it?'

She'd been speechless. He was right: every time they packed up the van and drove through the night to the West Coast, they fantasised about owning a huge house in the middle of nowhere. They'd turn it into a boutique hotel, a Scottish escape, fill it with log fires and whisky lounges. Jules would run the marketing and hospitality; Rob would instruct the outdoors pursuits. This was the dream.

Rob had massaged her temples in the van that night. He'd poured them both a whisky in plastic beakers. They ran through the finances, the hopes, the dreams. At the time, it had seemed that there was no reason *not* to put an offer in. They put their London flat on the market a week after that.

Six months later, they had been elbow-deep in plaster and paint, music blaring from the speakers as they worked, giggling every five minutes in disbelief at the fact that they'd actually done it. They'd made the move. They were living the life that they had dared to imagine.

Then she'd ruined everything.

Jules felt her face grow hot and rested her forehead against the cool window. Her stomach tightened as the familiar lick of shame reared its head. She stood quickly, tugging herself away from the memories. There was no use going over and over them, despite what the therapists said. The only way for her to survive, and she was sure of this, was to forget about her previous life. And if that took alcohol, pills and other distractions, so be it.

A car, a silver Mercedes, emerged from the pine forest at the end of the drive. It stopped just before the car park, as she'd predicted it would. New arrivals liked to take in their surroundings. The medley of baronial architecture, the loch, the mountains, the field of free-roaming Highland *coos*, promised a romantic start to any weekend break. She watched a man, probably in his late thirties, open the passenger door and edge towards the nearest cow.

He was wearing what most hotel guests viewed as "country chic": dark jeans, a jumper (most likely cashmere), a quilted gilet, and leather ankle boots that wouldn't last a minute on the estate walking trails. His hand hovered in the air, slightly apprehensive as he approached the huge, shaggy animal. Jules identified the cow as Fern; she was, like the whole herd, completely docile. The calves, Bracken, Heather and Thistle, trotted behind her. The man patted her forehead and he grinned, turning to call something back to his partner in the driver's seat.

Exhaling, Jules licked her lips and set her mouth into her best smile. The Mercedes was now parked, and the couple were taking their bags from the boot. She would make it work, she thought.

If it was the last thing she did, she would make this godforsaken hotel work. There was really no other option.

LUCAS

So far, so excellent. Lucas knew how smug he must look as he followed Sandeep through the huge, arched hotel doors. Give or take a few cows (who were adorable, actually) and that weedy gardener, nobody was watching him. He could enjoy a little bit of self-congratulation.

From the moment he had woken Sandeep up early that morning with a mimosa, a kiss, and a hint for him to pack clothes for "walks and snuggles", everything had gone according to plan. The cab had arrived on time, there'd been business flights available for an upgrade, the car he'd hired at Inverness was just as swish as he thought it would be.

Sandeep didn't seem to mind too much that Lucas had forgotten about having to drive from the airport to the hotel, so had been, let's say, a tad enthusiastic about the free champagne on the flight. Anyway, Sandeep enjoyed driving. He'd said so himself. Who wouldn't have loved speeding along those scenic roads, past ruined castles built on islands in the middle of frozen lochs, undulating mountains everywhere you looked? It was completely breathtaking. And Lucas had planned it all.

He did have to admit that the girl at reception was a bit of a let-down. She looked like she'd been weeping – either that or she suffered from a very unfortunate complexion. He'd hoped for something more befitting of the lofty surroundings. Certainly, they ought to get someone Scottish on the front desk. This woman sounded as if she was from across the road in Tooting.

She was also completely incompetent, clicking away at the old mouse listlessly, biting her chapped lip, glancing up and down at them. It had taken her an age to locate his booking, even though he'd repeatedly shown her the email, which was clearly labelled: *Highland Getaway Package*. For an awful breath, he'd been nervous she might ask him to pay full price. This weekend was all about treats and luxury... but he wasn't sure his credit card would stretch to this place's non-discounted rates. The Tornivan was properly exclusive – it even smelt expensive... what was that... lavender? – which is why he'd been delighted to see it on offer this weekend. They deserved only the best. Thank goodness she'd found the booking in the end.

Anyway, they were here! He and Sandeep. At a luxurious castle retreat.

'Could we please have some champagne brought up to the room?' The words spilt out of his mouth before he could stop himself. He then added, for good measure, 'Pink, if you have any!'

'Lucas, I think we've had enough...' Sandeep began.

'Nonsense!' Lucas presented his credit card to the receptionist, who observed it in a strange manner, before sliding it back to him and mumbling something about a room tab. She turned her back to them and opened a key cupboard, muttering something else about breakfast timings.

Lucas grinned as Sandeep moved closer to him, nuzzling into his neck. He could not remember the last time he had felt so relaxed. It'd been a long and tiring term at school; they really needed a proper break. He sighed and moved his face to meet Sandeep's, melting into the embrace.

'Seriously though, Lucas – champagne? We can't afford that. Just get some Prosecco.'

Lucas stiffened. Why couldn't he just lighten up? Life was for living, wasn't it? It wasn't as if they did this sort of thing all the time. And Prosecco! Was he mad? Everyone knew only people who knew precisely nothing about anything ordered Prosecco.

'Just getting into the mood!' he replied. He took Sandeep's hand and swung it into the air, spinning beneath it. 'This weekend is exactly what we need. Your wish, my love, is my desire!'

He had hoped that Sandeep would find his over-the-top display funny and endearing. Instead, he gave a very small, awkward laugh and hunched his shoulders forwards. 'I'm just a bit concerned about how much—'

'It's my treat!' Lucas heard his voice rise a little higher. He gulped, calming himself. Everything was fine. There was no need to lose his cool. This was typical Sandeep, which was precisely why he loved him. He was a planner, an organiser. He liked spreadsheets and numbers and tech and details and all those sorts of mind-numbing things. He was, let's not forget, a Computer Science teacher. In fact, this little frugal tantrum was quite cute.

He brought Sandeep into a deep hug and said, 'There's no need to worry about anything this weekend. I promise. I've got it covered.'

The woman at reception handed them their key, and, without offering to carry their bags, Lucas noted, led them up the wide mahogany stairs and along an impressive corridor lined with oil paintings.

'The, um, Dunmore Suite,' she said, opening the door.

Lucas's annoyance at her less-than-enthusiastic demeanour disappeared as he entered the room. It was simply stunning. An enormous four-poster bed, pulled tight with pressed white linen and a mound of decorative tartan cushions overlooked tall bay windows which framed the spectacular mountaintops outside. Two luxurious armchairs sat invitingly before a log fire and a magnificent mahogany platform beneath the main windows mounted a bronze bathtub.

'We check the fireguards periodically throughout the day, otherwise we couldn't allow guests to have log fires in the rooms,' said the miserable receptionist. 'It's just for safety reasons. I'll always knock, so don't be alarmed.'

Lucas fought a flutter of irritation as Sandeep met her with earnest approval. Why were they talking about health and safety? Why was she still here? He was ready to crack open the champagne (although he suspected she'd already forgotten), strip off, coax Sandeep into a bubble bath, and while away the rest of the morning in fluffy robes.

'Right! Well, if you need anything, then do let me know...'

The woman was clearly attempting to sound bright and cheerful, but her voice rose with a manic edge. Lucas moved towards the door to usher her out.

'And the champagne...?' He ignored how Sandeep shifted uncomfortably behind him.

'Ah, yes! I'll bring it up in a moment,' she said. She scratched her head, as if confused about something. Lucas couldn't help but notice the telltale signs of stress: raw, red, chewed fingernails, dark circles above sallow cheeks. He'd become quite apt at spotting this sort of thing in his role as Head of Year Ten. There was no judgement on his part, none at all, but didn't she feel the need to do herself up? This was a sophisticated place, after all.

'Just knock and leave it by the door,' he said, attempting to sound as cavalier as possible, as if champagne and boutique hotels were regular features in his life. He had to admit, he was taking to all this like a duck to water. If only he could get Sandeep into the groove. For the weekend's plans to really come into their own, he needed him to cut loose a little. At the moment, he was standing uneasily in the middle of the room as if he'd been asked to give an impromptu assembly.

The woman nodded and closed the door behind her. Lucas turned to Sandeep, his arms wide, his mouth spreading into a naughty grin. 'Time for a bath?'

'It's eleven o'clock in the morning...'

'Come on.' Lucas sashayed towards him, making sure to inject a cheeky glint into his eyes. Sandeep could never refuse him when he really turned it on. All it took was lowering his voice to a breathy whisper, hooking his fingers into the waist of Sandeep's trousers, and pressing against him, not too hard, but certainly suggestively.

As he expected, Sandeep relented. He sighed, hanging his arms around Lucas's neck.

'You're too much,' he said. Lucas watched the hesitance leave his face and give way to a softer expression. This was much better.

He gave Lucas a soft kiss and laughed. 'What am I going to do with you?'

Lucas could think of all sorts. He began to undress, trying to add a sense of urgency to the situation, pressing his lips hard against Sandeep's as he fumbled to rip his clothes off. 'A bath then?'

Sandeep nodded, and Lucas was relieved to see him finally crack a smile. 'Okay, why not? Hang on, she'll have brought the bubbly up by now, won't she?'

Lucas suppressed the urge to ask him not to say "bubbly" in such a nice place. He started to run the bath and sniffed the various bottles laid out on top of the towels. 'Fancy some sandalwood... whatever that is?'

'Mmmm...'

Lucas poured the whole of the tiny glass bottle in. He swished his hands around the tub and watched the foam rise higher. The water felt hot and exciting against his fingertips. He closed his eyes and imagined their bodies entwined together in the fragrant, slippery concoction.

Glancing behind him, he saw that the door was left a tiny bit open. Sandeep had left the room in search of their drinks. All it took was a little bit of persuasion and the man was gagging for the champagne! Lucas laughed to himself and lowered his body into the hot water. The steam rose about his head, and he reclined backwards, feeling weightless.

After a short while, the sound of distant shouts disturbed his peace. He couldn't make out the words, but they buzzed away like angry mosquitoes from somewhere outside. People honestly had no sense of decorum. He sighed in relief as the voices thankfully grew quieter, and let his head fall back against the gentle slope of the bronze tub. But the shouts started again.

Swearing under his breath, Lucas pushed himself to a seated position and looked out of the window. Wiping away the steam, he peered down at some stone buildings surrounded by what he guessed were allotments.

The woman from reception was holding the arm of a young man who looked like the gardener from earlier. She was tugging him towards her as he tried to pull away. His face was pulled into an uncomfortable grimace, his body language gravitating inwards, like he was trying to curl up and hide. She was screaming, but the windows' thick glazing made it impossible to hear precisely what she was saying. Her face was wrinkled up and ugly. She looked furious. What on earth was she so angry about? Didn't she know that places like this required hushed and measured conversations? She was behaving like she was in an episode of *EastEnders*.

Lucas rolled his eyes, before the familiar teacherly sensation took over. He didn't know the boy, but it looked like he was still a teen. Nevertheless, Lucas had no responsibility for him at all. Sandeep would be walking along the corridor with their champagne by now. They could spend the next couple of hours together in the steamy water... yet, there was that niggling urge to intervene. He hated ignoring those in need. Part of the reason he'd gone into teaching had been because he liked looking out for the hidden signs, the silent cries for help, especially from young people. The shouts grew louder, and this time, the young man's voice broke into a fit of desperate garble.

Lucas rose to standing, the water splashing down his legs, and threw a robe around his wet body. Perhaps he could alert the hotel owner, tell them what he'd witnessed? Better yet, he could casually walk by, pretend he was getting some fresh air. It would look a little unconventional in a dressing gown, but posh people were often quirky, weren't they? They often did eccentric things without batting an eyelid.

He was shaking his head and muttering to himself by the time he made it to the top of the stairs. He tried to picture the hotel in his mind's eye: if the windows faced that way, then he needed to turn... right at the driveway? He looked out for Sandeep, who should really have been on his way up when he heard the chuckle.

That chuckle – the one he hated, the one that made his world tumble and twist without fail. He stopped still before jogging down the stairs to reception, hovering on the balcony next to a painting of a particularly angry-looking horse. He could relate.

Sure enough, the laugh erupted from reception again.

Sandeep never reserved this laughter for him. He could buy

him all the champagne, business class flights, and hotel stays in the world, but he never gave him that delightful, flirtatious honour. Who was he talking to this time? Surely there weren't enough people here for his eyes to start wandering? They were in the *Highlands* for God's sake. Lucas had brought him here specifically so they could be alone. He needed Sandeep to focus entirely on him, away from external distractions. Otherwise, how would he persuade him? How would he win him over? They needed their own time, their own space. He needed Sandeep's undivided attention.

Lucas pulled his robe tight and, after taking a deep breath, trotted down the stairs, trying to ignore the slapping sound his wet feet made against the wood. He wanted to come across as serious, after all.

Sandeep leant on one elbow over the counter, looking as relaxed as could be, chortling sickeningly with a striking man who looked like he was in his early thirties. He was wearing those trendy trousers that tapered in at the ankles – the ones that made Lucas's own thighs look like misshapen caterpillars – and he had shoulder-length dreadlocks. He was, Lucas thought furiously, effortlessly attractive. What a prick.

'Darling, there you are! Where's our champagne then?'

Lucas interlocked his fingers with Sandeep's and planted a lingering kiss on his cheek. He felt Sandeep draw back, so he pulled him closer. When he had finished, he acted like he'd just noticed their new friend and blew through his lips, pretending to be embarrassed. 'Oh God, sorry, didn't see you there. This one's kept me waiting, as you can see... apologies, I'm Lucas. Sandeep's *boyfriend*.'

The man shrugged, a coy smile on his face. Lucas knew what he was thinking. He was imagining all the things he'd like to do to Sandeep. He was imagining the feel of his fingers running down his chest, the scent of his skin, how it would feel to press against him, taste his lips. He could back off.

'Zach,' the man held out his hand to shake his. 'I'm Zach. Hey, you don't know if reception's open? I've been waiting here for a while.'

I'm sure you have, thought Lucas, squeezing Sandeep's arm. Zach spoke with the sort of confidence that Lucas had only ever come across when out with friends who had a penchant for dating entitled, privileged arseholes.

'We checked in earlier,' replied Sandeep quietly, stepping away from Lucas.

Did he think Lucas couldn't see what was going on here? All it took was ten minutes. Ten minutes of taking his eye off the ball and Sandeep had disappeared from their perfect room with their perfect bath and thrown himself at the first available younger model. Had he bothered to consider how much planning had gone into this trip? How much Lucas had stewed and pored over the details, over and over in his mind, ruminating over the scenarios and the red-letter moments he had in store? No. He had not. Clearly, he had not.

Lucas was about to ask Zach how long he was planning to stay, when the receptionist turned up. He had forgotten all about the argument he'd seen from the window. Thankfully, the young gardener followed her in. He looked fine, and was carrying a large pile of firewood. He said good morning in a thick Scottish accent to the three of them before disappearing into the lounge.

Perhaps Lucas had overthought it. It had been an early and long morning. Maybe they hadn't been fighting after all. He just needed to get out of his own head. Relax. Enjoy his surroundings.

He grabbed Sandeep by the waist and squeezed him tight.

Jumping in ahead of this Zach fella, he asked the receptionist, 'So, when can we expect that bottle?'

ZACH

What was going on here? Zach watched the couple, the unhinged man in a dressing gown, and the nicer one who was fully-clothed, skulk up the stairs. The man in the dressing gown, Lucas, carried the champagne bucket, swinging it ostentatiously. Sandeep, his boyfriend, as Lucas had been so keen to announce, looked back towards the entrance hall's door as if planning his escape.

Christ, thought Zach. *Poor guy*. Although, there was something compelling about the pair of them, something electric about that power struggle, that controlling behaviour. There was potential there. He'd keep an eye on them.

The lady at reception seemed unduly flustered, given that he was the only person she had to serve. She couldn't find his booking, which was a problem, because he couldn't afford his room without the discount. He would need to ring his mother to make the payment and that would be... unfortunate. He could imagine exactly how the conversation would go.

She would be delighted, *darling*, that he'd made it to a new boutique hotel she'd (no doubt) read about in *The Times*. There would be a comment about the menu (there was always a comment about the menu): *I hear the food is superb, chef's from London, you see. Land to table, but elevated,* topped off with a disparaging remark about the interiors: *seems like the sort of place that could do with a dose of someone like Kit Kemp. Looking at the photos, you can tell they're going for Fife Arms, but lack the direction... potentially, dare I say, the taste?*

He wouldn't be able to get a word in edgeways to tell her about his predicament, which would mean she'd assume this meant he was *finally* working in a *noble profession, just like your father. You know, he was three years younger than you when he set up the consultancy firm? There for a little celebration, darling?* There would almost certainly be a hopeful enquiry about a *new squeeze,* by which she meant one of those god-awful women she was incessantly setting him up with (always daughters of her friends, always unsalvageably boring).

After all that, he'd need to reveal that, no, he was still filming documentaries and, no, he was alone. But, please, could she cover the cost?

It would be yet another *little favour* she'd use to dangle over him.

He took a lingering breath and raised his eyebrows at the receptionist, pulling the expression that usually persuaded women of her age (he guessed that she was mid-to-late thirties from the fine, papery lines appearing at the sides of her eyes) to do whatever he wanted.

'So, should I start gathering twigs for my makeshift shelter tonight?'

Her head jerked up at him as she continued to scroll on the computer. 'Errr, no, no. No. Mr... Williams, you said?'

'That's right! Zach Williams. You've found my booking?' He tried his best not to sound impatient. The sooner he could drop off his things and start work, the better.

She stared at her computer, her eyebrows drawing close

together, her mouth tugging into a surprisingly sensuous pout. Her lips were slightly swollen, chapped but moist, the sort that looked like they'd just been pulled away from a passionate kiss. Unexpectedly, he felt an excited kick of desire pulse low in his abdomen. She wasn't unattractive. Her body was almost slim, sporting curves where he liked them. Although her hair was pulled up into a frumpy ponytail, he could imagine it spilling across a pillow, wavy and thick. Her eyes were sad, which he had found a turn-on in the past. Listless, is how he'd describe her; he could maybe work with that. Listless could be a thing.

'Errr, yes, here it is, sorry.'

She clicked on the mouse and, meeting his eyes, looked like she was about to say something but thought better of it.

'Wonderful,' purred Zach.

She looked taken aback at his tone, but quickly averted her gaze to his luggage: his camera bag, his tripod case, and the two Aspinal travel bags that his mother had bought him a few Christmases ago. He reminded himself to take it easy; there was no rush. He had the whole weekend. He didn't want to scare her away. And anyway, he was still undecided. He hadn't yet managed to take in his full surroundings. There could be better, more worthy opportunities.

'You're a photographer?'

So, he had piqued her interest.

'Filmmaker,' he said, making sure he sounded as elusive as possible. 'I'm hoping to find some interesting footage here.'

She nodded and rang the bell at the front of the desk. 'It's a beautiful spot,' she said. 'I'm sure you'll find all sorts. We have deer in the woods, as well as pine martens and otters. You never know, you might get lucky and spot a Scottish wildcat. Some of the villagers have seen them. They're incredibly rare, almost extinct.'

Zach nodded, wondering what the hell a pine marten was.

But he didn't need to bog himself down with the details. All the greatest filmmakers didn't bother with that sort of stuff. They didn't hold themselves back, obstructed by making plans and research. They were adventurous. They were dynamic, like him. That's where the magic was: in spontaneity.

As soon as he'd seen the photo of this hotel in the middle of nowhere, he'd *known* that this was where he'd travel next. He could see it: *Zach Williams' Undiscovered Highlands.* He'd find the story whilst he was here. He had the eye, he knew that he had the eye. Plus, he had schoolmates in television who, he was sure, would lap up a mishmash of remote scenery, whisky tasting, and wildlife. He'd already lined up drinks with them back in London. A young lad gathered up his luggage.

'Calan'll show you to your room,' said the woman. 'Anything at all, don't hesitate to call the main desk. I'm here, mostly.'

Zach quickly wrapped his hand around the navy Aspinal bag before the boy could touch it. That one always remained with him, thank you very much. He didn't like to risk it.

'Oh!'

The woman scratched her head. 'There's a guided hike this afternoon if you're interested. A few guests have signed up. Calan leads the group.'

She pointed vaguely in the direction of the mountains outside. 'It's supposed to snow, but don't let that put you off. Tornivan's beautiful when it's snowing.'

'I'll let you know,' said Zach, gripping the bag's handle, eager to unpack its contents once he got into his room.

JULES

Jules watched Calan and Mr Williams disappear up the stairs. She hesitated, feeling like she ought to call something up to him, round the conversation off. Something about the entire exchange felt oddly unfinished. Her thoughts were broken by the main door opening.

He had arrived! Jules smoothed her hair down, wishing she'd thought to wash it that morning. Had she remembered to put her deodorant on?

She cracked a winning smile as he walked towards her. Tim was just as good-looking as he had seemed on their Zoom meetings. His cheeks were pleasantly rouged from the cold outside, and his hair – stylishly cut, although thinning at the temples – was slightly dishevelled.

He removed what looked like an expensive woollen coat while he waited in the middle of the entrance hall. 'Gracie, are you coming?' he called behind him.

It was rare for people to be confident enough to raise their voices in the hotel. Most guests adopted a reverent hush, like they thought they didn't quite belong. Tim Melrose was at perfect ease amongst the mahogany wood panelling.

'Gracie!' he shouted again, this time followed by an impatient grunt.

A woman whom Jules presumed was his wife emerged from outside. She was irritatingly stunning in a way Jules would never be. She had the shade of red hair that was usually only reserved for Instagram filters. Her skin was pale and clear, her face sculpted into the perfect heart. She looked like a gorgeous little doll.

'Coming!' The woman smiled, apparently unperturbed by the brusque tone of her husband. 'Couldn't work out the lock!'

Tim shook his head and approached the reception desk. 'Roads are a bloody nightmare.' His eyes narrowed as he looked at her more closely. 'Julia Spyres?'

Heat rushed to Jules's cheeks. Did she really look so terrible that he didn't recognise her from their calls? She straightened her back, sticking her chest out ever so slightly, and wetted her lips with a quick flick of her tongue. 'That's me...'

She lifted her arm over the desk to shake his hand. He looked at it momentarily before reciprocating. Her skin sounded like dry leaves when his hand touched hers. She should have moisturised. She should have gone to more effort overall. All her flattering T-shirts had been screwed up in her washing basket for well over a week. Had she known she would be coming face to face with someone like Gracie... well, she would have at least blow-dried her hair.

'I hope you had a good journey, Mr Melrose.'

He cleared his throat. 'Yes, thanks for sorting the hire car.'

He assessed the reception hall. She watched him nervously, wondering whether she ought to say something else, explain the décor or talk him through the history of the place. She'd spent the past week making sure every corner was scrubbed of cobwebs, every sideboard free of dust, every detail polished and waxed. The task had been enormous given there was close to no staff here. But, it had to be done.

First impressions were always important, especially when it came to securing an investment. She wanted Tim Melrose to feel as if he'd walked into an offer he couldn't refuse: an exclusive, luxury retreat. With only three bedrooms, it was a unique proposition.

The Tornivan was small enough to feel like a home away from home, yet grand enough that most guests mistakenly referred to it as a castle. She hoped, with the help of Melrose Investments, to turn it into one of the most coveted membership clubs in the UK. A world-class restaurant, an extensive whisky bar featured in specialist magazines, reading rooms... she'd even got grand plans about luxury cabins in the woods.

Tim was truly her last hope at turning this place around. She had not believed her luck when she'd received his email.

Her hand trembled slightly as she gestured to the door across the hall. 'Welcome, both of you. Please help yourself to a whisky from our lounge. It's complimentary and never too early for a wee dram... that's what they always say here!'

Tim sniggered at that and looked over his shoulder to his wife. 'Is that right, Gracie? They always say that here?'

Gracie rolled her eyes apologetically. 'Sorry about him,' she said in a Scottish accent. 'He's just playing. I'm from down the road, actually. This trip's a bit of an unexpected homecoming.'

Jules felt colour flare in her cheeks. She averted her gaze to the keyboard immediately. *Wee dram?* What had she been thinking? 'Ah, lovely...' she replied.

'I'll take one. Whatever you recommend.'

It took Jules a couple of seconds to realise Tim was addressing her. 'Oh! Yes! Of course...'

The way he'd said "recommend" sounded like a challenge.

Rob had always been the resident whisky expert. She tried her best, but there was a lot to keep up with. Leaving the desk, she hurried into the lounge and stood back to observe the bottles stretching to the ceiling. The top shelves were usually where the really good stuff was. She climbed the ladder, and reached for a random bottle: forty-year-old Macallan... no. It looked like she was trying too hard. Next to it was a twenty-six-year-old Glenfarclas. It was much lesser known, which might earn her Brownie points.

She popped it under her arm and grabbed a couple of glasses, before rushing back to her guests. 'Here you go...'

She poured the golden liquid out, making sure to give a liberal measure. 'Classic Speyside, sherry cask. Good for the daytime,' she gave a little breath, 'with its fruity and nutty undertones.'

Tim made a show of sticking his nose in the glass and swirling the whisky around before tasting it. Gracie raised hers gratefully before sipping, her pristine lips enclosing primly over the rim.

Jules took the opportunity to speak. 'The Tornivan is really pleased to have you here, Mr and Mrs Melrose. I trust you'll enjoy your stay – most guests do – but if there's anything special you'd like to see, or observe...' *Anything that might swing your decision to invest in my favour,* Jules thought, '...then please do just ask. There's a hike this afternoon, led by our groundskeeper Calan. If anyone fancies shooting clay pigeons, then I'm sure he'll happily oblige.'

Tim looked less than enthusiastic about the prospect. Gracie chuckled, although Jules was sure she noticed the faint lines of irritation twitch around her lips. 'Tim's a workaholic, I'm afraid,' she said. 'He's been itching to open his laptop all the way here. Instead, I forced him to talk to me...'

Jules smiled politely as Tim set his glass down with just a tad too much force. 'Well,' she replied, 'as much as I want you to have a good time, I suppose this is a business trip.'

'That's right,' said Tim. 'Where's our room?'

ZACH

Zipping open the navy Aspinal was always a sensuous experience. The leather gave way as the bag emitted a soft smell that promised the deepest and most vivid of memories. He checked the door again (one could never be too careful) and began to empty the bag's contents onto the shaggy sheepskin rug.

A ring. A hair clip. An acrylic nail. A lipstick. A notepad. A pen. A feather from a pillow. A bookmark. A half-used miniature bottle of moisturiser.

Zach closed his eyes as he touched each item and inhaled deeply through his nostrils. The name associated with each relic rolled off his tongue. This was his museum of conquests. It was tradition to introduce them to every new place in which he stayed. He liked to remind his surroundings that he was a winner. He got what he wanted. He knew how to make women, no matter what their background, their age or type, succumb.

A door slammed further down the corridor and the sound of footsteps running past his room distracted him. A woman's voice muttering, *'Fuck's sake'* invaded his space.

He shook his head, annoyed he didn't have more privacy.

The boy who had shown him in had described the room as "one of our nicest suites", which was, frankly, a joke because it was only one room with a queen-sized bed and two oil paintings which looked like they'd been found at the local charity shop. Still, the hotel provided an acceptable bottle of complimentary whisky, from which he'd poured himself a sizeable glass.

He stroked the pillow feather against his lips and tried to entice his memories to come flooding back. He liked it when he reheard the sounds. They spun around his skull in wispy, silk-thread phrases. He had perfected precursory conversation to an art form. The dance of persuasion: it never ceased to amaze him how low women's self-esteem could be. Offer them the most meagre of compliments, tell them that they were intoxicating, that they needn't be shy of their bodies, that they weren't just plain, boring pieces of flesh, and their self-control would buckle in an instant. Zach had worked it out years ago: all women were gagging to be dominated. They just needed convincing.

He took a sip of whisky and lay down on the rug. The fire crackled in intermittent squeaks and pops. Would this be where he'd conquer Julia? He'd googled her already, as soon as he'd got into his room: Julia Spyres. She was, surprisingly, the owner, not just the receptionist, which meant she was of a different calibre than he'd initially thought. She must have come from money, or married into it, or at least earned it at some point. Her husband Rob seemed to have disappeared from the hotel's social media updates about a year ago. This was intriguing. She was alone.

Zach checked his watch. There was a little time before the hike. He scrolled through his phone and found a good photo of her. Julia. Her face filled the frame. Her hair rippled past her shoulders. Her lips were curled in a small nervous smile. Unzipping his flies, he imagined the ways that he might make her beg.

JULES

Jules lit a cigarette and took a deep drag. She wished the rolling mounds of smoke erupting from her mouth into the freezing air would carry her away with them. The anxiety, the all-encompassing electric panic had seized her completely. The first in-person meeting with Tim Melrose had hardly been amazing. She didn't know what she could have done wrong already, but he seemed to have taken an instant dislike to her.

The tips of her fingers were taking on a purple tinge, but she couldn't move. The panic was incapacitating. She inhaled another pocket of smoke and let its warmth smother her lungs. Rob had hated her smoking. She'd done it secretly whenever she could, often here, on the kitchen steps. Now, there was no need to hide it from anyone. Yet, she still felt the need to.

It was at times like this when she barely recognised herself. She had told no one – not even her therapists – about her dark urges. Only Rob knew, and he had left her. She had disgusted him, that's what he had said. He had called her all sorts of names. She remembered each and every syllable. He had shaken her, shouted in her face. She could still feel the droplets of his judgemental spit spraying across her forehead. She hadn't said anything to defend herself because there was no justification. She was broken, clearly. There was something wrong with her, deep inside. Something shadowy lurked beneath her skin and she couldn't expel it, no matter how hard she tried. She couldn't help herself, and that was the problem.

In the distance, shots fired. Calan must have taken the guests clay pigeon shooting after the hike. She ground the cigarette stub beneath her heel, smiling. At least something was going well. He was so excited to finally guide outdoor groups officially, having completed his training a couple of weeks ago. It was great that he was eager to show off his repertoire: she was lucky to have someone so dedicated. Hopefully, the assortment of guests wouldn't be too much trouble for him. The talkative man, the one who had ordered champagne, Lucas, hadn't wanted to borrow the hotel's wellies. His suede ankle boots would be as good as newspapers by now. She had a feeling he wouldn't be shy about complaining.

Her hands began to twitch with cold. Letting out a low groan, she heaved herself up and opened the door to the kitchen. All the guests had opted for a packed lunch for the hike, so the chef, Marta, had taken the afternoon off. She'd be reading in her cabin on the other side of the courtyard. From the amount of packages that arrived at the front desk, Jules guessed she was a voracious bookworm. Between hiding out in her cabin and her bi-weekly visits to the village church (a commitment, seeing that the drive was just under an hour), Marta very much lived a life of solitude.

Jules reminded herself again that the woman had no obligation to socialise with her. She was an employee and could do whatever she wanted in her downtime. But it would be nice of her, wouldn't it, even courteous, to offer to share a glass of wine? The countless evenings Jules spent alone in her apartment might not seem so bleak if they were broken up by the occasional social visit. Perhaps things wouldn't have gone the way they did had she had a friend.

For a long time, she'd assumed Marta wasn't confident in her English, being Italian, but then she'd heard her chatting away to Calan about seasonal vegetables and how to grow them. Whenever Jules tried to strike up conversation with her, she was always met with stern, monosyllabic answers. She hadn't been Jules's first choice. They'd interviewed a surprising number of chefs from all over the world: the remote setting seemed to offer a certain appeal. Marta had boasted an impressive track record – Jules and Rob had even eaten at one of the restaurants she used to work at in London – but she had struck Jules as a little odd. Throughout the interview, she held a hand to her heart, as if in some sort of secret prayer. When Jules asked why she wanted to move here, especially after living in Milan and London, she had replied, 'It is difficult to explain, but I feel a part of me is here. I must find it and protect it.'

Neither Jules nor Rob had known what on earth to say to that. However, Rob rated her food and her references, which Jules had to admit were excellent. So, they had taken her on. She was so competent in the kitchen that she preferred to work alone, despite them offering to hire sous chefs. 'They will break my concentration. I work best in solitude,' Marta insisted.

Well, it was a good job, seeing that hiring an extra pair of hands now was completely out of the question.

Jules passed the kitchen. Only the orange rectangle of the oven glowed in the grey single window. That would be the slow-roasted ribs for dinner. The thought of roasting meat reminded her to check the guests had positioned their fireguards properly before leaving.

She listed the guests' names and their respective rooms silently. Lucas Croft and Sandeep Todi had the Dunmore Suite,

Zach Williams had the Benroman Junior Suite, and Gracie and Timothy Melrose had the Ruamor Room.

As she jogged up the stairs, rubbing her hands together to stop the numb tingling, she made a mental note to double-check the discounts she was running on the booking sites. Two guests had booked under a special offer, but she hadn't been able to find the code anywhere. She'd had no choice but to let them pay the amount they'd agreed to, despite it being criminally low. She hoped that she hadn't made a mistake somewhere, although, given her current mental state, it was likely. At least everyone seemed happy enough with their rooms... well, they should have been at the price they'd paid.

Everything was in order in the Dunmore Suite. As she closed the door, she thought back to the odd check-in experience she'd had with Zach Williams. He'd been so forward, so assured in his every gesture and word. She suspected, very briefly, that he'd been *flirting* with her. But that would be ridiculous, obviously. She was hardly looking her best at the moment, plus, she was sure a guy like him had an endless string of gorgeous twenty-somethings lined up.

With his soft-looking lips at the forefront of her mind, she opened his room's door. The fireguard was in place, but she allowed herself a little time to scan his possessions. They were neatly laid out about the room, his luggage stored correctly on the rack (most guests didn't know what it was for). She thought of the way he had raised his eyebrows at her, how his eyes had glinted ever so slightly... her gaze lingered on his bed. A tiny giggle escaped from her mouth. She clamped a hand over it, shocked. It sounded so alien. She hadn't giggled in months, no, years.

Stop it, she thought, closing his door behind her. *Stop it.* She was letting her imagination run away with her, beginning to paint all sorts of ridiculous scenarios. This was what she did.

There was nothing at all to suggest he was interested. He was a guest... honestly! She had to put an end to these fantasies. They never led her anywhere good. She should have learned that by now.

She hurried to the next room. Blood was beginning to pump properly through her hands, and she wiggled her fingers to aid the circulation. A creak of floorboards sounded behind her. She jumped and turned around, searching the dim corridor. There was no one there.

'Jesus,' she said to herself, turning back towards the Melroses' room. 'Just relax.'

As she turned the key in the lock, she heard another sound. This time, it was the unmistakable pounding of footsteps coming up from behind her. Before she could turn, a hand gripped her shoulder.

'What—?' Jules cried out, stumbling backwards.

'Oh! Sorry!'

Jules blinked at the shadowy figure, recognising her as Mrs Melrose. Ribbons of adrenaline fluttered deep in her chest. She forced herself to breathe slowly.

'It's dark in here,' Mrs Melrose said, squinting at her. 'I didn't realise...'

'No... no, no problem!' cut in Jules, keen to extract herself. How long had she been there, lurking in the shadows? Had she watched her poking about Zach's room? She hadn't closed the door behind her. Would she tell him? 'The lights are automatic, for the environment. They'll be on in a minute. Sorry, I was just about to check the fireguard.'

Mrs Melrose was nodding, a little too quickly. Her eyes looked red in the dim natural light, as though she had been crying. 'There's no need. My husband stayed back anyway.'

'I see, oh, sorry...' Jules began to back away. 'I thought everyone had gone out, you see. Otherwise, I wouldn't—'

'It's all good!' Mrs Melrose's voice glided up an octave. 'I thought he'd join me too. But he didn't.'

Her eyes widened and she set her mouth into a forced, stiff smile. She looked like a stunned gargoyle.

'Right...' Jules added, because she thought she ought to. 'Did you enjoy the hike?'

The lights finally flickered on, showing Mrs Melrose in multicolour. Her cheeks were, indeed, blotchy and puffy, and her lips were tinged blue. The bottom of her jeans were also wet and covered in mud. What had this woman been doing? She'd have to ask Calan – it was imperative the Melroses had a brilliant stay.

Mrs Melrose cocked her head to one side, as if she didn't understand the question. 'Oh, the hike. Yes, thank you.'

There was an awkward silence as neither of them moved before Jules said, 'Well, sorry again! Glad I didn't barge in!'

'No problem,' Mrs Melrose said in a tone that reminded Jules of a wounded dog. 'It's no problem at all.'

Just before Jules turned to leave, a gleam in the mirror at the end of the corridor caught her eye. She froze at what she saw. Mrs Melrose followed her line of sight and sniffed, her expression forming into a blank, cold stare. Behind her back, she was holding a long, sharp knife. Jules felt her limbs freeze with fear as Mrs Melrose raised the blade to her side and moved closer.

LUCAS

The thing about snow was, once it settled on your clothes, it made you all soggy and cold. It looked beautiful and everything – sure, this place was a winter wonderland – but Lucas was struggling to see the point of walking straight through it. He was absolutely freezing.

His foot made a squelching sound inside his shoe and he shuddered, before exclaiming through his chattering teeth, 'It's good for the soul, all this, isn't it? The Great Outdoors!'

Nobody replied, although Calan, the young gardener, who also seemed to be doubling as a hiking guide, gave him a small, encouraging smile.

The group had assembled at reception about an hour earlier. To Lucas's disappointment, he and Sandeep weren't the only guests attending. He'd only agreed to come because Sandeep had wanted to "earn" their dinner. It was obvious the afternoon should be spent in front of the fire in the whisky lounge. Also, Lucas could think of much better ways to work up an appetite.

However, this weekend was supposed to be all about Sandeep: loving him, treating him, sealing the deal. If he could just make sure it all went perfectly, then this would be the most memorable trip of their lives.

The ring was nestled tightly against his chest in his inner coat pocket. Tomorrow was the day. He would strike when the iron and Sandeep were suitably hot. That way, there would be less time for Sandeep to start making excuses.

Lucas gritted his teeth as the group paraded along the beach. He still couldn't believe Sandeep hadn't come out to his parents. He was almost forty! Did he really think they bought the whole "best friends living together" crap? Obviously, they suspected something. And what was the plan? To pretend for the rest of their lives?

He felt guilty as soon as he thought it. Sandeep's dad was still in the hospice, deteriorating a little more every week. Lucas couldn't ever quite remember the details of the disease. Awful words like "degenerative" and "rare" had been bandied about. It was enough to warrant around-the-clock care. He could see why Sandeep was reluctant to rock the boat... but... well, he'd have to when they were engaged, wouldn't he?

That wanker Zach had unfortunately tagged along too. Lucas had given himself stern words before leaving: he had to try to not be so possessive. Ugh, he hated that word. It wasn't like he wanted to be so suffocating. The problem was he always saw sense *after* the event. When his blood was boiling and the green-eyed monster was in full action mode, he struggled to contain himself.

He had apologised to Sandeep about the run-in at reception when they'd got back to the room. As always, Sandeep said he understood. He knew that Lucas's little outbursts came from a good place. Thinking about it, he probably found it endearing. It must be nice, really, to have a boyfriend who was so keen to keep him all to himself! That must be lovely. All he needed to do was ignore Zach, with his obnoxious expert country gear and stupid dry feet. He had not stopped going on about socks in the boot room earlier.

'*You really need proper welly socks, Le Chameau are the best, I find...*'

What a giant yawn of a man. He'd even dared to suggest that Lucas might want to change his shoes. Lucas had snapped back that he was fine, *thank you very much*, and that he always wore these boots on walks. This was true enough: although the walks usually amounted from his front door to Tooting Broadway station. But still.

At least Zach seemed more interested in his fiddly camera gear than chatting up Sandeep right now.

The other guest was a softly spoken Scottish woman who introduced herself as Gracie. She'd made them all wait an extra fifteen minutes back at the hotel in the hope that her husband might join, but, when it became clear he wasn't interested, she'd begrudgingly set off alone and was now having a strop at the back of the group.

Lucas fingered the hip flask of whisky ensconced in his pocket. He wondered when they would be stopping so he could whisk Sandeep off for a quiet drink. That would be a moment to remember, wouldn't it? *The time they drank whisky from a flask in the snowy Highland hills.* They'd reminisce about it in years to come... their engagement weekend! Sandeep would probably feel bad about all the effort and expense, but he shouldn't. That's what Lucas would tell him: he was completely worth it.

Lucas quickened his pace to catch up with Sandeep. These pebbles were an absolute nightmare to walk on. 'Hey, wait for me, gorgeous!'

He bear-hugged Sandeep as he launched forwards. 'Whoah! Isn't it beautiful here? What do you say...' Lucas opened his coat suggestively, letting the snow fall against his shirt, 'a cheeky snifter?'

Sandeep sighed and nodded in Calan's direction. 'Calan said we might have a go at shooting after.'

'Oh great! Sounds good!' *There he goes*, thought Lucas, *look at him getting into it.* Shooting? Who would have thought? Perhaps this could be their new hobby. He quite liked the idea of Sandeep the Hunter. Oh yes, he could definitely get on board with that.

'Yep, but obviously we can't drink if we're going to do it,' Sandeep confirmed.

Lucas nodded, fiddling with his zip which refused to budge as he tried to do up his coat. 'Right... right... no, of course, absolutely.'

'It's just clay pigeons,' Calan said, striding ahead. 'Back around the loch. Don't worry, you'll have plenty of time for drinks before dinner.'

Lucas had always wondered what clay pigeons were, exactly, but didn't want to embarrass Sandeep by asking. 'Ah ha, thanks. Do you live locally, then?'

Calan nodded. 'In the village about thirty miles east. It's what the house is named after: Tornivan. You probably drove past it.'

Lucas bit his lip. The boy's accent was incredibly strong, and he didn't want to be rude by asking him to repeat himself. He settled on changing the subject. 'So... it's a nice place to live?'

'I bet it's very peaceful,' said Sandeep.

'Yeah, I mean, it'd be good to have more going on. Been gardening and stuff on the grounds for a while. When I was at school I did a bit of casual work and since leaving college, I've been full time. I like it all right.'

Despite identifying only seventy per cent of what he'd just said, Lucas was convinced there was an undercurrent of anxiety beneath the boy's words. Well, not boy, really, because he'd left school, but he was still very young; closer in age to Lucas's students than to him. The protective instinct resurfaced. Lucas couldn't help but feel that Calan was silently screaming for someone to help him. Was he picking up on signs that weren't there? Certainly, he'd offered a lot of information without being prompted, which was common. People tended to garble when they had something to hide. He also avoided eye contact, which could, of course, be down to a number of reasons.

He squinted as a gust of white wind pummelled him in the face. Perhaps he was just assuming the worst. Anyway, he wasn't at school. This was his and Sandeep's special weekend.

'Wait, where are you going?' Zach's elongated vowels travelled through the snow from behind them.

'Everything okay back there?' Calan called down the beach. The snow had begun to fall in a thick, heavy stream, meaning it was impossible to see further than a few metres away.

They waited in silence for a few moments, listening to the moaning of the wind, when Zach's silhouette emerged. 'She's marched off. Tried to stop her. Girls will be girls, I suppose.'

It sounded like he expected them to laugh in response, but Calan stepped forwards, looking very concerned. 'Mrs Melrose? Weather's come in,' he said. 'Which way did she go?'

'Oh, just back to the hotel,' said Zach, rolling his eyes. 'Something I said, I suspect!'

Too bloody right, thought Lucas.

'You're sure she was okay? She knew the way?' Calan reached into his coat pocket. 'I'll phone reception to check...'

'We've barely left the drive,' said Zach in a haughty voice. 'She's fine, trust me. From these parts, she said.'

Calan swore gently. 'No signal.' He blew through his lips

and narrowed his eyes. 'Sorry, boys, I think we've got to head back. I can't risk her getting lost, not in this weather.'

'Oh, for God's sake.' Zach folded his arms. 'Look, look. Why don't I follow her? I saw where she went. Like I said,' he shook his head, 'the hotel is literally right there.'

Calan looked like he was about to refuse, but eventually bit his lip and nodded. *Most likely*, thought Lucas, *because he'd worked out that the plan meant getting rid of this intolerable arse.* 'You're a confident walker?'

Zach laughed. 'All the gear, right? Every idea. No, seriously, I've done my ski-guiding quals. This, believe me, is nothing I can't handle.'

Calan did a pretty sterling job of not cringing. 'Right, well, all right, as you say, we're close to the hotel. Just check she's arrived, yeah? Let reception know if she hasn't.'

'Roger,' said Zach, turning to walk away. 'Enjoy your walk, lads! Onwards!'

They watched him disappear back into the sheet of snow as Calan tried his phone again.

'I'm sure they'll be okay,' Sandeep offered. Lucas loved it when he put on this voice. It made him warm and fuzzy. He mostly heard it when Sandeep was at school. It was authoritative and calming. It made everything seem that it would work out just fine. 'Zach looks like he knows what he's doing.'

The warmth in his belly disappeared in an instant. Oh, *Zach knows what he's doing*, does he? Lucas felt the familiar pointed jealousy curdle in his chest. He clenched his hands inside his pockets. There was no need to get annoyed. Sandeep was here with him, wasn't he? It was just a thoughtless comment.

Calan made a tutting sound and pointed to the forest ahead. 'No signal,' he repeated. 'Happens with the snow. There's a circular path through there that leads to a nice spot, the bothy. People like taking pictures there, normally. Never know, the weather might die down by the time we reach it. That'll lead us back in time for a quick shoot, if you're still keen?'

'Sounds brilliant,' said Lucas, putting an arm around Sandeep's waist. 'Perfect.'

MARTA

Marta rocked back and forth, her hands pressed tightly together, her head bowed, kneeling at the foot of her bed.

'Loving Father, touch me now with Your healing hands, for I believe that Your will is for me to be well in mind, body, soul and spirit...'

She would pray the badness out of her. She would repent.

'Cover me with the Most Precious Blood of Your Son, our Lord Jesus Christ, from the top of my head to the soles of my feet. Cast out anything that should not be in me.'

She inhaled, shaking, sweat beginning to bead at her temples. 'Cast out anything that should not be in me!'

She closed the prayer book, the latest addition to her ever-growing collection. This one *had* to work. She could not hold the Devil in her for much longer. He – God – had proven Himself right. He had always and would always prove Himself right. But she had denied him. She had thought she knew better. She had waited too long. The shame caused her to double over on the quilt and let out a tight-lipped cry.

Here was the place where she could begin to make amends. She had worked so quietly here, started to build her way back into God's kingdom with neither pomp nor pride. This was her mission. She could not undo her remittances, her failings. She could not say the things she should have said. She could not bring the dead back to life.

A sharp pain vibrated in her chest, the same pain that came whenever she thought about that shining face. It felt like home.

The only thing left for her to do was carve a sliver of light through the darkness. Follow God's will in this tiny corner of the world. She could change nothing, she could not make good the past, but she could make good the future.

Marta's lips worked their way through the prayer one more time. Squeezing her eyes closed, she whispered his name, as she did every night. She said it again. Then again, until the last syllable was indistinguishable from the first. *Calan. Calan. Calan. Calan.*

She had followed him to the edge of the land. She would protect him from the evils of the world. She would throw herself between him and the Devil. She loved him, painfully so.

CALAN

The couple was nice enough, although Calan wished they'd stop treating him like a child. He was nineteen and had been for some time. Hadn't they noticed he was the one with the expertise here? Probably not. If it was up to them, they'd be struggling up an unmarked path by now, hiking in completely the wrong direction. The one in the suede shoes was a lot. He seemed all right, but, seriously, he liked to talk.

His boyfriend looked a bit embarrassed about him, to be honest, especially when Calan had needed to explain what a bothy was after about twenty minutes of Suede Shoe Guy going on about how much "he too liked sailing". They were clearly walking uphill... what sort of boat had he thought they'd find up here?

Anyway, they'd both seemed pretty excited about the small stone structure. It wasn't really a proper bothy. The old hotel used to let guests stay in it, so it had been decked out with a few luxuries. There was a nice wood-burner in the corner, as well as running water and an electricity supply to feed the fridge and the shower block. The beds were comfy and there was a working stove.

He hadn't been surprised when the Suede Shoe Guy had asked if they could hang back inside for a bit. The log burner was still emitting heat from last night, when Calan had slept here.

A familiar tightness gripped his chest. He'd begun staying over years ago when it had got too snowy for his dad to pick him up. He liked it. Out in the hills, overlooking the water. He'd often brought his school jotters along to do his homework by the fire. It had been his little hub. His little snug, his escape.

Until she had found it. Until she had found him.

He breathed out slowly, counting to ten, and reminded himself that he was an adult now, that he could make his own decisions. Then... why did he keep going back? Sometimes, it felt like his body wasn't his own. Like his brain was shutting down and this monster took over and made him do things that disgusted him. It was all his fault. He could have left. She told him that, showed him how their meetups were *his* choice, *his* desires. This is what he wanted to keep happening, over and over again. Otherwise, he would have moved, right? He would have left this place. It was a free country. Yet, he continued to treat the bothy as a makeshift home. It had even become known as "Calan's Bothy" semi-officially.

He had to get away. To make it stop.

Grateful for the sludge of the wet snow disguising his tears, he glanced back at the bothy. It crouched on top of the hill like it had always been there, like it had grown up with the trees and the grasses, an organic object. The dark stonework was black against the white sky. The windows glowed orange like two beady eyes.

He was pretty sure the couple were drinking whisky in there. That was all right. He hadn't wanted to say earlier, but most of the guests drank before using guns, especially the hunting parties. They had invited him into the bothy with them, and, although it was tempting to get warm, he knew it would be uncomfortable. Suede Shoe Guy seemed determined to find romance under every rock. Plus, Calan didn't want to be reminded of last night so soon. He'd made up an excuse about wanting to check out some animal tracks he'd seen on the way up.

He knocked on the bothy door. 'All right? I reckon it's time to head down if we're wanting to catch the last light for shooting.'

There was no answer.

He knocked again, this time a little louder. 'It's about time to be heading back.'

Still, there was no reply. He pressed his ear to the door to check that he wasn't about to barge in on them in a private moment.

He heard a loud crash and then the unmistakable shout of, 'She's dead! I need to find her!'

ZACH

He had to admit, nothing was jumping out at him yet. Yet. He was sure it was just a waiting game. How hard could it be to capture some half-decent footage of a... what was it again... pine marten?

Zach kept his camera ready, poised between his leather gloves as he stared over the water to the other side of the loch. It had been good fun secretly filming the group leaving the hotel. No one seemed to notice; they were all so wrapped up in whatever sad little issues were occupying them.

The couple – Lucas and Sandeep – seemed to have made up. Neither of them had a clue about what to wear for a country walk. It was as if they'd never seen a boot room before. A hotel like this had to be careful letting just anyone stay. The whole point of exclusive places was that they kept the undesirables out. Then, people like Zach could relax. Kick back. Stop pretending to be so bloody socially conscious all the time. As his mother said, *as soon as one lets the masses in, all good conversation dries up.* He didn't agree with much of what the old bitch said, but she was bang on about that.

Then there was the mopey Scottish girl, Gracie. She was fit, there was no denying it, but she had a strange manner about her. The way she moved, how she pulled on her wellies, or slid her arm into her wax jacket seemed overly thought through, too contrived. It was like her skeleton was robotic, a machine whirring beneath her pale skin. He'd filmed her walking behind him for a while, turning the hidden camera in his rucksack on via his phone. Their subsequent exchange had been captured too.

The loch stretched out silvery and opaque before him. He glanced over his shoulder to check the annoying gamekeeper wasn't on his back. The faint smell of logs burning worked its way through the cold air. They'd stopped off at the bothy then. Good.

Of course, he'd not bothered to check up on Gracie like he'd said he would. That would have been pointless: he knew precisely why she'd disappeared. He'd seen how her perfect lower lip wobbled with hurt as a result of what he'd said to her. The rest of the group hadn't heard their conversation, but he had it all on camera. It had been such a satisfying exchange that Zach immediately wanted to watch it back, here, by the water. He was lucky the guide had agreed to carry on without him. It would have been... disappointing had they all turned back and ruined his alone time.

Sitting down on a driftwood log, he took out his phone. Finding the secret footage from the walk, he hunched over the screen to protect it from snowflakes. There was Gracie in the centre of the frame. Even the way she walked was considered, each step across the pebbles an identical motion from the last. Her face was set in a pinched expression. He could see it a mile off: she'd been hurt. She was a woman scorned. Her husband – the man she was with, presumably, who remained in their room – had fallen short of her expectations. Unsurprising. Female expectations were always so far-fetched and immature.

'Much of a stalker then?' his voice sounded a little tinny through the recording. On the screen, Gracie bent down to touch something on the snow-covered grass: a small animal track.

Unlike most women, she didn't jerk her head up in a mock-surprised, coquettish way when she heard him approach. Instead, she very studiously settled her eyes on his walking boots and shifted her gaze upwards, over his legs, his chest, before finally meeting his face dead-on.

Zach paused the screen and then watched her in slow motion. She looked like one of those stop-motion cartoons.

'A bit,' she said. She looked behind her again, no doubt hoping her husband would be hurrying around the bend of the loch.

'Trouble in paradise?' There was a slight flicker on the screen; the moment he had changed cameras from the back to the one concealed in his front bag strap.

She rubbed some frozen soil between her forefinger and thumb and replied, rather pointedly, 'I don't think that's any of your business, do you?'

He listened to himself chuckle and marvelled at how good he was at this. Nobody could resist that deep and intimate sound. Gracie inclined her head at him and stood, rubbing her thighs with dirty hands. 'Do you have a... special someone?' she asked.

An odd way of putting it, thought Zach. A special someone. How quaint. Not a wife. Not a husband, a boyfriend, or a girlfriend. She cocked her head again like a tiny, wound-up, clockwork doll.

'Not me, no... married to the job, you see.' There was a sound from off-screen, where he'd tapped the main camera around his neck.

'I see.'

The icy beach crunched beneath their feet; the phone's speaker made their steps sound restless, quicker than they'd been in real life.

'Tim's married to his job too, apparently.' She offered the information freely, with no prompt at all.

'Oh? A fellow workaholic?'

'You could say that.'

'What does he do?'

'He owns an investment firm. Classic nondescript millennial sort of thing. I couldn't tell you what he does day-to-day, what's so *pressing* all the time. Money's always involved, obviously.'

They paused before the path turned. She faced him and the camera picked up the glistening tears in her eyes. Zach's heart began to beat a little faster. It felt so private, watching this back over. It gave him a greater sense of power. He had a piece of her, one that she didn't know he had.

'Do you work?' he asked.

She laughed at this for some reason. 'Yes, yes, I work. I'm a solicitor. Mainly family law, divorces, stuff like that. Fairly small-time.'

'Impressive.'

'Thanks,' she said, although she sounded vaguely sarcastic. 'But it doesn't keep me as busy as the lofty heights of property investment.'

'He stays late at work, that sort of stuff?' He couldn't help himself. He was like a sniffer dog for this sort of thing. He wanted – and he wasn't sure why, entirely – to make her hurt. She was so poised, so delusional. He was, in a way, helping her. Dragging her up from the dregs.

'Exactly, most nights. Then when he is home...'

'On his phone,' Zach finished.

'Yes, that's... that's exactly it.' He paused the recording

again. There was a look in her eyes. Was it suspicion? No, it was something deeper, more brooding.

Pressing play, he listened to himself inhale deeply as if he cared in earnest. He remembered thinking how this would be fun. There was something interesting here with which he could toy, something a little out of the ordinary. The opportunity was his for the taking. 'Can I be blunt with you, Gracie?'

There was a pause as she kicked a stone towards the water. 'I suppose... why not?'

'It sounds like our friend Tim is playing afield.'

She didn't answer. Perhaps she hadn't understood.

'Having an affair,' he added, helpfully.

Even through his phone, the depth of her silence was stifling. She choked on her words a couple of times, before spitting out, 'I...I would know that though. No, no. I would definitely know. I would always know.'

He shrugged, mimicking the gesture he remembered doing an hour and a half ago. 'No one plans for an affair, do they? They just happen. They're moments of passion. I mean, look, I don't mean to overstep the mark here, but it's a bit of a cookie-cut scenario, isn't it?'

This bit was magic. Her face, which had been muted for much of the conversation, lost almost all elasticity. It was as if a part of her had died. Her eyes grew larger like she was watching a secret film play in her head.

'Passion,' she repeated, although Zach had the impression that she wasn't talking to him.

'I wouldn't worry yourself about it. These things happen. I should know, look at my parents for starters!' He'd expected her to laugh at that but she hadn't. 'Look, look, Gracie...'

She stepped backwards when he said her name, a long, robotic stride into the shallow water. She was afraid of him. The moment was so identifiable. He could see it in the way that she clenched her fists tight. Her eyes searched beyond his shoulder looking for the rest of the group. As the snow whipped across her face, she looked like an ice statue, one that would melt in good time. 'We'd better catch up with...'

Zach stepped forwards. The camera picked up the fluidity of his movement, throwing the landscape into a blur of white and greys and browns and greens. Then, it focused on Gracie. Her eyes were scanning the beach rapidly – not wildly, he noted – she was too restrained for that.

Reflex seemed to cause her to step back again, deeper into the water. She gasped. It was a beautiful sound. The sound of hollow, frozen lungs.

'It's honestly nothing to worry about,' Zach continued.

He heard back in his voice how much he was enjoying himself at this point. He could feel the panicked scenarios spinning through her mind, stirring it up into a frenzy. She'd be imagining herself at the bottom of the loch with only the mountains as her witness. She would be telling herself she was being silly, but her blood would be pumping. She sensed danger. He loved it when they sensed the danger.

A violent gust of wind screeched down the beach and he bent even closer over the screen.

'Gracie, honestly. What are you doing?' His voice was the perfect combination of concern and mockery.

'I think—' There it was: the heave of the chest. He'd enjoyed it the first time around, but on camera it was so much more evocative.

'Just... *listen*. Listen, will you. Listen to me.' Haha! He was so commanding. The microphone picked up on her whimper, barely audible in the moment itself. 'Good. Good, Gracie, thank you. It's important to face up to these things, isn't it? Now, there's certainly nothing to cry about.'

'I'm not crying.' She was, she truly was. Her tears must have felt so hot and steamy against the cold.

'Hush, no really, hush. Affairs happen as a matter of course. It might not be what we want, but we must accept it. Where's Tim now?'

She didn't reply. He could see that her lips had begun to tremble, turning a very light shade of grey. 'Answer me, Gracie.'

'In our room.' Her voice hardened here. She was steeling herself.

He pressed on. 'He's probably messaging her now, isn't he? Wanking off to her photos, I imagine. He's thinking about all the ways that he can escape back to her...'

'You're a fucking creep.'

Gracie, Zach thought, *you've got spirit.* She harnessed the adrenaline rush, the fear. Not everybody did. It was amazing how much you could learn about a person when you took the time to really watch them.

She charged past him with astonishing force, the water churning around her legs as she ran. Drops of water sullied the camera lens. Before disappearing around the bend of the beach, she looked back at him. He paused the footage there. This was a moment to savour. She thought she was being chased. Her eyes were wide with fear. He zoomed in. Her chin was jutted forwards, tense. He wondered whether she would fight, if it came to it.

Zach turned off his phone and shoved it into his pocket, sitting very still for a few moments. On the opposite side of the loch, he spotted a doe. A killer instinct arose in him; he'd only ever seen deer before on hunting weekends. The impulse to shoot was fierce. The doe raised her neck and stared at him straight on from across the water. Perhaps it was her tracks that Gracie had been following. Zach shook his head. If only he found wildlife as interesting as he did humans. Trouble was, people didn't take very kindly to being filmed secretly. He'd obviously never be able to show his producer mates that type of footage.

He nodded at the loch, pleased with how the day had gone so far, and stood to walk back to the hotel. But then he spotted it. Nestled between two rocks, almost covered by snow. He almost ignored it but was glad that he didn't. Because when he opened it, things became more interesting than he'd ever dared to hope.

LUCAS

Lucas crawled around the bothy on his hands and knees, searching hopelessly. He had to find it. He couldn't have lost it. That photo was irreplaceable and one of the few memories he had of her.

'Lucas! Careful!' Sandeep knelt next to him as he tried to move the coffee table, accidentally sending the teapot and mugs laid on top of it flying.

Swearing loudly, Lucas felt the gust of freezing air enter the cabin.

'Everything okay?'

Calan stood in the doorway, looking understandably confused. Lucas's face burnt. He wrestled out of his coat, his breathing beginning to quicken. *For God's sake, why was it so bloody hot in here?*

'He's lost his wallet,' explained Sandeep.

'It's not just a wallet!' Lucas shouted, hearing the tremor in his own voice. Calan and Sandeep stared at him. 'Sandeep! Bloody hell! You know it's not the wallet! Can you just help me find it, please?'

Sandeep murmured to Calan, 'Sorry, mate, it's a photo of his sister, she...'

'Died,' finished Lucas, wiping his brow with the back of his hand. 'She's dead and her photo is inside the wallet. So, if you could help me find it quickly...'

Sandeep placed an arm around his waist and gave him the look they both gave students when they were behaving like idiots, but you weren't allowed to say. 'It's just a photo, you could get another one...'

Lucas honestly wanted to slap him. Obviously, he knew that he could print any old photo, but that wasn't the point. That should have been clear. Losing this, the irreplaceable one from her vintage Polaroid, just amounted to another failure on his part. He could see the image so clearly in his mind's eye.

They were at Dad's villa in the Algarve. She was holding a glass of red wine, tilting it at a dangerous incline. He had an arm around her shoulders. They were both grinning at the camera like they had done when they were children. Sandeep had taken it, making fun of how Lucas drew his cheeks up whenever he posed for photos. She had written on the back: *Let's remember the good times. Love you, Lu. Your Big Sis. X*

He'd never bothered to tell her how much it meant to him. He hadn't had the chance. Or, if he was honest, he couldn't bring himself to. It hadn't been her fault. None of it had been her responsibility. Lucas knew that deep down. He'd attended enough school pastoral care courses to realise it was always, always one hundred per cent the parents' fault.

God, those courses were tough going. All the other teachers sat down in their casual dress, ecstatic to be having a day off-timetable, taking random notes here and there. *What to do when a child discloses sensitive information. Never promise anything because you might not be able to follow through. Remember, it can happen in any household. No socio-economic group is immune. Abuse can take a myriad of forms. The signs aren't always as obvious as you'd think.* Lucas always tried to disappear into his own head for a bit, focus on the terrible clothing choices some people had made, doodle cartoons on his notepad. He didn't need to be told about the effects of child abuse, thanks very much. He was well aware.

The photo resurfaced in his mind. It was his last memory of her – for once, a simple, uncomplicated slice of their life – he had to find it.

Lucas marched out of the bothy and began retracing his steps. 'It has to be somewhere on the way,' he muttered, ignoring Calan and Sandeep stuttering behind him. 'I definitely had it when we left the hotel. Just keep your eyes open *if it's not too much trouble.*'

The sarcasm was aimed at Sandeep who, honestly, could not be behaving less supportively.

Lucas wound back down through the forest, his eyes raking over the path, old and unwelcome memories dancing in the back of his mind.

Little fists, hammering on his older sister's door. The absolute and innocent belief that she'd let him in, protect him from the smashes and screams coming from downstairs. The heavy footsteps, now climbing the bottom steps.

He slid on a wet rock, his arms shooting out in odd directions to balance him.

'Babe, are you all right? Wait, will you?' Sandeep called from behind. Babe? Really? *Now* he wanted to be affectionate? It turned out all it took to get Sandeep in the mood was a reminder of his dead sister. How romantic.

The snow had grown heavier; that wasn't helpful at all. He kicked at the path, trying to displace the fresh snowfall. It was useless. He skidded down to the lochside and groaned. There was no way he'd be able to find anything here. The pebbles were soggy and covered in snow. He took a step forwards, half-heartedly searching the ground with his eyes, when a figure emerged in the middle distance. They were hunched over, like they were rifling through something.

'Hey!' Lucas ran towards them. 'Have you by any chance seen...'

His voice trailed off: it was Zach, who appeared to be standing alone on the beach, looking through his wallet like no one's business. Lucas blinked, trying to work out whether he was seeing things. But no, as he stumbled closer, he realised he was right. Zach was holding his wallet, he could see, clear as day. He recognised the silver detail on the side of it, glinting in the white light. He watched for a few seconds before flinging himself forwards.

'Oi!' Lucas heard feet running behind him, Sandeep yelling at him to calm down. He absolutely would not. 'Oi, you! I'm talking to you!'

Lucas heard his accent slide back into a South-East London twang. He rarely found himself in aggressive situations but, just like when he'd had a few drinks too many, his childhood voice resurfaced. 'What are you doing with that? It's mine!'

But Zach didn't even look up. He held the wallet open, staring at the photo. The look on his face made Lucas stop still for a second. Zach's lips were curled in a thin sort of pout. His thumb was stroking his sister's face, and his head moved from left to right, as if he was lost in some sort of... fantasy? Lucas couldn't help but feel violated. This was private. The photo was private. And this creep was shitting all over it.

'Give it back!' Lucas pushed Zach with both arms; nothing more than a shove, just enough to make him stumble backwards. 'What do you think you're looking at, wanker? Give it to me. Give it to me now!'

Zach slowly gathered himself and met his eyes. Lucas was

reminded of the snakes he'd seen in wildlife documentaries, uncoiling themselves, patiently, venom hidden beneath their scales. 'I see. This is yours then?'

'Yes.' Lucas snatched it off him.

'Ah! You found it, thanks, mate!' Sandeep finally arrived at his side and patted Zach on the back. 'Sorry about the, er, commotion, long story, you see.'

He swivelled to face Lucas. 'But, look, you've found it now, eh?'

Lucas wasn't sure how to respond. He was seething. His breath felt like lava against the air. He didn't trust himself to open his mouth. The look Sandeep was giving him said, "Leave it" in no uncertain terms.

Clearly, his initial instinct had been right: something dark was working beneath the surface of Zach's oh-so handsome face. This wasn't normal behaviour. Something was very off and it made him uneasy.

Zach held himself with an awful, restrained arrogance. He shot Lucas an amused smile as he said, 'Right, time for a whisky after all the fun and games, I say!'

Jules watched in horror as Mrs Melrose wielded the knife towards her. 'Mrs Melrose,' she managed, her voice choking at the back of her throat.

'Oh, Gracie, call me Gracie, please, Mrs Melrose sounds so —' She stopped speaking mid-sentence and looked between Jules's face and the knife and then back again, as if something was dawning on her. 'Oh! You didn't think...?'

Gracie stepped back and placed the knife on the floor between them. 'Oh my God, I am so sorry!'

Jules felt her muscles relax. Her chest allowed her to take in a new gasp of air, but the relief was followed by a wave of embarrassment. Had she just genuinely thought that a guest was about to stab her? That was mad. Her cheeks flamed. 'Er, no, I'm sorry...' and then, 'Why do you have that?'

She gestured to the knife on the floor. Whether or not she had intended to murder her, she couldn't really let guests mill about the hotel with weapons.

'Oh!' Gracie looked taken aback.

Yet again, Jules had the impression that Gracie wasn't quite listening to everything being said. Standing in front of her, with her arms held stiffly at her sides, she couldn't help but feel that there was something unnatural about her. It was as if she had been forced to live in her own skin and was trying, concentrating, to make it work.

Gracie lowered her voice, looking at the floor. 'I... I was going to...'

She stopped, and shrugged a little too slowly. 'It's private. I wasn't going to... please, just take it. I'm sorry.'

As she spoke, Gracie rubbed her forearm back and forth. Was that a nervous tick? It didn't seem like it. The movement seemed more habitual, like she was in perfect control. The way she held her body didn't seem to match her broken words. Jules bent down and retrieved the knife. It was a thick bladed one she'd seen Marta use to cut root vegetables. Gracie must have stolen it.

She raised her eyebrows. 'Did you get this from the kitchen?'

Gracie shook her head, but it was obvious that she was struggling to come up with a decent answer. In fact, she seemed frightened.

In usual circumstances, Jules would have to ask her to leave. Stealing was obviously against guest policy... especially the stealing of knives. Purposefully trespassing into staff areas wasn't ideal either. But this wasn't just any guest, this was Tim Melrose's wife. That would hardly go down well.

'This is quite... er... irregular,' Jules said. 'I can't have knives going missing, you understand? It's not really... well, it's not safe...'

She felt so awkward saying it, like she was pretending to have authority over the situation. She'd never been good at this sort of thing. Rob had always dealt with difficult situations. He had that effortless way about him, managed to get everyone on side without making a scene. He would have known how to deal with this.

Gracie glanced at her room door. Jules was now convinced she was afraid of something. Perhaps Tim? If he was inside, it was odd he hadn't popped his head out.

'Oh!' Gracie's mouth flew open without warning and, again, Jules was reminded of a mechanism that wasn't quite human, like a ventriloquist's puppet.

Gracie let out a defeated sigh and stepped forwards. Her eyes had filled up – almost perfectly – with glossy tears. For the first time, Jules noticed how green they were. Against the dark wood of the corridor, they glittered as if trying to hypnotise. Ridiculously, she suddenly felt very aware of her own physical inadequacies. She felt so *big* facing this tiny woman. Her forehead, she knew, would be shiny with the sweat of doing chores. She could never get rid of that underlying greasiness, that dirtiness. Gracie, on the other hand, resembled a perfect little sculpture.

'I didn't want to say anything,' she whispered. 'But we, Tim and I, we like to use... sometimes...' She used her toe to nudge the blade a little.

'Sorry, I'm not following...' But then the penny dropped. Heat rose to the top of her chest.

Jules had no idea what to say. Even Rob would have stumbled over his words. It wasn't that she particularly minded; in fact, a certain part of her was thrilled to have come across such an intimate fact. But it was a bit odd to know so much about your investor, wasn't it? She was surprised Gracie had shared so openly.

Gracie continued to hold her gaze. She was almost defiant, daring Jules to be a prude. The sound of the bathroom door opening sounded from within the room.

With no warning, Gracie dipped forwards and suddenly her

cheek was next to hers, the warmth of her breath against her ear. 'Don't chuck us out. Just don't. It'll ruin everything, please, woman to woman.'

Gracie held Jules's shoulders. Jules smelt alcohol on her breath. Gin? No. Whisky. So, she'd been drinking. Maybe that explained her oversharing.

The entrance hall door opened and a freezing gust of air blew up the staircase into the corridor.

Gracie gently removed the knife from Jules's hand. It was a solemn gesture, and she flooded her eyes with gratitude. Even if Jules could have thought of the right thing to say, Gracie's exacting grip on the situation would have silenced her.

She slid the knife into her back pocket and said in a low voice, 'Thanks. Just this once, okay?'

Lucas watched Sandeep shoot at things in the sky and tried to muster a few half-hearted cheers. He was so cold by now that he couldn't feel his feet. At least Sandeep was enjoying himself.

He just wanted to disappear to their luxe hotel room and take a hot shower, perhaps with a whisky. That would be nice, that would calm him down after all the stress of the afternoon.

Still, as Sandeep fired and fired and fired, he couldn't shake the feeling of being violated. His hand tightened around his wallet, now tucked in his coat pocket. He sighed, bringing his shoulders to his ears, and tried to think of an excuse for the shooting to end.

'Won't the sound of the gun scare the cows?' he asked Calan, who was cheering along with Sandeep.

Calan looked back at him with a grin. 'Nah. The coos are grand. Used to it living here.'

'I wouldn't want to frighten them,' Lucas said, folding his arms irritably. 'Animal rights and all that...'

He stared into the field of shaggy beasts and willed them to make some sort of a noise, anything that might indicate they were perturbed. But they just stood there, a bloody hell of a lot warmer than him.

'Don't you worry, they're the best looked after ribs in the world, I bet,' Calan said.

'Hmmm,' Lucas replied, before actually processing what he'd said. 'Hang about, what?'

'They're well looked after, I said...'

'No, I heard that part.' Lucas fought against his chattering teeth. 'What did you say about ribs?'

Calan laughed. 'Where do you think we get the beef from around here? It couldn't be fresher, that's telling the truth.'

Lucas's mouth dropped open. He ate meat, and obviously, he knew where it came from. But this seemed barbaric. These cows were right here, in front of his eyes. 'But... but they're a *family*!'

The words burst out from him without any real explanation. He felt sick looking at the poor cows, standing there, waiting helplessly for the next victim to be chosen. It wasn't right. He stepped back, his arms swaying about him, horrified.

'No way, that's not okay...'

'Lucas, but you eat meat!' Sandeep was chuckling, clearly enjoying his meltdown.

'I didn't mean to upset you...' Calan started.

Lucas watched Calan level Sandeep with an awkward look. For God's sake.

He was acting like a lunatic, wasn't he? Even the teenager could see it. Ever since he'd seen that Zach bloke, with his arrogant smirk and creepy eyes, he'd been thrown off his A-game. Sandeep would never say "yes" with him behaving like a nutjob. He took a deep, shaky breath. It was just nerves, that was all. It was natural. People always got jittery before they proposed. This was all a part of the course. If anything, it was probably endearing him to Sandeep even more. He laughed, forcing the sound out.

'Sorry! Sorry, phew! Bit of a funny turn... losing my wallet, the cold, the flight...'

Both Calan and Sandeep stared at him. Bloody hell, talk about letting him stew in it. *Thanks a bunch*, babe, he thought.

'Anyway, reckon it's about time for a cheeky snifter?' He threw a look at Sandeep which he hoped said, *yes, it is absolutely time for a cheeky snifter. Right now, please.*

'Errrm...' Sandeep held on to his gun, showing no sign of wanting to stop any time soon. He deferred to Calan.

'We've probably got another half an hour while the light's still all right,' he said.

Fantastic, thought Lucas. Well, if Sandeep wanted space, then he wasn't going to throw himself at him like some desperate idiot. No. He'd paid for this hotel and he'd bloody well go for a drink if he wanted to.

'Fine, fine. Right, so I'll see you back in the room then? Shouldn't be too long.'

'Sounds good,' said Sandeep, already lining up his next shot, his back turned away from him.

'Cool, cool. Well, good luck!' Lucas trilled as he turned on his heel, sure his face was glowing a beetroot-red. Obviously, Sandeep should have come with him.

Would it hurt to show a bit of gratitude? This behaviour reminded Lucas of their first date. He'd booked the swankiest sushi place in London. The way Sandeep had pretended he couldn't remember the name had been funny at first: '*Flirty Flounder? Slinky Sea-bream, is it?*' but it had begun to wear a little thin the third time around.

Sandeep had as good as cringed when they'd arrived, complaining about the bright lighting and, worse, the prices. The literal price of fish: that's what Sandeep had deemed acceptable date conversation. He'd also begged Lucas not to post his selfies... what else had he thought he was going to do with them?

But, despite all this, they'd formed a deep connection. It felt like Lucas was showing him the ropes, introducing a bit of glamour into Sandeep's previously lacklustre life; he'd been happy to be the proverbial wind beneath Sandeep's wings.

They flirted whilst planning the Year Ten ski trip together. Squeezing their legs under the low classroom desks, their heads moved closer and closer as they puzzled over the paper name tags. He found out afterwards that Sandeep had already worked out a quick way to assign the student dorms on Excel – he just hadn't told Lucas. It was an excuse for them to stay late in the empty classroom. What was it about schools after hours? The locker-lined corridors, the dimmed rooms always felt so exciting, like living a teenage fantasy all over again.

Lucas had been the one to initiate the kiss. It had been in the alley behind the school on the way to the Tube. He'd pressed Sandeep against the wall, one hand behind his head. He could still remember Sandeep's body moving against him, melting into his mouth.

Lucas wasn't stupid. He knew the stuff with his sister, Bebe, was heavy-going, especially since it all reared its head so early on in their relationship.

It began with the phone calls. At that stage, Sandeep hadn't known much at all about Lucas's family and didn't press the topic. But she'd kept calling, and each time, Lucas would find an excuse not to talk to her. *I'm not in the mood. I've got too much marking. I'm exhausted. She's not easy, you know? It's complicated.*

Then, one night when they were walking home from the pub, Sandeep had noticed a well-dressed woman hanging around outside their intercom. Lucas knew he'd spot the resemblance. He and his sister had the same long, straight nose and defined eyebrows, as well as the red, full lips that pinched slightly at the bottom.

'Let's go out!' Lucas had grabbed Sandeep's hand and turned back towards the Tube. 'Come on, it's early! The night is young!'

He must have looked ridiculous. Sandeep stumbled with the force of his pulling on him.

'Lucas!' she'd shouted, waving towards them. 'Lucas! It's me!'

'Is... Lucas... is that your...?'

'Just fucking ignore her, will you?'

'But...'

Lucas had stormed forwards, dragging Sandeep with him. In his panic, he hadn't been watching where he was going. A car had screeched. Sandeep fell, narrowly missing being hit.

'Look what you made me do!' Lucas remembered rounding on her. 'I told you to stay away! What are you doing here behaving like a... a little stalker?'

'I just want to talk...' she said. 'Please...'

'No. No, Bebe. You don't come another step towards me. Do you hear?' As it replayed in his mind, the blood ran thick and hot to his head. They hadn't seen each other again until the villa, which was a whole other trauma entirely.

He'd been through a lot lately. One would think his boyfriend might muster a bit of affection.

Lucas shook his head and headed back towards the main driveway. He stopped to stroke one of the friendlier-looking cow's heads.

'Families are pretty dysfunctional, aren't they?' he whispered. 'Know how you feel.'

As he began to make his way back inside, he paused. There was that feeling of someone looking where they shouldn't again.

Was that the sound of footsteps? He was sure of it. His eyes darted to the corner of the hotel, from where he'd just come.

An outdoor passageway covered by a stone roof wrapped around the wall leading to the shooting huts. There! He knew it. The whip of a coat disappearing behind one of the columns. That weirdo Zach, again! He steadied himself, readying to really give him a piece of his mind.

Lucas jogged towards the main doors of the hotel as if going inside, then, before heading in, ducked down around the opposite side, hoping to catch Zach face-on. He jogged along the lochside and turned left into a sort of courtyard area containing a small cabin that looked as if someone lived there. He passed what he guessed was the back door to the kitchen, judging from the delicious smell of roasting meat. *Ugh,* he thought. *Poor cows.* Then, glancing at the back of the shooting huts in the middle distance, where Calan and Sandeep were still shooting, he entered a colonnade, his fists clenched, his jaw tight with anger.

The walkway was empty.

Lucas let out a long sigh. He was glad Sandeep hadn't spotted him. What was he doing, running about chasing imaginary people? Obviously, no one was following him. Why would anyone want to do that? He just needed to exercise a good bit of self-care. He'd wound himself up, clearly. Paranoia, possessiveness, jitteriness. These were all telltale signs. He pulled his coat tightly around him and put his head down, thinking eagerly about the hot shower waiting for him in the room. He quickened his pace, keen to get inside as soon as possible.

That was when he spotted it. Crouching between the passageway and the bushes was a black, hairy mass. He jumped back: he'd stumbled upon a wild animal! His chest tightened. His mouth opened to shout for help, but no sound came out. Fear had silenced him. He was nothing but a helpless bit of prey. Wolves didn't exist up here, did they? He'd never outrun it. But then... didn't they hunt in packs? No, no... of course it wasn't a wolf. But then what was it?

From the heaving mass of fur emerged a small, pointed woman's face. His brain began to churn, catching up with what he saw in front of him. Ah. It wasn't an animal. It was a woman wearing a large fur coat. What was she doing down there in the cold? Whatever it was, she was clearly not happy about being interrupted.

'Oh, sorry, I...' Lucas frowned. From where he stood it looked as if she had been spying on Sandeep shooting. What was it with this place? Could no one behave normally here?

'You shouldn't be here,' she snapped at him, her eyes darting nervously from side to side. 'Go away.'

She spoke in what he thought was a heavy Italian accent. Lucas felt like he ought to do something; clearly, she was deranged, hanging about in the bushes in the middle of winter. He'd tell reception. Surely, they shouldn't let types like her into a place like this. Honestly, he couldn't be bothered with any more drama today. She was still giving him daggers anyway. He looked past her to the silhouetted figure of Sandeep. The gunshots had stopped. They'd be heading back soon. He was pretty sure that a tiny middle-aged woman wouldn't do them any damage.

'I said go!' she hissed at him.

'All right,' he said, shaking his head. 'Nutjob.'

As he walked away, he sensed a movement behind him and, spinning round, he watched the woman scurry up towards the courtyard and disappear into the greying light.

MARTA

God, most merciful, God, most forgiving and most loving! She could not believe she had been seen. She was usually so careful, so covert. She often felt like she could glide between the walls of this place, melt into the stonework and covings, and dance amongst the shadows. Would the guest tell anyone? She hoped not, with all her heart, she hoped not. She doubled over her bed in prayer.

She could not be careless with this. She knew that. Although, the desire to see him, to watch him, grew so strong. Sometimes it felt like her insides ached for him, like she would explode if she didn't have him there. She bit her lip, rubbing her hands together. She needed to get to work. Jules would be in the bar, frantically mixing cocktails and climbing up the ladder to fetch the ludicrous, rare whiskies the guests here always ordered. She'd be expecting Marta to walk past the bar and give her a gentle nod, as she always did, to let her know that everything was prepared, that she had her kitchen in control.

'I'm working on everything,' she whispered in Italian softly. 'I hope you can forgive me.'

Stupid woman, Marta thought. *It cannot hear you. You ask a memory for forgiveness!* She placed the photograph back on her corkboard, carefully inserting the pin in the top centre. Then, forcing the tears to drain from her eyes, she left for the kitchen.

The bar was too busy for one person to run it properly but there was no other option. They'd got by whilst Rob was here, but with him gone, Jules was hanging on by the skin of her teeth. She knew this calibre of guests would expect a sommelier, a mixologist, and a whisky connoisseur, but that was out of the question until the investment came in. If it came in.

Her plan had been to train Calan as a bartender, but he'd been a little off lately, more stroppy than usual, so she hadn't got around to it yet. Luckily, so far, she'd had no complaints. Perhaps her chipping in might be regarded by the guests as novel, a sort of homely quirk. Hopefully.

She had to admit, despite the money issues, the bar looked in fabulous nick. She and Rob had done most of the work themselves. They'd exposed the oak flooring underneath the carpet (why on earth would anyone have covered it up in the first place?) and reinstated the wooden panelling around the walls. The seating was all upholstered in a tasteful tartan or leather hide and fires crackled at both ends of the room.

Mr Williams, Zach, made his way to the bar. She repressed an excited kick in her stomach, trying to push the image of his bedroom out of her mind. Guests weren't here to be flirted with. She knew this. But the way her blood raced, the way her skin danced whenever she thought there was even the tiniest chance someone might find her appealing was intoxicating. Validating. She felt human again. A therapist had once said that romance was her way of distracting herself from her problems. Jules appreciated the phrasing: romance made it sound so pleasant, like a scene from a 1950s musical. If only the reality was so wholesome.

'How did you find the GlenAllachie? Like I said, it's a classic Spey—'

'I liked it.'

Zach slid onto the barstool and placed his elbows on the counter. He was tastefully dressed in a white shirt and wide-legged trousers. He exuded the sort of style that looked effortlessly thrown together yet cost the earth. A heavy cross-shaped necklace hung low around his neck. 'It was smooth, like I'd expect from a Speyside whisky, but it had something in the undercurrent...'

He licked his lips, as if trying to taste something invisible in the air.

Jules showed him the bottle. 'Some people say they get a mineral taste at the back. It's less caramel, more earthy than—'

'Yes, yes, that's it. God, I like it salty, don't you?'

His voice rooted itself somewhere deep inside of her. Her eyes darted upwards as her heart fluttered, and she let out a short laugh.

'I'm more of a peaty girl myself, I'm afraid,' she replied, trying to sound as casual as possible, despite the familiar heat she felt rising to the top of her chest.

'Oh, by all means, show me the way.'

He gestured to the whisky bar behind her, although his tone sounded like he meant something else entirely. She nodded, shot him a quick smile, nothing unprofessional, and turned to select her favourite Talisker.

'If you want to go peaty without it being overpowering, I'd try this.' She brought the bottle down from the shelf and placed it on the counter. 'From...'

'Skye,' Zach finished, obviously very pleased with himself. 'I know it well. Family has a holiday cottage there.'

'Right.' Jules raised her eyebrows, suspecting he might be using the upper-class euphemism for "cottage", which usually meant a small estate. 'This one's a rare expression, though. Give it a taste.'

She poured a tasting measure into a glass and slid it towards him. He pressed it to his lips. They cupped the glass ever so delicately as he took in the liquid. She watched the whisky work its way down his throat, down behind the thin trail of dark curly hairs that pushed up above his open collar. He was so handsome. He met her eyes, as if to say: *enjoying yourself over there?*

Feeling herself blush, she turned to check on the rest of the bar. The Melroses were tucked into a corner table next to the fire. They didn't seem to be having a good time at all. Tim Melrose scrolled on his phone whilst his wife gazed into the dark window. She should go and check on them, make sure there wasn't anything they needed.

Jules cleared her throat. 'One of the Talisker then?'

'Delicious,' Zach said, and gave her back the glass, his fingers lingering over hers. She couldn't be imagining this. He was definitely flirting, wasn't he? Nobody came on this strong without meaning to.

As she poured the full measure, her hopes were confirmed. He leant forwards and whispered in her ear, 'I say we should crack open a bottle in private, don't you think?'

She pushed her shoulders back, satisfied. She still had it

then. She was desirable. To this beautiful man, she was an object of lust. The scene of his bedroom loomed vividly in her mind. She thought of his bedsheets, the fire. Where would he want her? How? The dull warnings of her therapists dimmed in contrast to the thrill of it. What did they know anyway? A warmth spread down the back of her legs.

Jules let her cheek touch his, allowing their skin to caress for just a second and replied, 'Sure, looking forward to it.'

A loud tut from behind Zach pulled Jules out of the moment. It was Marta.

Zach gave Jules a delicious and secretive smile, before returning to his table. Jules sighed, folding her arms, trying to look like she was busy with the bar. Marta eyed Zach with a dark suspicion.

Jesus, thought Jules, *you're not my mother*. Couldn't she mind her business?

'Marta?' she said pointedly. 'All okay?'

'*Si, certo.*'

Marta was still staring at Zach. She had always been a bit of an oddball, but she'd never behaved like this before. Something moved beneath Marta's eyes – what was that? It was like she was remembering something. Did she recognise him from somewhere?

'Is there anything...?' Jules stepped between them.

'I came to tell you that everything's prepped.' Marta spoke absent-mindedly, her gaze still set on the guest.

As if in a trance, she stepped closer to Zach's table. Her cheeks had grown slack, her mouth hung open.

Marta took another step towards Zach who, thankfully, seemed to be enjoying the show. 'Errr, can I help you?' he drawled, a small smile etching across his face.

'No, no, no, no...' Marta edged forwards, her hands hovering before her, reaching towards him.

'Marta...' Jules couldn't understand what the woman was doing. She was normally so quiet, what had gotten into her?

'Marta, stop it now.'

Marta ignored her and bent forwards, now only inches away from Zach's face. 'It cannot, my God...' She was shaking her head now, vigorously from side to side. 'It cannot be... it cannot be...'

The Melroses were watching the scene unfold. Jules felt her stomach flip: this wasn't the first impression she wanted Tim to have of the whisky lounge.

Zach leant back in his chair, completely relaxed, viewing Marta like someone might watch a bluebottle fly trapped between two panes of glass. He stroked his neck playfully, like he was trying to goad Marta into doing something even more bizarre. His arrogance was astounding. Jules had never seen anyone so confident in their own skin.

'I cannot... it cannot be real...' Marta continued, her hands moving up to her mouth. Was she mistaking Zach for someone else?

'Oh, I think, therefore, I am, I assure you,' Zach said, chuckling deeply. 'I am real, truly.'

It was like he was toying with the situation, eager to see which way it would go. Marta shook her head, mumbling something in quick, hushed Italian. Had she been drinking? Or worse?

'Marta, now that's enough.' Jules tried to make light of the situation. She looked towards the Melroses who were still staring. *Shit.* She slipped out from behind the bar and put an arm around Marta's shoulder.

'Sorry,' she said, loud enough so everyone could hear. 'Just a bit of a misunderstanding... let's just get you to the kitchen...'

Marta scowled up at her, her brow screwed up into deep valleys of flesh. If she was suffering some sort of an episode, then who the hell was going to cook tonight? She'd need to have a proper word with her, just not here. She gently pulled her backwards and began to lead her away. Thankfully, Marta yielded to Jules's touch and hung her head, continuing to speak quietly to herself. It sounded like she was chanting, reciting some sort of incantation.

'That's great, just through here...' said Jules. Marta mumbled incoherently. Her lips worked through the cracked Italian syllables in little, wet bursts. She continued to bow forwards, her hands pressed against her chest.

Before she left, Jules looked over her shoulder at Zach. He raised his glass to her and slowly, as if inviting her beneath, tucked the necklace under his shirt.

ZACH

Sometimes the universe conspired against you and sometimes you were placed, unabashedly, at the centre of it. Zach hadn't quite believed it immediately. He wasn't a fan of coincidences. People who believed in them were usually trying to justify the reasons for their own pathetic shortcomings. Being poor was attributed to coincidence. Being ugly. Being fat too. Being shy, or stupid, or boring. People just weren't willing to conceive that it was all down to them. *They* were the problem.

Although this, surely, was an exception. This had to be a coincidence, and a beautiful one at that. What else could it be? Here, in the middle of nowhere, in this snowy corner of Scotland, he had found her. One of his beauties. One of *his*.

As soon as he'd opened Lucas's wallet, and seen the photo, he'd been charged with an excited energy. The memory of their first night, his first night with her, flooded back to him. He had been unable to move, frozen by the loch. Nerves, excitement, the audacity of being here with – by the looks of the note on the back – her brother. Hah! It took his breath away. She and him, she and her brother, they shared the same genes. The same blood.

When he'd got back to his room, he had located her relic: the necklace he'd taken from her flat. He'd fastened it around his neck. It felt right. It felt balanced. It would have been rude not to, given the circumstances.

She had been a tricky one in the lead-up, that had been part of the fun. He'd seen her come into the same café for lunch a few times. He liked to work publicly. He enjoyed the way people looked at him: an industrious, brooding creative nurturing ideas behind his Apple Mac, fuelled by flat whites.

He'd been staring at his screen, scrolling through the images on his hard drive, when he'd smelt her. He remembered that. She was the sort of woman who emanated a constant, noticeable freshness. Some did and some didn't. He peered at her over his laptop. She was in the queue asking for a takeaway cortado, oat milk, and a black lentil salad with grapefruit. She had good taste then. She knew how to look after herself too. It wasn't just the healthy order that gave it away; it was the way her cashmere coat hung from her body. Clothes only hung like that if the body was firm underneath.

As if she had sensed him watching her, she turned to him over her shoulder. Her eyes were a dark brown, almost black. She had no qualms about staring directly at him. She was almost aggressive in the way she held his gaze. Stern, hard, and certainly interested. He knew the drill. Someone like her wouldn't respond well to straightforward flirting. She'd enjoy the hunt. She'd enjoy thinking she was in control.

So, he had looked back down at his keyboard, dropping her gaze instantly.

He listened to her collect her order and hesitate, just for a millisecond, as she passed him on the way out. The net had been cast. He watched her the next day and then the next. On the fourth, he was sure she would make her move.

'Working on anything interesting?' This was what she had opened with.

The laptop was such an under-appreciated pick-up tool. It was the perfect way in, an easy focus for women who were trying to start a conversation.

'Oh!' He gave her a nervous smile, as if he was surprised that she had approached him. 'Nothing much, more of a pipe dream...'

'You're here most days.'

She didn't pose this as a question. She spoke with a heavy sort of intonation, as if she wanted every syllable to land with gravitas. Why? Did she need to fight for authority in some other area of her life? Already, he had found a thread to unpick.

'Yes.'

He closed his screen defensively. This would create an air of mystery, make her imagine that he was working on something classified. Like he knew they would, her eyes hovered momentarily over the closed laptop, her lips pressed together. Good. He had irritated her.

'How do you know that?'

He laboured over the word "that", making sure that the insinuation wasn't lost. *You've been watching me, have you?*

'I wouldn't flatter yourself.' She made an effort to sound condescending, but Zach spotted the small twitch of a smile at the corner of her mouth. The snare was set. All he had to do was allow for the passing of time.

Sure enough, she had become his, and much more seriously than he would ever have presumed. He usually limited the time frame of his conquests. It didn't do for them to become too attached. But she had resurfaced intermittently, perhaps every couple of weeks, over the course of the year. The way she looked at him was intense, like she wanted more but was too proud to ask.

He was surprised not to hear from her in a while. He was even more surprised to learn of her death. But, like with most tragedies, there were silver linings...

Back in the present, in this unexpectedly tasteful whisky bar, he sipped on the Talisker that Julia had suggested for him. She was turning out to be unexpectedly tasteful too, in some ways. She had something about her, a deep restlessness which she seemed to try and fight but couldn't quite shake. He'd noticed her hands shook very slightly when she poured whisky. When she blinked, she sometimes kept her eyes closed for a fraction too long, as if trying to suppress some part of herself. He would enjoy playing with her throughout the course of the evening, seeing how keen he could make her. The bar was the perfect setting for the build-up. The fire provided a seething, hot tension, not to mention a flattering light. He presumed she must live here, somewhere in the grounds. He was certain he could secure an invite into her home.

The day was turning out to be much more stirring than he had planned. And that was before that crazy old cook had turned up.

He stifled a snigger and took another sip of whisky. He was accustomed to having a certain effect upon the opposite sex but she'd been something else. The old cook had looked at him like he was a miracle apparition, a deity or something. Her eyes had bulged as she'd staggered closer to him. He'd half expected her to squeeze his cheeks and plant a crusty, stale kiss on his lips. What a character. Hopefully, her culinary skills would be fuelled with the same gusto.

As he laughed to himself again, Lucas and Sandeep entered the bar hand-in-hand. Zach could hardly believe he hadn't spotted the resemblance between him and his sister before: it was striking, really. Lucas was wearing an outfit he probably thought was sophisticated – tight, cheap-looking chinos, a blazer jacket that looked like nylon, not wool, and a ghastly, poorly fitted linen shirt. He could smell the nouveau aftershave from where he was sitting. Lucas shot him a filthy look as he walked past, whilst Sandeep gave him a small, apologetic wave. What an absolute pair.

Behind him, he listened to the awkward murmurings of evening greetings occurring between the two sets of couples. They were so stupid, choosing to stagnate like that. Tonight, he'd have more fun than any of them.

Julia re-entered the bar, looking flustered, like a shivering lamb.

LUCAS

Sliding into the empty corner sofa, Lucas reluctantly let Sandeep's hand slip from his. The bar was everything he'd imagined: roaring fires, heavy curtains made up from tartan fabrics, and a wall stocked tall with whiskies he'd never heard of.

The setting was perfect, but not much else. Sandeep had barely said a word to him all afternoon. He was acting like it was *his* fault that creep had been snooping about in his wallet.

'He was just helping you out,' Sandeep had said earlier. 'He found it for you, didn't he? He was just checking whose it was. You should be grateful.'

No. He would absolutely not be grateful. Sandeep hadn't seen the way that Zach fellow had been staring at his sister's face. It was like he was hungry for her, perverted and disgusting. There was undoubtedly something wrong with him. Lucas drummed his fingers on the table. Why was no one taking their drinks order? They'd been here for at least two minutes.

'What are you thinking?' He winked at Sandeep, nodding in the direction of the bar. Surely, a few expensive drams would loosen him up? That's what they were here for! Lucas grinned, beginning to feel a little better at the thought of his fireside Highland fantasy taking shape.

Sandeep, however, didn't meet his eye. Instead, he folded his arms and seemed to shrink back into the armchair. 'Might lay off the booze tonight, Lucas, all right? Bit of a long day and I'm shattered to tell you the truth.'

A whip of anger lashed in Lucas's belly, but he did an exceptional job of keeping his smile fixed and pleasant. Anything to keep Sandeep happy. 'Okay then...' He waved the receptionist down, wondering why on earth a place like this didn't have a full bar staff. 'Well, I'm going to enjoy myself!'

The words, which he'd meant to sound light-hearted and frivolous, came off as strained even to him. Sandeep said nothing and studied the window panes as if plotting an escape route.

It was rude, that's what it was. Couldn't he at least pretend he was having a good time? If he didn't brighten up, then this weekend would be a total failure. All that planning, all that plotting, all wasted because of Sandeep's inability to go with the flow.

The receptionist (and, apparently, bartender) approached their table, dragging her feet as if this wasn't her literal job. Lucas jutted his chin a little higher; she'd been incredibly unsympathetic when he'd complained about that madwoman earlier, basically just shrugging and behaving like he was making it all up. He raised his eyebrows and flicked through the leather-bound whisky menu, giving the air of someone who knew exactly what he was looking at.

'I'll take one of these!' He tapped something on the list that cost over £20 a measure.

She frowned and bent over to see what he was pointing at. 'The Macallan 21 Fine Oak?'

'That's the one!' he tolled, wondering whether he ought to

have gone for something more adventurous. Macallan was a good one, he was sure, but she didn't sound too impressed.

'Anything else I can get...?'

Her voice trailed off at the end and, instead of finishing her sentence, she actually looked over her shoulder to give Zach what appeared to be a flirtatious pout. What the hell was happening? Lucas felt his mouth fall open at her audacity. She probably thought she looked sexy, but in all honesty, she seemed a tad desperate. He almost wanted to advise her to play it cooler. No, he wanted to advise her to stay away from that creep.

Zach, who was sitting alone and flicking through his camera, didn't even notice her. She turned, her cheeks a little red, back to their table. 'Anything else...?'

'No, thank you,' Lucas said, staring at Sandeep, secretly hoping he'd change his mind and join him. He continued to stare out of the window. 'Drinking solo tonight, apparently.'

She nodded, clearly preoccupied by whatever vibe she thought she had going on, and returned to the bar.

'So...' Lucas flexed his palms, his arms outstretched in front of him. If he needed to start the chat, then he would. He was used to these silent spells from Sandeep. Usually, he could bring him back without too much trouble. Once, on holiday in Santorini, they'd had a fight about something not worth remembering. Sandeep had behaved in a similar way then: begrudgingly coming to dinner, moping here, moping there, being a general downer. Little had he known that Lucas had organised for the restaurant's band to serenade them upon their entrance! Sandeep had had no choice but to buck up his ideas once Lucas began dancing. Unfortunately, there didn't seem to be any such band available here, which was fine. Lucas could rely on his sparkling conversation.

'...the weather looks like it's coming in, doesn't it? Better wrap up for this winter picnic tomorrow, eh?'

Sandeep grunted, but at least dragged his eyes away from the window to look at him. 'I'm sure they'll provide blankets.'

'Oh yes, hopefully!'

The receptionist returned with his whisky and he swiped it off the table immediately to give it a sniff. 'Mmmm...'

Sandeep actually rolled his eyes. 'I didn't even know you liked whisky.'

'When in Rome!' He gave it a quick nip. To be fair, it tasted a lot smoother than the supermarket stuff he'd been swigging from the hip flask. Maybe he was a whisky person after all?

Tension began to ebb from Sandeep's shoulders and he managed a weak smile. Lucas grinned – he knew it – all it took was a little tickle of encouragement. 'Sure you don't want a drink?'

Before Sandeep answered, a man's shout erupted from the adjacent sofas. 'Will you just drop it, for Christ's sake!'

Gracie, the miserable Scottish girl who had got lost earlier, and a man, whom Lucas presumed was her husband, glanced up simultaneously as if they were afraid of being overheard. Gracie was gripping the soft leather of the chair with both hands, her knuckles white. Her eyes were wide and glassy like she was on the brink of tears.

Lucas raised his whisky to her, hoping to diffuse whatever was going on. 'Cheers. Found your way back then?'

Gracie began to answer but she bit her lip as her husband cut in. 'Sorry about all that. She can get a bit... manic sometimes. Obviously, I should have come along. Hope it didn't ruin your outing?'

Sandeep cleared his throat uncomfortably. Lucas agreed: the man's tone and manner seemed, at least on the surface, demeaning and controlling. He tried to catch Gracie's eye but she was resolutely staring at the fire, lost in her thoughts. His gaze shifted to the husband again. He was one of those men who looked like they would have belonged to a "sports club" at university, without actually playing any sports. He held himself with a confidence bordering on arrogance in the way his lips curled ever so slightly up at the edges, the way his eyebrows drew closer together as he awaited a response.

'Sorry, I'm Lucas, and this is my boyfriend, Sandeep. I don't think we've met?' He made sure to make his tone as neutral as possible. In his experience, men like him could flip at the smallest of things.

'Tim.' The man held his own whisky up and dipped his head before turning his attention back to his wife 'Oh, Gracie... Gracie... will you just pull it together.'

How he spoke to her made Lucas's skin crawl. Clearly, Sandeep had a similar opinion – he turned his back to Tim and shot Lucas a meaningful look.

Gracie showed no sign of responding. Lucas held his tongue, deciding to mind his own business. There was enough to focus on this weekend without getting caught up with whatever marital disaster was going on over there. And, anyway, he told himself, he didn't really know anything about these people at all. There could be a hundred reasons behind Tim's attitude.

'Nice meeting you both.' He shifted back into his armchair to face Sandeep, who was browsing the drinks menu. Lucas smiled. 'Change of heart?'

Sandeep smirked. 'Oh, go on then...'

'Twisted your arm...?'

'Something like that...'

'Know your whiskies, boys?' Tim was calling across the room in a voice that was just a tad too loud for comfort. The creep Zach turned to watch him, an odd, enraptured expression on his face.

'We're just browsing,' Sandeep responded curtly without turning around.

Lucas gave a small nod, planning to follow his lead, when Tim continued. 'Let me know if you want some help with navigating the menu. Thinking of investing in this place, so I know my stuff somewhat.'

He sniggered in a way that suggested he was very pleased with himself as the receptionist brought him another drink. 'Of course, being the money man brings a few perks...'

The words were clearly meant as bait. Gracie's eyes flew towards the receptionist as she set the glass down, her cheeks flaring pink with embarrassment. It was the reaction Tim seemed to be going for. When he'd made a show of looking the receptionist up and down for his wife's benefit, he waved dismissively for her to leave, and sniffed at the whisky, his eyes closed. 'I meant the whisky, Gracie, darling. The free drinks are the perks. Don't look so alarmed...'

Gracie looked like she would quite happily strangle her husband right on the spot, and Lucas did not blame her one bit.

Sandeep tapped the menu, signalling he'd chosen what he wanted. 'She looks busy,' he said, eyeing the receptionist as she giggled with Zach, who had returned to the bar. The upper half of her body pretty much splayed over the counter.

'And would you like that clean or dirty?' She fumbled over the words, like she could barely believe she was saying them. It was the most cringeworthy attempt at flirting Lucas had ever heard. He caught Sandeep's horrified face and they both gave a delighted snort.

Lucas wiped his eyes and shook his head as he composed himself. Good. They were back on track. *We're laughing. We're having a bloody fun time. That's what we're supposed to be doing. That's how it has to be.*

CALAN

Calan finished sweeping up the smashed mugs in his bothy. If he'd found Lucas annoying on the hike, he was now pretty certain the guy was, as his dad would say, "a few chickens short of a run". The way he'd raged about dropping his wallet had been something else. And then he hadn't even thanked the other guest for finding it! He was used to *types*, but they weren't usually this bad.

The snow was about as heavy as it got, so he'd be staying here tonight. He'd started storing some stuff under one of the beds. His toothbrush, a book, Scrabble (which he liked to play alone) and the shoebox. He slid it out carefully. It was beginning to fall apart.

Instinctively, he checked over his shoulder. The early evening was the best time to hang out in the bothy. He was most likely to be left alone, while everyone was busy, but the door could open at any time, really. Since the bothy was intended to be used by guests for when they were hiking, no lock had ever been installed. He noticed his hands trembling and glanced up at the wood-burner. It was blazing.

Closing his eyes, he rested his forehead against the foot of the bed. Recently, the flashbacks had been getting stronger, more vivid, like it was all happening again in horrible multicolour. He used to be so good at blocking it out. While he was still an apprentice, he'd worked out how to compartmentalise everything. There was work. Then home. Then sleep. Then *that*.

Fingers laced at the back of his head as he pulled away. Low and breathy whispers filling the heated space. Moans that he wished hadn't come from his lips, but had.

Shaking his head, he placed the box on his lap, and began sorting through the information again, as he had done so many times before.

The photograph of his birth mother lay on the top of the pile. She was young in the image. Her smile seemed nice and her eyes twinkled like she knew he'd be staring at her all these years down the line. He put the photograph to one side and removed the thick pile of paperwork from the box. The letters between his parents and the agency written about eighteen years ago were mainly just administrative. Over the years, Mum and Dad had sent them updates about him: his first day at nursery, school, his birthdays, his National 5 results. For as long as he could remember, he'd always known he was adopted. The fact had just never really featured significantly in his life. He'd never thought about it too much.

Until now of course.

Work was tight in the area. He was lucky to have this job. It was relatively well-paid and, as his mates reminded him, the free kegs of beer were amazing. They didn't know about what happened here, though, did they? They didn't know how much working here made his teeth ache with guilt and embarrassment, and whatever that hot feeling of suffocation was. They didn't know how his stomach trembled and flipped every time he found himself alone, how he always knew it was just a matter of time until the next ordeal.

These papers now symbolised his only way out of here.

He'd requested his birth mother's address just under a couple of years ago, thinking she might know of a job going, wherever she lived. After a few months, the agency responded stating that his "birth mother" would be happy to "receive correspondence" from him and provided her address.

He'd never expected her to be loaded. However, after googling the area in which she lived, where she worked, and scrolling through her active social media accounts, he'd realised she had money. Bags of it. She might be able to *really* help, he'd thought. Mum and Dad worked in the local Scotmid; they didn't have the sort of funds to help him move away. And anyway, they'd ask all sorts of questions about why he wasn't happy at the hotel and Mum would start getting nosey and, well, he couldn't think about what they'd say if they found out the truth. His heart thumped in a fit of anxiety just imagining it.

It was a matter of getting all his ducks in a row. You couldn't just ask people for money, *especially* rich people. They were a selfish bunch. He saw how they behaved every day. All the cash most people could only dream about, and they squandered it on half-arsed hunting trips, congratulating themselves when they managed to shoot something, when really the set-up, the trail, everything, had been done by him. Afterwards, they celebrated by drinking the most overpriced whisky he'd ever seen without even batting an eyelid. If this was the world of his "birth mother", then he had to tread carefully, or his one chance would be blown. It's not like she'd ever reached out to him, was it?

Gathering the papers and placing them back in the box, he stood and wriggled into his coat for the evening jobs. He had to perform his nightly security check on the rifles, before popping into the kitchen to see if help was needed serving. He opened the door to the outside. The snowfall was now nearing a blizzard and the wind slammed it closed behind him, making him jump forwards in surprise. Hunched over, his face taking the brunt of the icy wind, he had the familiar feeling of being watched. As he approached the main hotel building, he stopped for a second to look out over the loch. Through the fits of snow, the moon beat grey and restless on the thin ice, giving the impression of tiny, shadowy mouths gasping beneath the glassy surface. Breathing out in a cloud of steam, he made for the gun room just by the main entrance.

The door swung open easily, and he swore beneath his breath. He'd forgotten to enter the code again. It must have been unlocked for hours, even though Jules had repeatedly told him to keep the room secure at all times. He wasn't sure what she was so worried about. They were in the middle of nowhere here, and the guests were the sort that probably struggled making their own breakfasts, let alone stealing a rifle. He hit the light switch and stood back to count the weapons. He'd cleaned them all earlier and put them all on their correct display hooks. Usually, this was a twenty-second job.

Calan swore again, this time more loudly. He stared into the room and blinked, hoping he was seeing things. This wasn't how he'd left the rifles. His forehead grew clammy and cold. There was a vacant space on the wall.

Somebody had taken a gun.

LUCAS

Three whiskies down, and Sandeep was beginning to get with the programme. Lucas moved his fingers in happy, sensuous circles along the back of Sandeep's hand, the smell of the burning logs mixed with alcoholic goodness sending every muscle in his body into a satisfied lull.

He wondered whether he ought to order some champagne before dinner. They had half an hour before he'd made the reservation, so there was probably time. Would that be too obvious though? Two bottles in one day? He didn't want to give the game away, nor, he mused, give Sandeep another excuse to get all weird about money.

'Another bevvy, we've got time...' He raised his eyebrows suggestively.

Sandeep sighed and pulled his face into something between a smile and a grimace. 'You're really pushing it this weekend, hmmm...'

Lucas kept calm, but couldn't help but feel yet another twinge of irritation. Pushing what, exactly? Fun? Excitement? Spontaneity? How awful that must be for the poor man! Sometimes, he thought Sandeep had no idea how lucky he was to have a boyfriend like him. There weren't many people who'd put up with his attitude. He'd better react with at least medium enthusiasm tomorrow. Surely, it would be impossible not to?

He was going to head out early to find the perfect spot: he was thinking about doing it by the loch. He'd hide a champagne bottle somewhere in the snow and pretend he fancied a little stroll along the shore. He even had a little speech prepared: *Remember when we first met? All that sneaking about, secret drinks, and covert kisses after school in my office? I didn't think it would turn serious! You were quiet, I'm... well, apparently I talk too much (PAUSE FOR LAUGHTER). You like staying in, I don't. But... well, there's something in what they say about opposites attracting, isn't there? Because, despite our many differences, I love you, Sandeep. I can't think of another...*

'Why are you smiling like that?' Sandeep prodded him and Lucas gave him his best, mysterious expression.

'Let's just say I'd like this weekend to be memorable,' he purred in a low and sexy voice.

Disappointingly, Sandeep didn't bite the bait. He frowned and looked over his shoulder towards Gracie and Tim. Lowering his voice, he said, 'Locked in a remote castle with that dickhead? I'm sure "memorable" won't be a problem.'

Lucas chuckled, secretly irked at Sandeep's incessant ability to focus on the negatives, and looked up to flag some more drinks. The receptionist, who was still embarrassing herself with Zach the creep, caught his eye, and began to approach their table but was distracted by Calan who burst into the bar, breathless and panting.

'Jules!' He scanned the room wildly before settling his eyes on her. Lucas hoped she'd have the sense to serve her guests before dealing with him, but, of course, she rounded back.

Groaning impatiently, he downed what remained of his

whisky. 'I'm going to the bar, hopefully she'll take the hint. Your wish is my command!'

He flicked his hands theatrically in what was definitely a very amusing impression of a genie. Sandeep met him with a weak smile. 'Just a glass of red then—'

'We'll have wine at dinner—'

'Lucas, I want a glass of red. Nothing too pricey. Just the house stuff.'

Lucas bit his tongue. If he wanted cheap wine, then he could have cheap wine. Their differences were their strengths... oh, hang on! He wondered whether he ought to insert that line into his proposal speech.

He strode purposefully towards the bar and leant over it, drumming his fingers on the dark wood surface. The creep, who was still sitting on a stool, levelled a gaze at him. 'I think it's table service only, mate. She's run off her feet.'

He spoke with such an imperious sneer, as if Lucas needed educating on how to behave properly, that he felt the red flush of anger rush up his neck. Nevertheless, he pushed the image of this guy ogling over his sister's photograph out of his mind. Sandeep wouldn't react well to another confrontation. 'Thanks. But I'll wait here.'

Zach shrugged and continued to stare at him as the staff exchanged, quite frankly, off-putting whispers on the other side of the room. Lucas pulled out his phone and tried to focus on scrolling, but couldn't ignore the weight of this guy's eyes on him.

'Look,' he said in a very quiet voice, hoping Sandeep wouldn't hear. 'I don't want any trouble, but what's your problem?'

This seemed to amuse Zach greatly. His lips curved into a smooth and calculated smile. 'You tell me.'

Lucas opened his mouth to respond, but realised he had no

idea what to say. Clearly, he was dealing with a complete narcissist, perhaps a sociopath, maybe even a psychopath. The way Zach's eyes glittered, set dead and cold, was truly arresting. He wouldn't be sucked into whatever game he wanted to play. He shook his head, relieved the receptionist woman was now slipping behind the bar. 'A glass of—' Lucas began.

Calan followed closely at her heels. Now that the red slap of the outside had faded from his cheeks, he looked pale and worried.

'Calan, I said I'll look into it.'

The receptionist woman – Jules, as Calan had called her – waved her hand in the air dismissively and forced a smile in Lucas's direction.

Lucas tried to order the drinks again, but Calan barged his way behind the bar and grabbed her shoulder. She turned towards him, her face set into something that resembled a smile, but was more of a baring of teeth. 'Go and help Marta!'

'But...' His eyes grew wet. 'I don't understand why—'

'Calan!' she hissed and grabbed him by the arm, leading him out from behind the bar and through the arched doorway to the hall. Lucas groaned.

'Told you,' Zach said next to him, back to looking at his camera. 'Table service only. Can't get the staff these days.'

Lucas glanced at Sandeep, who seemed completely content alone, reading that weird self-help book he'd brought with him (why, oh why would you bring a book to a bar?) and followed Jules and Calan into the entrance hall.

'I wouldn't...' the creep called behind him.

Their voices drifted from the other side of the wide staircase. He gathered himself as he approached, ready to apologise for interrupting, whilst sounding understandably annoyed – as any guest *would* be – before demanding his drinks.

At this rate he and Sandeep would be moving into the dining room before they could finish.

Something about the tone of Calan's voice made him stop out of sight at the foot of the stairs.

'She won't stop!' His words were wobbly. He sounded helpless, much younger than someone who had already left school.

'Keep it down, Calan.' Jules's voice was soothing, yet firm. 'I'll talk to her, okay?'

'No!' The fear was palpable. 'No. I just... I wish she'd leave me alone. I can't stand the thought of...'

'I understand.'

Lucas nodded approvingly to himself. Jules was saying the right things. She was reassuring and sympathetic. It's exactly how he spoke to students when they were disclosing distressing information. He hoped she was being genuine, because it sounded like someone in Calan's life was causing him significant stress.

'What if it's her?' Calan sounded more sure of himself now, and he sighed loudly. 'You should be worried too...'

'I said I'll speak to her.' Jules cleared her throat and it sounded like Calan was blowing his nose.

They were around the corner before Lucas could disappear back into the bar. He froze for a second, taking in their surprised faces.

'Oh!' He sprang into action, noticing how dry his mouth had become. 'Sorry! There you are! I was waiting to order some drinks?'

Calan shot him a stormy look and rushed out of the main door. A horrible gust cut through the warmth, sending a shiver down Lucas's spine, before it shuddered closed. He looked at Jules, expecting an explanation, but she visibly drew herself up, her face erupting into an exaggerated smile, her hands clasped before her stomach.

'Now, what was it you were after?' She walked towards the bar, and beckoned for him to follow.

Lucas stared at the door. Was it worth telling her he had experience with teenagers? How well would that go down? As an employer, she should know how to support vulnerable staff members. It sounded like Calan was really going through something and she was the person to whom he'd decided to turn. That was a serious responsibility. He pursed his lips.

'Um, what red wine do you have by the glass...?'

MARTA

And so, this proved they had a most special connection. A connection approved by God. Marta knew something beyond the human, beyond the physical world had caused Calan to stop before the loch this evening. She had watched him look out over the hardened water, still and perfect. He had sensed her watching him, she knew. He had sensed her presence, which meant he needed her, as she had always needed him.

God moved in ways nobody was meant to understand. Yet, sometimes, for a special few, the signs revealed themselves with the most beautiful clarity. To behold what she had in the bar earlier! That was intervention. It had to be. His Holiness had sent her a signal, a token, an encouragement to carry on with her mission. She should not have reacted so obviously, but she could not help herself. It was a shining example of His divine guiding hand. God was clearly reaching out to her.

Why else would He have sent a man wearing that very necklace? She would have recognised it anywhere, since it was one of a kind. She had made it herself in a lacklustre church hall in a lonely bid to fill one of her first weekends in London all those years ago. The bright-red stone, the way she had bent the metal clasps above it to form her initials: M.V., the volute crucifix designed by her own hand. She thought she would never see it again, yet, here it was in the hotel. It had made its way back to her. God had sent it back to her as a sign. That meant he blessed what she was doing. He was on her side, as she had always known He was.

Of course, God understood there were all sorts of love, although not all of them were cherished by non-believers. But God clearly approved what she was to Calan, and what he was to her. There was no denying it. And now she knew what she had to do. If she was his protector before, she was now his guardian. Sin manifested everywhere in this place. Sin manifested everywhere in the world. But what she and Calan shared was pure. Guard him she would. Now, she had a divine mandate to use whatever means were available to her.

As she sprinkled the finishing garnishes onto the first table's starters, she thought about the rifle hidden beneath her mattress and nodded in grave observance.

JULES

She and Rob had decorated the anteroom as a tasteful reception area. They'd sanded the wooden panelling and floorboards, revarnished, bought a cheap Persian rug from an old manse sale, sourced oil paintings from the local charity shops, hung them, and fitted a huge stone fireplace. It had taken a lot of sweat, a few tears, but they had both thought it would be worth it.

The plan had been to use it as a cocktail station for when the hotel was hired out for weddings. There had, to date, been only one, which suffered the onslaught of the Scottish rain and a twenty-five per cent refund due to the food caterers breaking down on the way and missing the wedding breakfast. That 1* review – scathing of the "incompetent woman who purported to run the place" – still made Jules cringe with shame.

Neither she nor Rob had ever envisioned the room being used for the purpose it was at this moment. Zach held her waist with both hands as she perched on a side table. His forehead pressed against hers, his dark eyes drinking in her every pore. He was a phenomenal kisser. She allowed him to move from her mouth, to her neck, to the tops of her breasts.

'Okay...' She breathed, loving how rough and ragged her voice sounded. 'Okay, I need to get back to work.'

'Let them wait.' His voice would have been enough to make parts of her tighten with desire, but he also moved his hands to the top of her trousers.

She let out a stifled gasp of delight and moved closer to him, pushing her hips towards his. She nuzzled into his neck. All the guests would be in the dining room by now. She really should get to the kitchen to help Marta, but... would it be so terrible if she skipped tonight? That inebriated sensation, the elated and breathless feeling of being desired, took hold. The scent of his skin, so close and intimate, made her toes tingle, made her bones ache. She giggled and rolled her head backwards, exposing her throat to him.

'I'd love to stay,' she murmured.

He nodded in silence, dragging his eyes along her upper body ever so slowly. 'I'd like to have you,' he said.

The bluntness of the statement was almost too much for her. There was something potent about his elongated vowels, the way he carried himself in a cavalier, offhand manner. She tugged him closer, but he pulled back.

Her eyes widened with confusion. Had she missed something? 'What is it?'

His lips moved into a seductive curve. 'Not in a hurry. I want to take my time with you. I want to have you for the whole night.'

She nodded, understanding his meaning, and leant in for a long kiss. His lips worked against hers with the skill of a man who knew exactly what he was doing. She moaned, pulling at the front of his shirt, her hands finding her way beneath it to his chest. She fingered his crucifix pendant. 'Are you very religious?'

She'd meant it as a little joke, given their current

entanglement, but he didn't laugh. For a split-second – she was sure she imagined it – she saw a darkness move behind his eyes. A strange impulse to run shuddered in the pit of her belly, but then it was gone.

He cocked his head to one side, as if considering the question ever so carefully. 'Not in the conventional sense.'

She slid off the table so that her torso pressed against his. He didn't move back. Placing her hands on her hips, she mirrored the angle of his head, injecting a playful glint into her eyes. 'Why do you wear a crucifix then?'

He slowly brought his hand to the chain around his neck and drew the pendant out. He held it gingerly, like it was his most prized possession. He must have been kidding himself – he was acting about as devout as they come. 'Kiss it.'

'What?' She laughed aloud and smacked a hand against her mouth. God, she felt drunk on this exchange. It was electrifying.

'Kiss it.'

He was dead serious. His face almost seemed stone-like. The only movement was a light twitch at the corner of his eye, barely perceptible. He reminded her of the big cats she'd seen in wildlife documentaries, how they existed in a moment of almost complete stillness before the concentrated sprint towards their prey.

She smiled, playing along with his game. 'Why?'

'Just kiss it.'

His words were calm, yet insistent. She giggled again, although she wasn't quite sure what she was supposed to find funny. Her heart gave a soft thud behind her ribs. She frowned, feeling her smile falter for a moment, before drawing in her lips.

'I don't think so.'

He stared at her, unresponsive. Then, he slowly moved the crucifix closer to her face. It almost touched the tip of her nose, and she breathed in the metallic, musty smell. From this angle, it was impossible not to judge the thing in more detail. It certainly wasn't her style of jewellery. Gothic, volute palmettes of tarnished silver wrapped around the figure of Jesus, who hung, his face pulled in anguish, his arms outstretched. In the centre of his chest was a dark, blood-red stone. She didn't know Zach well at all, but the piece didn't seem to match the rest of his style, which was best described as metropolitan elite. It was too dark for him, too grounded, like something you'd find in an old coastal junk shop.

'Do as I say.'

She'd never really been one for games like this, but he was very attractive. Plus, there was a certain elicit excitement attached to becoming entangled with a guest. Fleetingly, she wondered how she'd explain this in her next therapy session. She locked eyes with Zach. She didn't need to explain anything. Why did she always feel like she had to validate herself? Maybe the therapists were wrong. Maybe Rob was wrong. Maybe she wasn't destructive or masochistic or sex-obsessed. Maybe she was the normal one and *they* were abnormal. What was wrong with a bit of excitement? It made her feel alive, didn't it? It stopped her feeling dead inside. It made her feel *something*, at least.

She gently pressed her lips against the metal, grazing Zach's fingers as she kissed it. It wasn't an entirely pleasant taste. It was old, earthy and bitter. She drew back and he sighed as if he was relieved. Stepping to one side, she smoothed out her clothes.

'I need to get back,' she said, trying her best to sound as nonchalant as possible. Then, because she couldn't help herself, 'That was fun.'

He took his time, tucking the necklace under his shirt, a small smile forming. 'It was. I still want you though.'

The words were everything she needed to hear. He wanted her. She was desirable. He – this random man – wanted her. 'All right. Later – I'll come to your room. It shouldn't be too late. I just need to finish dinner service.'

He nodded and, almost so quickly that she thought she'd imagined it, licked his upper lip with a serpentine tongue. 'Your place, not mine.'

She nodded, enjoying the demands he placed on her.

'It's on the floor above yours. Follow the stairs at the end of the corridor, turn left, and it's the unmarked double doors. Wait for me there. I'll leave it unlocked.'

With that, she left him in the anteroom, a heat emanating from the base of her spine.

ZACH

Julia had been precisely as he'd imagined. That energy she carried beneath her skin, jittery and nervous, had reached through her kisses. She was desperate for touch, thirsty for it. Usually, he wouldn't have cared for her body. Her flesh gave way beneath his fingers, soft and pliable, soon to be saggy. But the way she held herself interested him.

She had no business being so sexually confident, yet she was. There had been no attempt at all to suck in her stomach. She hadn't tried to move her chin to stretch out the first signs of jowls. No. She had stood before him as if she was proud of herself. It was as if the promise of pleasure, of him, had filled her with an insatiable sense of abandon. She'd even left her staff in the lurch at dinner service... all for him.

The young Calan was hovering around in the bar when Zach emerged from the anteroom, pacing up and down, asking after "Jules" in a terrible panic. Zach silently thanked his lucky stars he'd never been in this boy's unenviable position... to be forced to waste his time on pointless, meaningless tasks. No wonder the lad looked so downtrodden.

'I heard... thought I heard... I just needed her... to talk...'

Calan mumbled, looking at his feet, and then at the anteroom door with telltale embarrassment. Zach suddenly realised why the boy was so ruffled: he'd obviously spied on his and Jules's rendezvous whilst searching for his boss. Perhaps he'd watched for longer than he ought to have? Got a little bit out of it himself? Zach didn't blame him. Between scrubbing floors and clearing up after people all day, he'd have done the same.

'I'll take a quick martini,' Zach replied, changing the subject to spare the poor boy's awkwardness. Calan had looked like he might protest, but he'd eventually obeyed. Thinking he was being sly, he got out his phone to search how to make the drink.

'Vodka,' Zach offered. 'With a twist.'

Calan bit his lip, his pale cheeks stained with a red blotch on either side, and nodded. He measured the vodka clumsily, his hands all over the place. It was a wonder, really. A boy his age must know about sex by now? There was no reason for him to be so shaken.

Calan slid the drink over the bar towards him. 'Um, there you go.'

Zach nodded and took a quick nip. He smiled. 'Pretty good.'

Calan performed a strange shuffle like he didn't know what to do with his limbs. He was uncomfortable. Something was really bothering him, making his blood itch. What could it be? Zach settled his gaze on him. He always wanted to *know*. He always had an insatiable desire to possess, to chew all the anxieties that pulsed beneath people's skin. It seemed like Calan had something to hide.

'Do you enjoy working here?'

The question caught him off guard. He took a shallow breath and Zach noticed a thin film of sweat form on his upper lip.

'It's not too bad.' Calan cleared his throat and looked

towards the door which led to the main hall. The faint sound of cutlery scraping on plates drifted from the dining room. What was making him so nervous?

'Must be lonely working in a place like this. There can't be many people your age about.' Zach was fishing. He held his breath to see if he would bite the bait.

Undeniably, he'd hit a nerve. The sweat on Calan's lip thickened, his cheeks reddened into a deeper shade. So, there was a story here then... perhaps an illicit lover? Someone from the village? Maybe he snuck them into the hotel when he wasn't supposed to? He had a secret, that was for sure.

Calan grit his teeth and smoothed down the front of his apron. 'Sometimes wish I could get a minute more to myself, actually.'

A laugh followed, but there'd been a palpable tension in his voice. Before Zach could answer, he nodded to the martini. 'If you'd like anything else, just ring the bell, or help yourself to the whiskies in the decanters. They're complimentary.'

With that, he headed out of the bar, shoulders hunched, head hung low. How intoxicating other people's burdens were.

In the dining room, Zach let a lump of tender steak sit on his tongue as he watched Julia hurry around the tables taking dessert orders. It was perfectly rare and bloody, which was surprising. Julia had secured a half-decent chef in that mad old bat. Lucas and Sandeep were ordering the chocolate fondant to share. What was it with poor people over-enunciating that word? 'For *dessert*, I'll have...'

Where Zach came from, people said "pudding". "Dessert" was so pretentious, so try-hard. This pair's entertainment value was getting better and better though. Sandeep displayed so many obvious signs of disinterest. He averted his eyes whilst Lucas was speaking to other people as if embarrassed; his legs were tucked firmly beneath his chair to create as much distance as possible between him and his boyfriend; when Lucas made a joke, his laugh was flaccid and limp.

Of course, Lucas didn't notice any of this. He was so preoccupied with the image he wanted to portray to the world that he seemed oblivious to how he really came across. Zach smirked and swallowed his food. Hopefully, he would get to watch it all blow up in their faces. He'd seen Lucas patting the top left-hand pocket of his coat earlier. Did he have a ring, per chance? Was this meant to be a very special weekend? Oh, Zach hoped so. He really, really hoped so.

Julia sent him a particularly desperate glance before she disappeared into the kitchen, laden with dirty plates. He downed his wine ready for the night ahead. The 24mm lens would be required for later. When he'd first started this project, he'd assumed it would be difficult to persuade people to have their photograph taken. Actually, the opposite was true. It turned out post-coital women were particularly camera-confident. He'd only ever had a few pushbacks, and these had been placated with a few strategic compliments.

Walking up the stairs towards his room, he heard the sound of raised and angry voices. The Melroses had enjoyed a disastrously short dinner. Neither of them had spoken much at all, and Gracie had appeared deliciously sullen. Interestingly, Zach had watched her slip a steak knife under the long sleeve of her velvet top instead of leaving it to be collected from the table.

'Naughty Gracie...' he whispered as he passed their door, the shouts getting louder. 'What are you planning to do with that?'

'*Just tell me the truth!*'

'*You have the truth, for Christ's sake! Or do you want to be wound up? Is that it? You want to be driven mad?*'

'*How dare you say that to me—*'

'*You're fucking insane! You know what you get like...*'

Closing his door, he rested his head against it for a few seconds. It was relaxing to allow his face to drop, the guise to fall. When he was around people, he had to perform. He had to insert a light into his eyes, he had to tense his facial muscles. He had to make sure he looked like one of them. It was good fun, most of the time. But, like all masks, it wore thin eventually. The first few moments of being in his own company were always bliss.

Kneeling before his trunk, he lay out his camera equipment on the floor. He ran his fingers over the black metallic parts, wondering in what position he would ask Julia to arrange herself. She would probably be willing to go topless, if not completely nude, given how easy she'd been to manipulate so far. He licked his lips, intrigued by the prospect of her naked body.

He was about to leave for her flat, when he spotted the note written on hotel stationery. It was on his pillow, balanced carefully. He opened the card and smiled.

Let's be adventurous tonight. Meet me by the loch at 11pm. There's a fishing hut down the path. About a ten-minute walk.

Zach slumped on the bed, his imagination racing. This was entirely within keeping with her character, of course. She would have been plotting all night, wondering how she could push the limits, groping about for ideas to make herself seem more alluring. He'd need access to her room eventually. How else would he obtain his souvenir? But there was a whole weekend for that. And this fishing hut sounded good.

He didn't mind if he obliged at all. Not one bit.

The fishing hut was, as Julia had said, just along the way from the main lochside path, right on the shore. It felt a long way from the hotel from here; clearly, she intended for them to enjoy some privacy.

Inside was a wood-burner, which was crackling brightly – a nice touch. He'd never actually been fishing before, but was fairly certain most huts weren't equipped with leather armchairs, a mini-fridge, and a sheepskin rug. Zach helped himself to a glass of Chablis and put his feet up. Predictably, she was running a few minutes late. She probably thought she was being fashionable. No matter. He wasn't in a rush.

The door swung open very slowly. From where he was sitting, the dancing shadows of the flames made it impossible to see Julia's face.

'Aren't you coming in?'

He took another quick sip, and blinked into the blizzard outside, eager to see her again. She didn't reply.

'Playing it coy, Julia? I like it—'

The sound of the gun was startling. He didn't have time to react. He was aware of his mouth hanging open but his brain was unable to keep up with the pain in his chest. He felt his eyes bulge, and heard a glass shatter. A horrible wet wheezing sound filled the space around him.

Footsteps. They came towards him. His vision was already fading. The world was tinged with grey and whites. He was cold. So very cold.

He felt the work of nimble fingers unclasp the crucifix from around his neck. There was a voice exclaiming something in quick, frantic Italian. Then, before another thought could form from the confusion, everything faded away.

CALAN

The sun hadn't fully risen and the sky was a brilliant gauze of orange snow clouds. Calan stood shivering in his swimming trunks on the decking, ready to jump into the water. Jules had instructed him to get the lochside firepits ready for the pic 'n' dip this afternoon, which had made him realise that a cold plunge was exactly what he needed.

He breathed out in three exaggerated whooshes, closed his eyes, and stepped into mid-air. The cold wasn't immediate. It was more of a numb shock for a few seconds, the water submerging his head, enveloping his whole body, before it seized him. Kicking to the surface, a roar escaped his lungs as he gasped for air. The release of frustration felt incredible.

How could Jules have not taken the missing rifle seriously? She was the one who was always banging on about guest safety and all that. Did a missing weapon not strike her as a problem? She was so patronising, treating him like a child. Well, he wasn't. Did he have to *spell* the Marta situation out to her? Jules ran this place, didn't she? She was the boss. Shouldn't she have the sense to read between the lines?

He hauled his weight up the steps and flung the towel

around his shoulders, shivering violently as he dried himself. The abrupt change in temperature brought a bit of clarity at least. He would take things into his own hands.

Tonight would be the final time. No question. The decision was made. He was putting an end to this horrible, messy affair. For the last time, he'd let her do whatever she wanted; he'd grit his teeth, then he'd put a stop to it. He'd put his foot down, say whatever he had to say. There would be no more surprise meetings, no more whispers from the shadows, no more knocks on his door in the middle of the night.

He patted himself dry, his face set with grim determination. One last time. He could take it one last time.

MARTA

'*When you're near me, I see the world in technicolour. Your smile melts through the coldest winter. Our love will last a thousand years over, when you're near...*'

The sunrise cast a narrow shard of yellow light over the courtyard. Marta rocked back and forth as she sang in her cabin, her eyes closed, her head tilted upwards as she immersed herself in the memories. It was so easy to return to those nights. She could conjure the laughter, the aimless conversations, the warmth, the gentle touches and caresses. All she needed to do was think of their song. The lyrics they'd sung together on many a wine-drenched night were like a prayer transporting her back to another time.

London hadn't been easy when she'd arrived all those years ago. The slow pace of her hometown in coastal Calabria couldn't have been further removed from the constant noise, the churning, the spitting, writhing, relentless city. Her parents hadn't wanted her to move.

Marta, what about friends? You know no one. What about your family? Are you not worried about money, Marta? Why not cook here? Open a restaurant here. It will be far cheaper. Why leave us? Why leave your home?

For a while, she suspected they were right. Her English was sufficient, but the people in this city weren't patient with her. An insidious sneer followed her about the place, like there was a secret code nobody was telling her about. For example, it took her about a month to realise that it was pointless changing at Charing Cross underground station for Embankment, where she worked in a chain burger restaurant, since they were a mere twenty seconds' walk from each other. The whole city was a frightening mystery to her. The sprawling, endless myriad of grey stone and Tube stations and glass skyscrapers and buses and commuters was impenetrable. She was, for longer than was bearable, an outsider.

Eventually, she secured a job as a kitchen porter in a small Italian restaurant in Highbury. She moved from her sad hostel room in Bloomsbury, which smelt interchangeably of urine and weed, to the top floor of a townhouse in Holloway. She had no friends and no social life to speak of, so dedicated herself fully to her craft. She studiously watched the senior chefs at play, committing how they moved their fingers around their knives, how they gently slurped almost-reduced *jus* to check its consistency, how they judged pasta to be ready from the colour of the water to memory. She volunteered to clean up when the dishwashers called in sick. And, when she got home long after midnight, she opened her kitchen cupboards and laid out her modest ingredients before practising what she had learnt that day until the early hours.

She began to enjoy her own company. Within six months, she had been promoted to commis chef, and it seemed impossible she'd even be able to find the time for friends. That was until Rebekah walked into the restaurant.

It was a rare, crisp blue Tuesday in November and the

lunch rush had just begun to quieten down. Apart from two businessmen finishing their wine, the dining space was empty. Since the waiting staff had already left for their break, Marta took the lead.

'Hello, table for one?'

She smiled like she was supposed to. She knew service wasn't her forte, preferring to work behind the scenes, but doing an exceptional job – whatever it was – was important.

Marta remembered how the customer had glanced around the space, her eyes widening, before shooting her a nervous grin. 'I'm Rebekah... I'm... testing the menu.'

She sounded embarrassed, as if she'd got something wrong. 'I'm from the PR firm? Er... the CEO was supposed to be here, but she's been held up... so it's just me.'

Marta felt the space between her eyebrows crinkle. Surely, this woman, barely a year older than her, wouldn't be receiving a free meal? Three courses with wine came close to £150. 'Let me just check.'

She opened the booking system, and, sure enough, she was entered as a gratuity meal with the note *Our new PR company – impress!*.

'It should have been confirmed...'

Rebekah had been so unsure of herself, which struck Marta as odd. She was the sort of girl who exuded a weightless, careless beauty. Her hair was long and fell in waves over her shoulders. She wasn't wearing obvious make-up, but her skin was luminous, with a deep caramel undertone. Someone who looked like her surely never felt self-conscious?

Realising she was staring, Marta cleared her throat. 'Yes, absolutely. It's fine, right here.'

They got chatting almost immediately after Marta took her drinks order. Rebekah even offered her a glass of the Gavi di Gavi, which she declined, but throughout the service, their conversation moved from small talk, to where they lived, how they liked London, and what they were doing that night.

Marta remembered how she had looked at her feet, suddenly shy. She was confounded by how this vivacious, bright thing would want to spend more time with her. 'Oh, I'm working.'

'When do you get off?' Rebekah handed her a company credit card, her finger grazing the back of Marta's hand. She felt a light flush rise up her cheeks.

'I...' She had been planning to try laminating dough again that night. Over the last couple of weeks, she thought she almost had the process perfected, but wanted to see whether the bread flour she'd used in the last batch made it any easier to roll thin.

She met Rebekah's eyes, which seemed so patient and accepting. 'Do you like pastry?'

The next few months were magical. Both of them were too poor to go out, so Rebekah spent wonderful night after night in Marta's studio flat. They drank whatever the restaurant gifted Marta after busy shifts. Rebekah slid into the role of Marta's at-home sous chef, growing giddy on wine as Marta worked. The 2am tasting test became their ritual, before they both more often than not slumped, exhausted, onto the futon.

They sang.

Sometimes, they sang so much that the neighbours downstairs rang the doorbell to ask them to shut up.

They danced.

Rebekah was so good at moving. Marta loved how she intermittently closed her eyes and let her arms move freely to the music, before catching herself, her mouth pinched into an embarrassed pout. She held Marta's hands and encouraged her to dance with her, showing her how to twist and shake and wiggle. They always fell onto the floorboards in fits of giggles afterwards, both of them gasping for breath.

Their first kiss happened early on. Marta could still feel the rush of excitement, the taste of Rebekah, the electrifying moment when they committed to the embrace and allowed their hands to go where it felt right. It happened again the next night, and then became a regular occurrence.

A few months later, when they were snuggling in bed, a delicious buzz of alcohol and passion whirring through her brain, Marta plucked up the courage. 'So, what do I call you?'

Rebekah laughed. Such a joyous and pure sound. It still rang through Marta's heart all these years later. 'Errrm, Rebekah. That's my name.'

'I know...' Marta bit her lip, struggling not to show her frustration. 'But are you... are we...'

Rebekah turned towards her and pressed her nose against hers. 'Girlfriends?'

She laughed again, which made Marta worried. Had she said the wrong thing? She'd been so stupid to bring it up – it didn't matter what they called each other, as long as they were together. As long as it always stayed the same. After Rebekah stopped laughing, a more serious expression clouded her face. 'Would you like that?'

Marta didn't reply straight away. Something about the way Rebekah asked made her hesitate. 'Is it your family? You said your parents were Catholic too? I think if we—'

'It's not that.' Rebekah smiled and took her face into her hands. 'It's not that.'

'What is it then?'

Rebekah shook her head and turned away from her, pulling her knees to her stomach. 'Can we talk about it another time? I'm knackered.'

Marta's lips moved over the conversation as she remembered it in her cabin. '*Certo,*' she replied. 'Sweet dreams.'

Pulling herself out from the memories, she wiped her

cheeks dry. There were jobs that needed doing. The winter picnic was that afternoon: she needed to prepare the hampers and the mulled wine. Of course, the most important job was keeping a close eye on Calan. He seemed more wound up than usual. Of all people, she was able to sense it. She could see it in his mannerisms. She'd seen how he shivered and screamed this morning in the cold water when he thought nobody was watching. She'd heard his anguished cries.

Now, however, she was armed. She had for a long time suspected the danger he was in. And now God had paved the way for her to protect him however she saw fit. Already, she had put her plan in action. She was watching more closely than she ever had before. Already, she was walking the righteous path.

'Do not worry, Calan,' she whispered. 'My love will last a thousand years over.'

LUCAS

Lucas slipped on yet another patch of ice and swore loudly. It had been near impossible to drag himself out of bed this early (especially during half-term!), but it was worth it to find the perfect spot. Things were looking up, after all. Forgetting the miserable start, last night had actually been an unmitigated success. Sandeep and he had enjoyed a wonderful meal. The conversation had been flowing. It had been obvious that Sandeep was really hanging off his every word.

Lucas smiled, patting the ring in his pocket. He was so lucky to have such an attentive boyfriend... soon to be fiancé!

Yes, sure, Sandeep could be a little dense when it came to emotional intelligence. And, yes, he was also a bit flirtatious with strangers. He was definitely a prude... and frugal to a fault. And sometimes too serious for his own good. And a coward when it came to his family. But, none of that really mattered, did it? Not when you *loved* someone. And Lucas was certain he loved Sandeep for all his glaring faults, which would hopefully be ironed out over the coming years. That was marriage, wasn't it? Making little (sometimes big) improvements here and there.

Sandeep had certainly made it clear what he thought Lucas

needed to improve upon. *Possessive.* Ugh, it was such an overdramatic word. As he'd suggested many times before, *jealous* would be more suitable. Or *enthusiastic.* He wasn't anywhere near possessive, even though it might occasionally come across that way. Anyway, he'd explained all about why he disliked Sandeep's wandering eyes so much. After that first confrontation with the oh-so *perfect* Bebe, he'd been forced to. He specifically remembered how the conversation had gone in the pub at the end of their road.

'I just don't understand why you hate her so much,' Sandeep had said, taking a sip of a pint at their local. 'She seemed okay.'

'I don't hate her.'

Lucas was well aware the venom in his voice suggested otherwise as he skimmed over the shitshow that had been his childhood, but he didn't care. Sandeep could believe him or not. 'I just wish things could have panned out differently,' he finished. 'I'm not an idiot. She was young too, but that doesn't stop me wishing she'd protected me.'

He shrugged, the familiar puppet-like indifference taking over like it always did when he talked about his upbringing. 'I can't help how I feel and she can't change what she did or didn't do. Dad could have apologised for being an abusive arsehole, but that's not going to happen now he's gone. So, it's best for me and Bebe to keep our distance. I'm fine with it, honestly. But it's why trust is so important to me.'

He imitated his therapist's voice, trying to make light of the conversation. 'You felt let down as a child, so it makes sense you expect those you love as an adult to eventually let you down too.'

Sandeep didn't speak for a minute or so, and instead stared at his pint. Eventually, he replied with, 'Families. Complex, aren't they? But with everything going on with my dad... I don't know. She's still family. Maybe you'll work it out.'

It wasn't precisely the hug-in-a-mug Lucas was expecting, but at least Sandeep didn't employ the faux *"omigod that's awwwful"* that previous boyfriends had. He didn't like focusing on the details anyway. His father had been angry and belligerent. He'd focused all his rage on his son... because of... well, who knew? And it didn't matter anyway, because he was building a new family with Sandeep. What was in the past was in the past.

Little had he known then that he and Sandeep would find themselves trapped on the world's most depressing family holiday only months later. He blinked, trying to dispel the vivid images that surged behind his eyes. Placing a foot on the ice, he applied a little pressure and watched it crack in long, insidious branches.

The early sun pressed against the heavy sky and the loch glowed golden underneath it. Lucas squinted at the strange expanse and bit his lip. The champagne bottle had grown so cold that it was starting to make his fingers sting. He shook his shoulders, forcing himself to focus on the task at hand. Now, where was a good place to hide it? They would want some privacy for the Big Moment, obviously. Trouble was, that involved risking his life on this ice rink of a path. He gritted his teeth, telling himself that the ruined suede of his shoes was a small price to pay for the perfect proposal. Spitting out the snow which insisted on filling his mouth every time he took a breath, he scanned the middle distance.

Ah ha! Was that a hut? Another one of those bothies, or whatever they were called? That would actually be the perfect location! Especially if there was a fire like the one yesterday. He hugged his arms around his middle, wishing he'd put a proper coat on. The hotel's dressing gown felt a little flimsy in this weather. Putting his head down, he soldiered on, grimacing. This would make a hilarious story once the ring was on Sandeep's finger and the champagne had been popped!

The hut looked even more perfect close up. It was perched on the shore like it was just made for cosy, romantic escapades. If the weather cleared up, the Insta photos would be next level. Pushing open the door, wondering how much of a big deal it was that he couldn't feel his toes, he poked his head inside.

It was just what he'd hoped. A warm slice of luxury in the rugged landscape... and a fridge! He popped the bottle in and scanned the space more carefully. There were two armchairs and a very expensive-looking sheepskin rug – ideal for what he had in mind after Sandeep said yes.

He frowned, cocking his head to one side as his eyes fell on a dark stain in the corner. He crouched to try and wipe it off, but the substance was encrusted onto the fluffy sheepskin. It was a bit unsanitary, wasn't it? Probably some blood from a pheasant or something... or worse: fish guts. His lips twisted in disgust and he frantically wiped his hand on the dressing gown.

It was fine, he thought. Completely fine. There was no need to panic. He just needed to find someone to clean it up – he'd explain what a special occasion it was, and his plan could still come together nicely. After performing a quick, excited spin on the spot, he hurried back down the lochside path.

JULES

Opening her eyes, Jules rolled over in bed and groaned. Her mouth tasted of whisky, and wine, and the other ten drinks she'd downed before sleep had finally put her out of her misery. There was something particularly destabilising about waiting for a knock on the door that seemed less and less likely to come. Was it her fault? Had she misunderstood Zach somehow?

Rob had always told her how prone she was to misinterpretation. *That's not what I meant, Jules. No, you're hearing things. You're making stuff up again.* She shook her head and flinched at the all-too-familiar throb. No. Zach had been keen. She was certain of it. He had agreed to meet her. Nobody kissed like that unless they really meant it.

From the light outside, she could tell she'd woken up at least an hour later than she'd meant to. Holding her phone above her face, she confirmed she'd slept through her alarm. It didn't matter: she was still too fragile to move. Hopefully, Calan and Marta had remembered to prepare the pic 'n' dip.

As she sank back into bed, a rustling noise sounded from beneath her pillow. She fumbled between the sheets and pulled out a wad of paper: sheets in varying degrees of size, torn in manic shards from her notebook. This was something she did when she was hammered. Some reaction between alcohol and her pills sparked a deep compulsion to scrawl out her feelings, however random. She rubbed the notes between her fingers, her dry tongue moving over the words.

Where is he?!?

Hate myself. Hate myself. Ugly. Fat. Hate. Hate. Hate.

An embarrassed flush crept from the base of her spine. Oh God, she'd got it wrong, hadn't she? Clearly, Zach had meant her to be a bit of fun, a secret fumble. He'd just been playing a part and expected her to go along with it. He hadn't *actually* ever intended to come to her room at all. It had all been role-play. Thank goodness she hadn't knocked on his door as she'd almost convinced herself to do about twenty times.

She couldn't look at the notes anymore. It made her feel like a madwoman, like a person who didn't know her own mind. Nausea melted into a hollow depression. She inhaled gingerly, afraid the slightest of movements would cause her to vomit, and scrunched up the pages, tossing them onto the floor.

A thump from beneath her room was so violent that it made her bed tremble. Muffled shouts emanated through the floorboards. She rearranged herself as gently as she could to get a better listen and her stomach flipped dangerously.

It was unmistakably a male voice. Directly beneath her was the Ruamor Room, where the Melroses were staying.

'What the hell are you doing?'

Gracie gave what sounded like a whimper in response. Jules stared at the ceiling. Should she intervene? It was difficult to tell whether this was a standard couples' argument or if Gracie was in real danger. She swung her legs off the bed and placed both feet on the floor. The movement made her dizzy.

'Answer me! You think you can just behave like this and I

won't say anything? You think you're clever, do you? You know what, I don't care what you think!'

There was a definite sob from Gracie and some mumbled words that Jules couldn't make out. Tim started shouting again.

'Are you just fucking stupid or have you lost it? Because I can't tell! What's wrong with you? What's going on in that mental—'

There was another thump and then a scream. Tim was bellowing now.

'Are you even listening? Is any of this going into your thick—'

Was that... was that the sound of choking?

Jules couldn't wait any longer. She pushed herself up, pausing for a moment to steady herself, pulled her dressing gown around her and flung herself into the hall. Her head pounding, she burst into the second-floor corridor and threw her body weight against the door. She hammered against it with her palms, wishing she'd thought to get the spare key from reception first.

Another crash sounded, followed by a scream.

'Mrs Melrose! Gracie! Hello?' She pounded on the door with her fists. 'Open the door! Open the door now, or I'll call the—'

The door swung open and Jules's words caught in her throat, her hands still clenched into fists before her. Gracie stood in front of her. She was wearing a silk nightdress that came to mid-thigh – the kind Jules had always assumed no one wore in real life – and a matching embroidered kimono. Framed by the door, she looked tiny, like a Christmas decoration wrapped in a box ready to hang on the tree. Her eyes were glassy, almost like she'd been crying, but her lips were pulled into an exaggerated, cookie-cut smile. Tim was standing at the bay windows, his hands on his hips, his back to them.

'Uh, apologies for interrupting.' For the second time that

morning, Jules was filled with the gaping dread of having completely misread yet another situation. Was this just a part of the games Gracie had alluded to yesterday? She felt heat rush to her face. 'I heard... well, I thought I heard shouting so I wanted to check everything...'

Jules made sure to hold Gracie's eye with as much gravitas as possible. Games or not, it was worth making sure she was all right. Tim didn't bother to turn around. Gracie gave a soft, nervous giggle. The sound was disarming, yet also heartbreaking. 'Oh God, I'm so sorry. Did we disturb the other guests?'

She was holding a laptop in her arms as if she'd been in the middle of work. Jules was beginning to feel exceedingly stupid. She backed away. 'No, no. No worries about that. Like I said, I was just checking in.'

Jules turned to go upstairs, but Gracie called after her, 'Better to look in the wrong place, than not at all. You never know what's hiding beneath the covers.'

Jules turned back to look at her. She was leaning against the door frame, the laptop clutched to her chest, her eyes wide and dreamy.

Without wanting Tim to hear, Jules gave her a thumbs up. *'Are you okay?'* she mouthed.

The gesture seemed to fill Gracie with glee. She breathed in and rested the back of her head against the panel of the door. 'Of course, sometimes when you go looking, you find things you don't like. And when you find things you don't like... well...' She moved her toe in a small circle on the carpet and watched as one might watch a small animal, like her foot was a completely separate entity. 'Well... it's difficult.'

Jules frowned but nodded politely. If they'd been any other guests, she would have asked them to leave. Based on this behaviour, she wouldn't be surprised if they'd brought recreational drugs into the hotel with them. Thankfully, they seemed to be keeping themselves to themselves and there was only one more night to go.

'Of course,' Jules replied. 'Please just let me know if you need anything.'

'Oh, I will,' Gracie said, swinging herself melodramatically back into her room. 'I certainly will.'

LUCAS

Where the hell were all the staff? So much for this being an exclusive place: guests deserved, at the very least, someone at the front desk at all times. Well, it was past 7.30am and there was no sign of anyone. Lucas would definitely be emailing a complaint when he got home; the service had been crap from the very start.

He dithered in the main hall, conscious he was still in his bathrobe, then strutted through the door marked as *staff only* which led him to a room full of stainless steel. The kitchen was bloody freezing, with no sign of breakfast preparations, apart from a basket of what smelt like freshly baked croissants in the centre of the clinically clean island.

'Hello?' he called, inching forwards. 'Um... I'm looking for someone to help me? Is anyone...?'

He sighed, frustrated, then snatched a croissant from the basket. Taking a bite, he sauntered around, hoping someone would turn up soon. It was bloody delicious, he had to admit.

Resigning himself to the fact that no one was coming, he turned to leave, when he heard a shuffle from around the corner. A section of the kitchen was cordoned off by those creepy translucent PVC curtain strips. A shadowy figure moved in the dimly lit area. 'Hey! Hi... sorry, I wondered if you could help...'

Unbelievably, the figure completely ignored him and disappeared out of sight. Swearing quietly under his breath, he pushed the PVC strips out of the way. Oversized refrigerators and freezers lined a narrow room, which was bathed in a weird green light. Lucas marched forwards, his temper beginning to flare. His feet were sodden and time was running out for him to make things perfect.

'I said hello? I know you're in here, I just saw you...' His voice trailed off.

'When you're near me, I see the world in technicolour. Your smile melts through the coldest winter. Our love will last a thousand years over, when you're near...'

Someone was singing. He vaguely recognised the song as something he'd danced to at school discos in the early 2000s. The voice behind it was ragged and wispy. 'Excuse me?'

Really, he'd have expected better service at Nando's. The voice continued to sing the same lyrics over and over. It didn't look like the room led to anywhere else, which meant whoever was singing was behind the largest fridge at the end. He pulled the cord of his robe tight and strode forwards, ready to give a piece of his mind.

'Oh great!' he said, laughing and clapping his hands together in disbelief. This was just perfect. 'Following me again, are you?'

The woman from the bushes yesterday gazed up at him. She was sitting hunched in the corner, her back pressed against the fridge, hands clasped tightly against her chest, rocking slowly. She continued to sing as she stared at him, finishing the phrase, before she replied, 'That's impossible. I was here before you.'

He frowned, annoyed by her logic. Rubbing his arms to

keep warm he gestured to somewhere vaguely in the direction of the hut. 'I need some help cleaning—'

'I'm a chef.'

She said it like it was all that was needed. Her eyes narrowed when he didn't leave her be, the deep-brown irises scrutinising him. He shuffled on the spot, searching for the words.

'Look, I haven't been happy with the service here at all. I booked this for a special occasion and things have unfortunately fallen short. All I'm asking is—'

'I'm a chef,' she repeated, interrupting him. She gave an apologetic shrug and looked at her hands, which were still clasped before her chest. With her black shirt and trousers, she looked like a giant praying mantis.

A distinct feeling of unease trickled down Lucas's spine. He shivered, waiting for her to add something. A few moments of silence passed with only the hum of the fridges as a backdrop. He held his hands up. 'Can you at least point me in the direction of the manager then?'

The woman seemed to have forgotten he was there at all. She began rocking gently back and forth again, her lips curving into a serene smile. She hummed the tune of the same song as before, and then moved her hands from her chest to her forehead.

He considered getting help; clearly, she was suffering some kind of mental breakdown. He hoped she was lying about being a chef – he certainly didn't want her anywhere near his food.

'Jesus Christ...' he muttered underneath his breath, beginning to lose his patience.

'Yes, He's here. You can feel Him too?' She didn't open her eyes, too caught up in her musical trance.

He shook his head and turned to leave. 'Errrrm, no.

Although if you could ask him where your boss is, that would be useful.'

A high-pitched cry made him turn back to her. Her eyes were screwed up with distaste. She moved her hands slowly away from her forehead, so they hovered just in front of her nose. Then, she opened them, slowly, to reveal what looked like a very ugly piece of costume jewellery. He recognised it as one of those ornate crucifixes. Why on earth people wanted to wear an image of a man hanging from a cross baffled him. This one was particularly gruesome, with a bulbous red stone stuck in the centre of it.

'*When you're near, when you're near, when you're near...*'

He shook his head, backing quickly out of the cold room and into the kitchen. Swiping another croissant from the basket he hurried into the main hall, irritated she'd driven him to stress-eat. His teeth chattered over the buttery pastry as he shoved it into his mouth.

Calan as good as ran into the side of him, almost causing him to choke. 'Oh for God's sake—'

'Shit! Shit, sorry, sorry...' Dropping a clatter of firewood onto the floor, Calan patted him on the back as he doubled over to dislodge the mouthful. After a couple of heaving coughs, it was fine. Lucas regained his composure and remembered his mission. This was good. Calan was precisely the sort of person who could help him.

'It's all right, no, no... it's fine!' Lucas pulled himself up and placed his hands on his hips. 'I was actually hoping to run into you.'

'Me?' He looked far too worried than he ought to have, almost like he was being accused of something. Lucas thought back to the conversation he'd overheard last night, how afraid he'd sounded then.

'Oh! No, nothing big, don't worry.' Lucas gave him an

encouraging smile. 'It's just…' He lowered his voice breathlessly. 'I'm planning to propose to my boyfriend, Sandeep, you know, who was out with us yesterday…'

Calan nodded, then, when Lucas didn't continue, added, 'Congratulations…'

'Thank you very much! I have it all planned out actually. I got up early today to put some bits and pieces in place and, well…'

Lucas got the impression that Calan was only half-listening. His eyes kept drifting back to a spot over his shoulder, towards the kitchen door.

'…if you could just clean it up, say, within the next hour or so, that'd be lovely. You know, I want it to be as perfect as possible. Start of the rest of our lives and all that.'

Calan nodded again and gave a weak "hmm" sound.

'So…' Lucas pressed. 'You'll sort it? Tell the cleaners or something?'

For some reason, this made Calan laugh. He moved his eyes back to Lucas's face and replied. 'Sounds good. I'll get that done right away. Is there anything else I can help you with?'

Lucas checked over his shoulder. He knew it wasn't his business but this boy had seemed so stressed last night. That woman in the kitchen was clearly a screw or two loose; who knew, perhaps she was dangerous. 'Look, er, Calan, I just wanted to say I'm a teacher, so… well, I heard you talking to your boss last night, something about someone following you? There's a strange woman I keep seeing around here – you probably know I complained about her.' He lowered his voice. 'She's in the kitchen right now. Is she the one bothering you? Nothing to do with me, but if you wanted help or… advice…'

He let his voice trail off as Calan's eyes widened with horror, before adding, 'Oh, sorry, like I say, I shouldn't have brought it up. It's just because I overheard—'

'I'd stay away from her,' Calan said. His face moved into a dark scowl. 'She's...'

His bottom lip quivered. Lucas was used to young people being upset, but Calan's reaction tugged insistently at a niggling instinct that something really terrible was going on. He was genuinely shaken, Lucas could tell.

'I know you don't know me,' Lucas began gently. 'But if you need a listening ear, then I'm about for another day. I work with teenagers all the time. Nothing shocks me.'

'It's all good.' Calan knelt down to retrieve the firewood. His tone was definitely defensive. 'I'll get that stain cleaned for you.'

Lucas watched him for a few seconds, unsure of what the right thing to do was. He wasn't a child, and he certainly wasn't in Lucas's care. Unless he wanted to talk, there was nothing he could do to help.

He shivered and remembered how much he was looking forward to a hot shower. 'Great, thanks.'

MARTA

The body looked at home in the freezer. Marta had transferred the old game meat elsewhere, of course. The large oblong shape functioned surprisingly well as an icy coffin. She slid the door closed with a satisfied nod and entered the main kitchen. Chopping. That's what must be done. Chopping. She could easily focus on the methodical task. The rhythm, the soft lick of the knife through the carrots, the scrape against the board. Over and over again; there was no need to think about anything else at all.

She had completed her duty. And she had taken back her relic, her necklace, her most beautiful link to the past. Her link to Rebekah. It swung gently against her skin, tucked under her shirt, resting in between her breasts as she worked.

Her eyes flicked to the kitchen doors. She should have locked them earlier. She had been careless and stupid. That guest, that Godless man, could easily have ruined everything. The way he trespassed her space, her sanctuary, as if he had any right to set foot in here. This was where she answered her calling. This was her church, her temple. She heard His Holiness through the catch of the hob's flame; she saw Him in the rise of the dough, felt Him through the steam and the purr of boiling saucepans.

His Grace, certainly, had brought her here. He allowed her, due to her dedication and selflessness, to journey as much as she liked back in time to her old studio flat. Every time her knuckles cracked whilst kneading dough, she was transported. When she whisked her marinades, she remembered Rebekah's lips around her finger, tasting. Every time she sliced and grilled and washed and stirred, she journeyed back to those happy, blissful days.

She closed her eyes and the past took hold. The bump had begun to push through the layers of Rebekah's clothing. Marta had known before Rebekah said anything.

In bed, she refused to take her clothes off, pretending that she was cold or tired. Eventually, while Marta was practising cheese soufflés, the question spilt from her lips.

'When is the baby coming?'

Rebekah gave a sharp intake of breath. For a long time, the air in the tiny kitchen hung heavy and thick. Marta continued whisking, each flick of the wrist becoming more vehement, more desperate for an answer.

'Five months.' Rebekah mumbled the words.

Marta placed the bowl on the counter and turned to face her. She was crying. Big silent tears coursed down her cheeks. Marta pressed close against her and placed her palms on her belly. 'That's soon.'

'I'm sorry.' Rebekah stepped away. She folded her arms around her midriff, almost protectively.

Marta smiled, shaking her head. She moved to hold her. 'Sorry? You don't need to be sorry, Rebekah, my love – it's beautiful.'

Rebekah's hair had smelt beguiling that night. She'd recently swapped conditioners and it gave off a coconutty scent, with a hint of lime... and nutmeg. Yes, nutmeg. She buried her nose in those long, dark locks and inhaled deeply.

Rebekah pushed her away. Only gently, just a soft pressure on her shoulders, but it was enough to make Marta worried. 'What's wrong?'

She held herself awkwardly, like she wished she was anywhere else. She looked at her feet, rocked forwards on her toes and then back on her heels.

'My love...?'

'Don't call me that.' Rebekah's voice trembled. 'Don't call me *love*. It can't be love, so don't say it.'

Marta frowned. 'But I love you. You said you loved me.'

'I do—' She cut the phrase short, like a serrated knife severing a thick crust. She finally raised her eyes to look Marta in the face. Those dark irises were wet and frightened. 'Please don't make me explain myself. I feel horrible enough as it is.'

This was the moment Marta had truly felt the divine move within her. It was as if God had wrapped around the recesses of her mind and planted within it the most simple and wonderful of explanations: this baby was *theirs*. Rebekah was her reason for existing. She was her only friend, her one love, the only person with whom she shared the mundanities of her day. There was no way, no chance that she'd been unfaithful. She would never. Because Marta would never. They were in love. So, this baby was a gift. A glorious and immaculate gift.

She smiled, feeling her eyes shine, her cheeks tighten with elation. 'If we love each other, then everything will be fine.' She placed her hand on Rebekah's belly and rested her forehead on hers. 'This child is ours.'

Rebekah's eyes widened. She inhaled quickly, as if about to say something contrary, but Marta placed a finger against her lips. She kissed her forehead, her cheeks, and whispered, 'God moves in ways we don't understand. He's brought us together. That's enough for me.'

'I don't believe in God.'

Marta smiled and held Rebekah's face in her hands. 'But you believe in us.'

It was like magic, watching her anxiety disappear. The tension in her forehead smoothed, her mouth relaxed into the crescent shape Marta loved so much. 'You know I believe in us.'

'Then, it's like I said. It's enough.'

Marta returned to whisking the soufflés, her heart filled with rosy images of what their future, the three of them together, would look like.

Morning yoga in the library was Jules's idea. Rob had thought it wouldn't suit the vibe of the hotel, that it would make it seem too much like a "boring wellness retreat". By then, Jules didn't know whether he was just arguing with her for the sake of it or not. She was more than qualified to run the classes, having been practising for years, and it cost next to nothing.

This morning, Gracie stood at the end of her mat, her demeanour rigid and timid again, at complete odds with how she'd been earlier. Sandeep was taking the breathing work seriously, his eyes closed and his limbs relaxed and grounded. Lucas kept checking his phone.

'Try to relax, forget about all other commitments...' Jules reminded him, ever so pointedly.

'Sorry...' He stood up straight and exhaled irritably, shooting Sandeep an exasperated look. 'We just have a walk planned...'

Thank goodness Zach hadn't decided to attend. Jules turned her back to the guests to demonstrate which leg to bring forwards for the Warrior Two position. She breathed in, setting her eyeline on the bottom of the clouds where they grazed the tops of the trees. This side of the building overlooked the forest stretching up into the hills. The weather had turned the pines into white and stoic figures, a silvery light dancing through them with the movement of the wind. The landscape stretched almost impossibly far, giving the impression that The Tornivan was the only habitation for thousands of miles.

The wisps blended with the white-dusted pines to produce a scene that looked painted over, airbrushed and drained of colour.

'Breathe,' she said. 'And bend your front knee, inhale as you draw your arms up and...'

She listened to her guests' breathing with a quiet satisfaction. One of the reasons she enjoyed instructing was the small sense of power it gave her. Her students trusted her to say the right things. Their eyes followed her body as they tried to imitate her.

'Bring your hands to your chest and...'

A sniff followed by a whimper sounded from behind her shoulder. Jules looked back to see Gracie wiping a tear away from her cheek. Sandeep still had his eyes closed, although his chin was set forwards with dogged determination. Lucas cleared his throat again and glanced down at his phone meaningfully.

'Okay...' Jules said in a soft voice. 'Sometimes this practice can bring all sorts of emotions to the forefront.'

Gracie didn't react. Her palms pressed together with what looked like a worrying amount of tension. The shouts from earlier this morning resurfaced in Jules's mind.

'Sandeep, I'm just thinking, if you want to make the picnic, then I think we should get going for a shower now...' Lucas shuffled closer to his boyfriend and nudged him gently in the ribs.

'For God's sake...' Sandeep mumbled.

'Right!' Jules turned to face them all again and bowed her

head. 'Wonderful. We'll leave it there for today. I'll be here tomorrow, same time, if any of you...'

Lucas had already rolled up his mat and was tugging Sandeep's arm towards the door. Gracie knelt down delicately. She observed the corner of her mat, her head tilted to one side, but made no move to clear up.

Jules waited for Sandeep and Lucas to leave before approaching her. With the tall, dusty bookcases behind her, she would have looked like a sad, gothic heroine, were it not for her expensive yoga clothes. 'Mrs Melrose?'

Gracie's eyes flicked up, almost surprised at another's presence. 'Oh.' She gave a small gasp and attempted a weak smile.

'Is, uh... everything okay? Sorry to interrupt you this morning.'

For some reason, Gracie gave a low and broken laugh. 'I understand. We were probably being too loud.'

Jules nodded, pulling her jumper over her head. Gracie was still kneeling on the mat, her hands rested on her thighs.

'Did you want to stay here for a bit? The library's left open anyway.' She nodded at the books. 'Lots of reading material, although I can't make any guarantees about how good it is. Most of the books were scavenged from charity shops... mainly for the antique aesthetic than anything else.'

Gracie sniffed, before shuffling round on her knees to look at the bookcases. 'Must have cost a fortune.'

Jules walked across the room towards the tall rows of books and ran a finger over their spines. She nodded. 'The money pit. That's what we called it. *Just digging it a little deeper.*' She stopped for a moment, remembering the optimism with which Rob had spent their life savings on stupid little details like this.

'We?'

She turned to realise Gracie was standing right beside her.

Jules picked a random book, and slid it from its place. A cloud of dust followed it. Coughing, she replied, 'My husband and I bought this hotel a few years ago. We threw everything we had at it really. Maybe too much.'

She shook her head and waved her hand in front of her face to disperse the dust, remembering who she was talking to. 'Sorry,' she added. 'Too much information.'

'No, it's all good. *The Changeling*... I used to be terrified of that!' In a childish gesture, she brought her hands to her mouth. 'It's creepy, have you heard of it?'

Jules looked at the book in her hands: it was entitled *The Changeling and Other Scottish Legends*. 'Oh, sorry no, I haven't. Probably should have, living here...'

Gracie giggled and took the book. 'I wouldn't have expected you to – it was just some silly thing we learnt in primary school...' She flicked through the pages and smiled as her eyes fell on what she was looking for. 'See, here! Oh my God, I remember!' She lowered her voice dramatically as she read. '"Legend has it that the faeries would slip down from the hills, past the streams, over the lochs. They'd steal a human child and replace it with the Changeling... an identical-looking creature, but one of their own. Often, the Changeling would display abnormal tendencies..."'

She lowered her voice at the end of her sentence, screwing her face up to resemble the terrifying faeries. A stream of laughter burst from Jules's mouth. She was so surprised that she gave a little squeal, which made her laugh even more. Gracie joined in and the two women giggled like teenagers, until Jules took a deep breath, wiping her eyes.

'It's been so long since I've laughed like that,' she said, her mouth still twitching.

'Me too.' Gracie put the book back on the shelf and grinned. 'Guess it's a bit remote for much socialising?'

Jules turned to look at the vast sprawl of white trees. 'How did you find it, growing up here?'

'Fine,' Gracie replied. 'Quiet, but it's what you know, isn't it? School was good for meeting people. I actually suggested moving back here not long ago, but Tim wouldn't dream of it.'

The mention of Tim put Jules on edge again. She watched Gracie carefully. Her face remained composed and pleasant – there was no trace of anguish. 'Is he from London originally?'

Gracie lowered herself to the ground and sat cross-legged before beginning to stretch from side to side. Jules joined her. 'That's right. He wouldn't be able to do his precious job from here, that's for sure...'

'Investment? You can't do that remotely?'

Gracie laughed, shaking her head. 'Not the way Tim sees it. Anyway, if he worked remotely, then what opportunity would he have to get out of the house and away from me?'

The comment was so abrupt and bitter that it took Jules a few seconds to fully comprehend. Gracie stopped stretching and suddenly looked Jules square in the eye. 'I think he's cheating on me.'

Jules knew that this was her cue to politely get up and remove herself from the conversation. She needed Tim's company to work its magic on this place, and, for that to happen, he had to be on side. Entering into a conversation with his scorned wife about him cheating seemed very misguided, to put it lightly.

But there was something about Gracie's honest green eyes, so wide and trusting, that made her stay. She drew her knees up to her chest. 'Is that... is that something he's done before?'

Without replying, Gracie rapidly pushed herself to standing. She rolled her shoulders back and looked down at Jules, her arms folded. 'He's out running now. I think you can help me with something. In our room.'

She offered Jules a hand to pull her up.

'I...' Jules stared at Gracie's outstretched hand. There were a few hours left until the pic 'n' dip and pretty much all of the preparation had been done. She had to admit that she was curious to poke around the Melroses' room.

She smiled and accepted Gracie's hand. 'Of course, what is it?'

'Oh...' Gracie said, absent-mindedly, as she made her way to the door. 'Just a technical issue.'

MARTA

Marta crouched behind the tree, clutching the crucifix. She watched Calan carry the bucket of soapy water into the fishing hut. She was sure she'd cleaned up the mess thoroughly; in her panic, she must have missed something. And now her beloved was doing the dirty work for her. The thought made her whole body ache. He moved gracefully, his arms fuelled by that youthful strength she knew so well and she loved so much.

'Rebekah…' She whispered her name into the freezing air. Perhaps a snowflake would carry it to wherever she was in His Kingdom. Maybe, she would hear.

A gust of wind slammed the door to the fishing hut closed. Marta imagined Calan inside dipping the sponge into the bucket, squeezing, scrubbing. Dip, squeeze, scrub. He was such a good boy. So laborious. So diligent.

'Rebekah,' she whispered to the sky. 'Do you see him? Tell me you do. Please, tell me you do.'

While she waited for Calan to re-emerge, she rested her head against the cool bark of the tree. Sifting through the many conversations, the touches, the silences, the kisses, she closed her eyes and settled on the one she both hated and loved revisiting. The last time she had spoken to Rebekah. The last time she had felt her touch, her breath against her lips.

The baby was due any day. Marta had been putting in longer shifts at the restaurant in preparation. They'd bought a crib, various pastel-coloured baby grows, what seemed like a thousand nappies, and a buggy. The plan was to move to a bigger flat in the suburbs in a few months' time, when they could afford the deposit.

Rebekah's ankles were swollen and her joints ached. She complained about having to walk up and down the steep stairs to Marta's flat, but acknowledged it was a better option than her flatshare. On the way home from shifts, Marta borrowed library books about pre-partum nutrition and spent her evenings devising and executing meal plans. She would kiss the baby, beneath Rebekah's bump, each night, and whisper, 'We're ready for you, little one. We're ready for you, my love, my love, my little love.'

Rebekah said her lips tickled her belly and would laugh, causing the baby to kick in response. These were truly the happiest of days.

One night, Marta was carrying the ingredients for stuffed aubergines up the stairs. Rebekah had been up for most of the night previously with cramps, and she deserved something rich and rewarding to eat. They were planning on watching their favourite television programme about a forensic scientist who specialised in bones. Marta was thinking about how she would give Rebekah a foot massage before bed when her eyes fell on the packed bags.

Her heart jumped with indescribable excitement. 'It's time? It's now! Let me call the hospital—'

'No.' Rebekah wasn't writhing, nor panting, nor rocking, nor doing anything she'd read about. In fact, she seemed calmer than she had been in months.

Marta nodded at the bags. 'I can't believe I didn't think of it – it's good to be ready… any day now!'

Rebekah shook her head, her damp eyes catching the dim, orange light from the street lamp outside. 'They're not for the hospital.' She placed her hands on the small of her back and let out a whoosh of air. 'I'm staying at a friend's—'

'A friend's?'

'Yes, Marta, a friend's house! I have other people in my life, you know. It's not only you… much as you'd love it to be.'

Immediately, she surged forwards, taking Marta's hands into hers. 'Oh my God, I'm sorry. I didn't mean that, my head… it's just…'

Marta held her hands in return, but it felt like some phantom spoon had begun to scoop out her insides, bit by painstaking bit. She was light-headed. 'You're leaving me?'

'Marta…' Rebekah squeezed her hands even tighter. Her bottom lip was trembling. 'Marta… this is a lie, it's all a lie. I thought I could… because I love…' The word caught in her throat, like it was something distasteful, something she wanted to be rid of, to spit out. She took a deep breath. 'You *know* what I did, don't you? Really? I know you talk about this… this immaculate miracle, this conception, but, Marta? You can't believe it, truly. You know I cheated. You know this baby isn't—'

'Stop!' She covered her ears, backing away. 'Stop, stop, stop. This baby is everything! You are everything!' She felt her hands shaking like an electric, panicked current was racing through her. She didn't know what to do with herself, where to put her body, how to be. 'I've prayed. I've heard Him. He's told me…'

Her voice sounded tiny to her, helpless and alone. She looked around her flat wildly, groping for something that would change Rebekah's mind. There was nothing. What would keep her here? What used to be their cosy little paradise now looked like a grimy, inhospitable hovel. A sound halfway between a wheeze and a sob escaped her lips. She fell to her knees and wrapped her arms around Rebekah's legs.

'Please...'

She buried her face in her scent, desperately trying to commit it to memory. 'Please, please, my love... we can talk about it. We can—'

'Marta, we can't.'

Her voice was so final and determined. She looked up at Rebekah's face as she continued to speak. 'Everything we've built here is based on a lie. I let it happen. I let you... I let you fantasise or believe or... whatever it was. It's not fair on you. I can't keep doing this to you. Soon, there will be a reminder.'

She caressed her stomach. 'Every day, a reminder of what I did.'

She moved to arrange her bags. 'My friend will be here soon.'

Marta felt as if her body was floating above her, looking down at this alien scene happening from the ceiling. She shook her head wordlessly, failing to find anything to say. Her hands moved to her neck and she fumbled with the clasp of her necklace. 'I... I thought we'd be a family,' she said.

Rebekah let out a short sob and nodded. 'I'm sorry.'

Marta held the necklace out to her. It swung gently in the space between them, to and fro, just like cruel, inevitable fate. 'Would you take this? Take it for me. At least, if I know you're wearing it, it will be...'

'Less painful,' Rebekah finished.

'No. Nothing could make this less painful. But I'll feel closer to you, to our baby, even if I'm not.'

Rebekah tapped her chest, intimating she wanted Marta to place it around her neck. Marta stepped close to her, feeling the baby between them, and leant over her shoulder to fasten the clasp.

'I love you,' she whispered.

'You too,' Rebekah said, her voice hollow and thin.

Marta stepped back as the doorbell rang. The necklace looked nice on her. Jesus hung magnificently just above her breasts, and the bright-red stone contrasted beautifully with Rebekah's dark, tumbling hair.

LUCAS

'Look, it's just a bit further. I thought you liked the Great Outdoors?' Lucas fought to keep his tone light and airy, despite his growing annoyance at Sandeep, who didn't seem in the least bit interested in their walk.

Sandeep blew through his front teeth and folded his arms even tighter. He was trudging on the pebbly beach as if he could think of no worse activity. There was no winning with him!

'The snow's really coming in.' He eyed Lucas with suspicion. 'Aren't you cold?'

Lucas waited for him to catch up and wrapped his arms around Sandeep's waist. 'What's it they say? There's no such thing as bad weather if you're with the one you love.'

'I don't think that's a thing...' Sandeep chuckled, which was something at least. 'Come on then. I suppose I'd better make the most of this new-found enthusiasm for walking...'

'Hey!' Lucas couldn't help but progress with a spring in his step. An electric excitement was dancing in his belly. Sandeep had absolutely no idea what was coming.

They meandered along the loch for a few more minutes. A

strange mist had settled a couple of metres above the water, slicing across the landscape.

'Ooooh!' Lucas tried to suppress his grin. 'Do you see that? What is it? A hut or something...? Shall we...?'

He took Sandeep's hand and led him further down the path before he could object. 'Lucas, are you sure—'

'Just go with it,' Lucas cooed, barely able to contain himself to a walk.

Thank goodness, Calan had cleaned the hut. It was completely spotless. The wood-burner was roaring and the armchairs had been plumped. He'd even placed a couple of crystal champagne glasses on the coffee table.

'What's...?' Sandeep pursed his lips into a small smile. 'Have you been making plans?'

Shutting the door firmly closed, Lucas wrapped him in another hug as they luxuriated in the warmth. 'I might have something up my sleeve...'

'Oh?' He drew himself away from the embrace and scanned the small timber interior. 'It's cosy in here, isn't it? A nice idea for walkers.'

'Absolutely...'

'Why are you smiling like that?'

'Like what?' Lucas held the ring box behind his back – the tension was close to killing him.

'You're beaming, Lucas.'

He was down on one knee, the box perched on his palm, his face upturned and ready to witness Sandeep's surprise. 'Sandeep, I want you to know that this past year and a half has been the most amazing...'

'Lucas—'

'Hang on, I'm not finished... don't worry, the champagne's in the fridge!' He paused, trying to remember where he was in his speech. He hadn't planned for interruptions. 'Errm, you're the constant in my life. When things are crazy – and I know they often are with me – you're there, bringing me back down to earth, whether I like it or not...'

He paused for Sandeep to laugh, but was met with silence. His heart skipped a beat. Sandeep was so shocked that he couldn't bring himself to react!

'You accept me the way I am, and I love you for that. I know things aren't always easy. I know my family is... well, you stayed with me after that horrible holiday, which is more than most people would do...'

'Lucas, don't...'

'No, it's true.' Lucas was surprised to feel himself blinking through tears. He realised with a shock that this was the first time he'd ever properly thanked Sandeep for being there for him during that terrible time. Most people would have run a mile after that trip. Most people would have wanted nothing to do with all that sadness, that heartache, that history. But Sandeep had stayed. For all his quirks and forgivable faults, he had stayed.

'Sandeep, I can't tell you how much you mean to me...'

'Lucas, I'm serious.'

It occurred to Lucas that Sandeep's reaction had been, so far, unconventional. He hadn't smiled yet, which was disappointing. And he hadn't done the thing he'd seen in films, where the person says "yes" before the speech is fully over. In fact, he looked almost panic-stricken.

'Babes, I'm serious too,' Lucas said gently. 'I know this will be difficult to navigate with your family, but—'

Sandeep was massaging his temples. 'It's not my bloody family, Lucas. They know I'm gay, I just... I just didn't want you to meet, after—'

'What?' Lucas began to feel ridiculous. Here he was, on his knees, midway through his beautifully composed proposal.

What did Sandeep think he was doing? 'What do you mean? They won't like me?'

'No! It's not like that.' Sandeep paced to the other side of the armchair and placed his hands on the back, hanging his head. This was the most highly strung Lucas had ever seen him.

'You're going to need to explain—'

'Okay!' Sandeep interrupted, not meeting Lucas's eye. It was like he was speaking to someone else, someone inside his head. 'I didn't want them to think it was serious. With my Dad how he is... I can't lie to him, Lucas. He's got enough on his plate. I can't deceive him like that... not when you don't know... I thought maybe you might never know... and so how could we be...'

'Sandeep! Just spit it out!'

Lucas felt himself trembling. The small space which had felt so cosy before was now claustrophobic. Although he'd taught the word "foreboding" many times in his English classes, he'd never truly experienced the sensation himself. However, here it was. The air tasted bitter. The crackling of the logs grew louder and urgent. There was a palpable sense that something awful was about to happen, but he didn't know what.

Sandeep raised his face to look at him. His expression was ashen, his eyes reddened at the corners. 'Lucas, it was me. I killed your sister. I killed Bebe.'

JULES

'That creepy man confirmed what I already think I know...'

Gracie slid the laptop out of its jacket onto the coffee table. They were sitting on the floor in the Ruamor Room. Six expensive-looking silk kimonos were spread out neatly on the bed. *Almost performatively*, Jules thought.

The way they were arranged confirmed her initial impression of Gracie as being an extremely clean and tidy person. She had that fresh look about her that a lot of women – including herself – would just never achieve. Obviously, her gorgeous red curls helped her, as did her perfect little face. But she also carried herself in a prim and careful way, like every movement was somewhat considered... apart from first thing this morning, of course. Those blurry eyes and that haphazard laugh belonged to a different person entirely.

'Creepy man?'

She nodded, tapping at the keyboard to turn on the screen. 'Zach, I think it is? He's another guest. You must have seen him skulking about. He's got those shifty eyes... know what I mean?'

Jules gulped down a wave of embarrassment and nodded, feeling heat rush to her cheeks. So, not only had she got the wrong end of the stick, she'd seemingly thrown herself at a creep. Brilliant. 'Now I come to think of it... um, what did he say?'

Gracie gestured at the computer screen, her eyes glowing from its light. 'He was for some reason obsessed with this idea about Tim having an affair. It was literally the first thing he said to me. See, that's strange, isn't it?' Jules found it hard to disagree. Gracie continued. 'Super weird. Anyway, what he didn't know is that I *do* actually think Tim's cheating on me.'

Her shoulders visibly tensed and she rocked back on her legs, stretching out her arms. Her voice dropped low. 'He's done it before.'

That much, Jules believed, but she was treading on dangerous ground. She cleared her throat. 'Gracie, I'm really sorry to hear that, and... well, if you need anything during your stay, please come and find me. My room's just above yours. But, you know Tim's a potential investor? This whole trip is supposed to give him some ideas about how to help the hotel. I probably shouldn't...'

She was halfway to standing up when Gracie's hand shot up to grab hers. 'I just need you to help me find something on his laptop. I think I saw him looking at some pictures once when he didn't know I was watching. Pictures of *them.*'

Jules extracted her hand. 'I don't really think that's for me...'

'It's on the company drive, I'm sure. That's where he keeps his... private documents.'

She punched the keys petulantly, her voice wavering between angry and broken, and something much darker. For the second time that day, Gracie's perfect doll-like image was bent out of place. Jules remembered how she'd caught her wielding a knife. The hairs on the back of her neck bristled.

'I should be going. Will I see you at the picnic?'

'Don't leave.'

Her words were suddenly laced with a venomous undercurrent. Her face transformed with no warning. The beautiful edges of it suddenly became jagged. Her cheekbones sharpened, her chin jutted in an elfish, insistent angle.

Jules took a step away from her. 'It's a busy day for me, unfortunately. Lots to be getting on with...'

Very slowly, Gracie got to her feet. With a meticulous sense of purpose, she knelt beside the bed and reached underneath. She drew out a long chopping knife. 'He makes me do things. He makes me.'

Jules stared at her in horror. Why had she got herself involved with this? Tim was a potential investor. She had absolutely no desire to hear about the details of his sex life. She wished she'd ignored their shouting this morning. 'I... well, I'll see you later.'

She began to make for the door but heard footsteps behind her before she got there. A tight panic seized her chest as Gracie's small form slipped between her and the way out. She forced herself to remain calm, remembering something about how panicking in dangerous situations risked escalating things.

'I'm sorry, Mrs Melrose, but I really have to start getting everything ready.'

Gracie blinked in silence, as if she hadn't heard, then eventually cocked her head to one side with interest. 'Back to Mrs Melrose now, am I?'

Jules reached for the door handle but Gracie grabbed her wrist.

'I'm just a guest asking for help,' she said. She was suddenly too calm, too collected. Jules's stomach gave a frightened flip. 'You wouldn't want me to tell Tim how the owner of this place, this expensive place, refused to help me, would you? If you can't even help your investor's wife, then I'd say that spells trouble.

It's unlikely he'll put anything into such a shitshow, wouldn't you say?'

The pressure tightened around Jules's wrist. She grimaced and shot Gracie a furious look. How dare she threaten her! In her own hotel. But the quiet triumph in Gracie's smile proved what she already knew – she couldn't afford to lose the investment. She needed Tim's favour, whether she liked it or not.

'What is it you want?' she said. She didn't bother to disguise her rage. The girly, butter-wouldn't-melt routine was an act. And she had fallen for it. This was the real Gracie: calculated and cold.

Gracie flashed a prim smile, released Jules's wrist, and nodded, twirling a curl between her fingers. 'Like I said, he's hiding something on his work drive, which I don't know the password for. It's a shared portal, isn't it? His recipients have access to it? Potential ones too?'

Jules's stomach sank. She had, indeed, already been on-boarded into the system. She'd had to upload her business plan and other documents. Her mouth turned dry. 'I have access to the recipient area, which includes some of the drive, yes. But if he's hiding something, then I doubt he'll have put it somewhere so accessible. He'll have it in a private folder, surely?'

Without replying, Gracie beckoned her back to the coffee table. She pushed the laptop towards Jules and closed her eyes, as if reciting words from memory. 'The thing about Tim is he's an idiot. He's always been told how brilliant he is, how special he is. He's never *actually* had to be special, not really. He's never had to display any *real* intelligence.' She shrugged, nodding at the laptop. 'Passwords are a weakness for Tim... Not Nice, Very Dim. They always have been.'

Jules nodded, flinching at Gracie's poisonous expression.

Before Gracie continued, she pulled a small, folded piece of paper out of her sports bra. 'He writes his credit card PINs on this and keeps it in his wallet, as well as some prompts for his website passwords. And, look here...' She unfolded the paper and showed it to Jules. '*Private company files in main server – fake email addresses in KEY CONTACTS FOR BUSINESS PARTNERS.* I assume you have access?'

Jules vaguely remembered the folder. She sighed, keen to be out of there as quickly as possible. Before she pressed enter after typing her password, she shot Gracie a look. 'Not a mention of this to him? I have your word?'

'Of course,' she replied, seeming angelic as she waited patiently.

Jules located the file quickly and scrolled down the short list of email addresses. Sure enough, there were a few funny-looking ones interspersed with the email contacts she recognised. She would have written them off as typos had she not known better. She turned the screen to face Gracie. 'There. Is that all?'

Gracie ignored her as she typed furiously, trying one amalgamation, followed by another. She was mechanical, almost ruthless. It was obvious this wasn't anything new to her. Jules thought about making a run for it, but the threat of losing Tim's investment was too big a risk. Plus, a part of her was intrigued. Is this what Rob had felt like? Is this how she had made him feel? Paranoid, manic to the point of madness? It was fascinating to see how it must be like on the other side: the cheated, instead of the cheat.

Gracie's fingers stopped, rigid, hovering over the keyboard. Her face remained expressionless for a few moments. Then, her lips pressed together so tightly that they turned almost white.

'I knew it. I knew it. I knew it. I always know. The bastard.' Her eyes dragged down the screen as she scrolled. It was as if she was hungry for it, like she was addicted to whatever images she was seeing on the screen.

Jules couldn't help herself. She moved behind Gracie to take a look. Just as Gracie had thought, the file was full of photographs of Tim and another woman. There were hundreds of them: at restaurants, embracing in parks, on holidays in Paris, Rome, Copenhagen. This had been – perhaps still was – a full-blown affair.

'Gracie, I'm sorry...' Jules shifted awkwardly behind her.

'Don't be.' She slammed the laptop closed and walked to the door, opening it to show Jules out.

'It's nothing I didn't already know. And I like being right.'

MARTA

Marta eyed the hampers on the kitchen island. They were ostentatiously over-the-top; luxurious to the point of tasteless. Lined with tartan fabric, each one contained smoked salmon sandwiches, complete with condiments packed into separate miniature glass jars. Pickled red onions, capers, dill-infused jelly. It was as if the guests' tastebuds wouldn't be spoilt by the fumes from the firepits.

A bottle of champagne was tucked into each, even though she would be doing hot toddy runs between the kitchen and the lochside throughout the afternoon. The aim seemed to be to keep the guests permanently inebriated.

She stepped back to admire her work, but her eyes trailed to the freezer room. The body couldn't be kept there forever, of course. It could stay there until this evening though. This was when she planned to reveal everything to Calan. He would finally know the extent of her love. He would, she hoped, wrap his arms around her. Surely, he would express his own love for her? At the very least, his gratitude. She smiled, fingering her crucifix. He was such a good boy. Such a good, good boy.

A year after Rebekah had left her, Marta had spoken to nobody except colleagues. She was promoted again – she was *chef de partie* – and her life was her cuisine. Without Rebekah to caress, her hands embraced the kitchen. She was driven, dedicated, and very much alone.

But then she saw them. It was on the way home. Marta was walking through Highbury Fields, her hands shoved into her pockets, hood up, mind busy with what she would be cooking that evening. Rebekah crossed her path pushing the buggy and stopped a few metres ahead. The baby's soft gurgle reached out through the air. Marta stopped walking. She remembered how her heart had thudded, how she'd wondered at how Rebekah had not heard its beat. She looked the same, just as beautiful and wonderful as a year ago. She was a natural mother – at least, it had seemed so. She bent down towards the buggy and made a cooing sound, which turned into a song.

Marta's throat tightened at the sound of it, hardly able to believe her ears.

'*When you're near me, I see the world in technicolour. Your smile melts through the coldest winter. Our love will last a thousand years over, when you're near...*'

It was beautiful. Yes, she had considered approaching them. She thought about singing along, giving Rebekah a hug, wishing her well, meeting the baby. But she didn't. That image of them was enough. She could live with it. They were well. They were happy. It was all she wanted; all she had hoped for.

She respected Rebekah's wishes. She didn't want to intervene. She just wanted to know they were okay, so she secured Rebekah's new address through her work, explaining how she needed to forward her post. It wasn't too far away, just down the road in Farringdon. She used to sit in the pub opposite her flat, just to check that Rebekah was getting enough fresh air with the baby. She would watch the lights flicker on inside, and saw when she was watching television, putting the baby to bed.

At times, Rebekah seemed sad. One night, she forgot to pull the curtains closed. She rested her head in her hands at the kitchen table, visibly weeping. Marta was so close to ringing the buzzer; it was a physical pain to see her love like this. But how would she disguise her wine-drenched breath? What reason would she give for being alone and so close to her new house? Rebekah would get the wrong idea. No, it was much better to protect her from afar. From here, she could be a part of everything.

She started to use up her holiday days from the restaurant – something she'd never done before. By midday, she was waiting outside the pub for the staff to unbolt the doors. As the first customer, she was able to secure her preferred seat: the barstool at the window. They knew her well enough by now and brought her usual bottle of *Valpolicella* promptly. From there, she stared at the ground-floor flat opposite. She learnt that time passed incredibly slowly when you're waiting for a glimpse of the one you love. She thought that this might be just how God feels, constantly watching his children, his creations. She loved it there, in her corner. And when Rebekah emerged from her front door, her hair messy from sleep, her mouth slightly opened with rushed breaths, one hand fumbling to lock the door, the other trying her best to rock the buggy, Marta's heart sang with their song.

It was a Wednesday when the unfamiliar couple arrived. They were dressed for the countryside and looked out of place against the row of London townhouses. The man knocked on Rebekah's door and when she appeared, she wore an odd expression of both fear and relief. They stayed for about half an hour that day.

They returned about a week later. This time, they stayed for an hour.

Two days later, they returned with a lady, dressed more smartly, who was carrying a briefcase. They were inside for forty-three minutes.

The wine glass shook violently in Marta's hand. The couple re-emerged from Rebekah's flat, the official-looking woman following them, holding the baby – Rebekah's baby, *their* baby – in her arms. Marta stood, her hands pressed against the window. Her ragged breath blew in panicked steam against the glass. 'No!' she shouted.

'Everything all right?' the barman called out.

'No! No! No!'

Marta watched in horror as the couple climbed into the woman's car and drove away. Rebekah remained in her doorway watching them leave. She stared at the end of the road for almost ten minutes. Then, she wiped a single tear from her cheek and shook her head, as if she could shake off what she had just done. She had given their baby away. She had *given their baby away*!

She wanted to run outside and scream at her. She wanted to take her by the hair and drag her along the street and point at where the car had gone and tell her to get it back! Get the baby back! *Get our baby!*

Instead, she watched Rebekah go into her house and did nothing. She finished the bottle of wine, her hands trembling, tears tumbling down her face. She pulled her hood tight and crossed the road towards Rebekah's bins. She recycled her old post, Marta knew. Crouching down, she sifted through the envelopes until she found what she was looking for: adoption agency papers.

A high-pitched, animal wail escaped her lips as she scanned the words. It was all here: the baby, a baby boy, single mother struggling with mental health, depression, a loving couple in need of a child. She heard the front door open.

'Who's there?' Rebekah sounded like she'd been crying. Good. She had done the most stupid, unthinkable of things.

Marta stuffed the letters in her coat pocket and ran without looking back.

CALAN

It was too early for knocks on the door.

She usually waited until everyone was asleep so nobody would see them. Calan pushed himself up from the bed, half-awake. He'd slipped away to the bothy for a quick nap. The afternoon was likely to be an endurance test in patience. He'd be required, firstly, to persuade the guests to try cold swimming. After a painstaking back and forth, some of them would finally jump in, before screaming at him to get their towels ready. Then, they'd struggle getting out of the water, before needing him to pull them up and wrap them in their dry robes. Obviously, they'd then demand a cocktail be mixed, so they could huddle by the fire and screech with laughter at just how *ridiculous* they were.

More knocks.

He wasn't ready for her yet. He'd prepared himself for this evening, told himself he would finish it then. He was ready to stand up to her... but not right now. He didn't have the energy, plus, the timing was off. It was the start of a busy afternoon. He had stuff to get in place, he had other things to be thinking about. He couldn't have this conversation now, nor deal with its fallout.

The knocking sounded again, quicker and louder.

'Okay!' he called, pulling his own dry robe over his boxers for ease. 'Wait a second.'

Why she had to do the dramatic knocking *every time* was beyond him. The door swung open.

There she was. That disgusting smile slithering over her face like she owned him. Like she was entitled to him.

'I'm busy now, Jules.'

She raised her eyebrows, probably because she thought it looked sexy, and entered. 'Looks it.'

He checked the surrounding area before closing the door. The sooner he could put this behind him, the better. And that meant keeping it a secret. She rolled her shoulders back.

'Can it wait for later?' He hated how his voice sounded, so cowardly and small. Why didn't he just tell her what he really thought? That she was a dried up old desperate mess who could only get some by forcing her employee to sleep with her.

She sighed and arranged herself on the bed, one hand above her head, the other stroking her thigh. 'I'm not in the mood,' he insisted.

She laughed at that and it was a horrible, throaty sound. Then, she made a show of rolling her eyes before settling her gaze on him. 'Jealous?'

He shook his head, not understanding what she meant. 'What have I got to be jealous of?'

She shifted positions, sighing as she removed her coat, and shot him a knowing smile. 'I saw you watching me last night, Calan, through the crack in the anteroom door. Oh, don't be embarrassed...' She slowly pushed herself from the bed and moved towards him. Bringing her face close to his, she said, 'I quite liked it, actually.'

Her breath smelt of cigarettes and booze. Heat crept up Calan's face and his hands clenched into tight fists. 'I wasn't *watching* you...' he mumbled. He breathed, trying to level his voice. 'I told you – I'm worried about Marta. And the missing rifle, in case you'd forgotten? I came back to get you to actually *do* something.'

Jules shrugged and moved away from him back towards the bed. He couldn't believe he used to like the way she swung her hips as she walked. Now, she just looked so embarrassing and fake. She slipped back down onto the duvet. 'And I've told *you* this weekend is critical, haven't I? I can't have news of a missing gun circulating. You think Tim would hand over any money then? Do you?'

Calan looked at his feet. 'He's got enough, I bet.'

She sighed in the way she did when she thought she was teaching him something.

'I bet. But companies like his don't tend to invest in chaos. And a missing gun is chaos.' She flipped onto her side and looked at him squarely, before adding, 'Anyway, I'm sure it's fine. Is Marta still following you about?'

He folded his arms, suddenly more exhausted than before his nap. 'She's ramped things up, all right. She was spying on me by the fishing hut earlier. You shouldn't have come during the day, Jules.'

She nodded, apparently thinking very carefully about something. Then, she patted the mattress next to her. 'Did you want to...?'

In that moment he truly hated himself. There was nothing about this woman he liked. She was so full of it; constantly preoccupied with her self-importance, the fantasies she told herself. She complained about her husband leaving her to run this place alone, but whose fault had that been? Predator. That's what she was. A full-blown predator. Still, a small part of him, a part that only reared its head in moments like this, wanted her. She had a knack of reducing him to nothing more than primal desire. He wasn't a person when he was with her. He was just a body. He removed his dry robe.

'We can't do this forever.'

Her eyes raked over his body as he approached the bed, satisfied and greedy. She stroked his hair as he lowered himself down. 'Don't think about that now.'

Her lips moved over his. She tasted of coffee and cigarettes. He closed his eyes. *One last time*, he told himself. *One last time*.

JULES

She knew she shouldn't have been so reckless... in the middle of the day! She couldn't help herself. The phrase reverberated through her skull as she walked back towards the hotel from the bothy:

You can't help yourself, Jules. You're unwell! You need help, do you understand that?

She'd been lucky Rob hadn't told anyone about her and Calan. Instead, he'd packed his bags and left in their van within half a day. She would never forget the look on his face when he'd found them; it still made her shudder. He shouldn't have been anywhere near the bothy. Calan had finished all his chores, and she'd said she was checking on the cows. She hadn't even heard the door open, which meant he would have seen everything. It was summer and they'd been on the floor, completely naked, no blankets, nothing. She'd tripped up over her clothes in her hurry to run after him.

Don't touch me! Don't follow me... finish yourself off, why don't you... with that child! A child, Jules!

She gritted her teeth. There was no point replaying it all over again.

Zach's rejection had set her back. He'd lifted her up, teased her into thinking she was worth his time, then left her cold. She had *needed* Calan today. He was always so dependable, always so careful with her. And anyway, it wasn't as if she was doing anything wrong. He was nineteen years old! He was an adult! He was perfectly capable of making his own decisions. If he no longer wanted her, then he was more than able to say it.

The force hit her from the side out of nowhere. She was flung down onto the ground, her head narrowly missing a rock. Before she could open her mouth to scream, she was wrestled onto her back. As she blinked into the snow, a face emerged above her.

'Marta, what—'

Marta's hand moved with almost supernatural speed. It slapped across Jules's face with unbelievable force. She lost focus in the midst of the pain, her cheek slamming against the freezing ground. Gradually, the stars from behind her eyes began to disperse and she groaned, confusion setting in. She sensed an object being wielded above her and moved her face towards it, wincing at a sharp pain which was spreading beneath her left eye. As her vision sharpened, she realised she was looking into the barrel of a hunting rifle.

Her stomach spasmed with fear, and her mouth opened and closed silently with shock. Marta pressed the barrel gently against her forehead.

'Do as I say,' Marta whispered, barely audible.

Jules widened her eyes, too scared to nod against the weight of the rifle. '*Okay,*' she mouthed. '*Okay.*'

Marta peered down at her, and, for a moment, Jules thought she was going to spit in her face. Instead, she just licked her lips and glared. 'You're corrupting something very precious to me. Something I promised to protect.'

A necklace dangled low from her neck: an opulent crucifix.

Jules was too scared to think clearly, but she had seen it before. Yes! Yes, Zach had been wearing it last night. But that didn't make sense. A dull throb began emanating from the side of her face. None of this felt real. She was disoriented. Marta's words settled over her like a dry ash cloud.

'You and your godless ways are infecting him. The one I love! I cannot allow it.'

Jules felt her body begin to shiver in small, jerky convulsions. She was lying in the snow. She needed to move soon. But she was struggling to follow what Marta was talking about. An infection? She gulped, filling her lungs with cold air. 'Marta, if we can just go inside, then we can talk...'

'Shut up!' Marta's power showed itself in full. Her eyes blazed like two coals in her sharp, bird-like features. Against the white sky, she was like some mythological demon.

Marta pressed the gun harder against Jules's forehead. She whimpered. 'Please...'

'I said shut up!'

Jules had never seen Marta like this. Her rage, her prowess was at complete odds with the eccentric little woman who kept herself to herself. It was as if she'd been possessed. The wind blew a gust of powdery snow between them. When it cleared, Marta had her eyes closed and was murmuring beneath her breath.

'Marta...' Jules spoke carefully. 'Marta, please, just put the gun down.' The metal was brutally cold against her skin.

Marta opened her eyes and stared down at her. Her face was blank but her eyes were still filled with fury.

'Listen carefully,' she clipped. 'Never touch him again. Never touch Calan again, do you hear me? I suspected something, but never... never the extent of this filth!'

Jules watched the woman ruminate silently, her face crinkled and pained.

'If I'd had any idea what you were doing to him, I'd have stopped you sooner. He is a boy! He is to be protected! Do you understand?'

Jules did not understand. She did not understand a word Marta was saying. But she nodded, her whole body now shaking with either cold or fear. 'Y-yes. Yes, I understand.'

Marta looked at her for a second then removed the gun from her head and watched her scramble to her feet. Jules held her hands up in front. 'Please, I won't see him again. I promise, Marta, I promise.'

'You defile him,' Marta spat back. 'You mock me. You mock God. I was supposed to watch him, to keep him safe. I was supposed to guard him from evils like you.'

'Okay...' Jules's shoulders sagged with relief as Marta lowered the rifle. 'Okay... I'm sorry...'

Marta started to back away down the path. Her feet were unsteady but she kept her eyes on Jules with a dogged determination. 'I won't keep your secret,' she said, her thin voice carrying through the cold air like a serpent. 'Don't tell anyone about this, otherwise everyone will know what a pathetic godless slut you are.'

As if already confident of Jules's reply, Marta carefully picked her way down the hill path. Jules nodded anyway, her limbs now trembling uncontrollably. She hugged herself, letting a long whoosh of tension release from her lips. She brought a hand to her cheek, realising she was bleeding.

'What the...?' she whispered to herself. 'What the hell was that?'

MARTA

Her heart felt like it was about to explode from her chest. She could not unsee it. She could not dispel that hideous act she had watched through the bothy window. How could that woman have done it! How could she have polluted such a pure and perfect child? It was unconscionable. It was revolting.

'Rebekah...'

Marta skidded down the icy scree to the edge of the loch. On the opposite side, she could just about make out the orange lick of the firepits ready for the guests. Nobody was congregating yet. 'Rebekah, I'm sorry. I'm sorry.'

She knelt on the thin ice and it shattered around her. The cold water submerged her legs but she didn't move. Perhaps she deserved to be numb. She had kept tabs on him for so many years; she'd even caught a flight from Milan once to visit this remote, grey place. She had moved here, given up her restaurant, her accolades, her life's work all with the noble purpose of keeping a watchful eye on him. Their baby was her real life's work. Her true calling.

'Rebekah, I failed... I am so, so, sorry. I failed our child, our son. I tried. I tried to make sure your mistake didn't ruin him. I tried to keep him safe for us. I should have come long before. Long, long before.'

'When you're near me, I see the world in technicolour. Your smile melts through the coldest winter. Our love will last a thousand years over, when you're near...'

The song came from behind her. It was a soft voice which wove through the trees and infiltrated her ears, warm and comforting. She twisted her head quickly but lost her balance. Her hands splayed flat as she fell forwards into the shallow water. She spluttered, slipping on the rocks beneath the surface, trying to get up.

'Rebekah? Is it you? I can hear you...'

'Your smile melts through the coldest winter...'

The song continued but there was no one to be seen. She breathed out, and felt her foot slide from beneath her again, this time throwing her weight completely off back into the floating shards of ice. 'Oh...'

She kicked her legs, the sensation of needles beginning to pierce them. With difficulty, she pulled herself back onto the scree and sat there for a while, breathless. She ought to be getting back to work. The guests would be ordering drinks soon, and she needed to start preparing dinner. It wasn't wise to leave the kitchen unattended for too long.

'When you're near...'

Hoisting herself up, she shuddered at the feel of wet clothes against her skin. Now she would need to change before she got back to work, which meant she was already behind schedule. She clapped her hands, as if telling herself to hurry along and turned towards the trees from where she'd come.

The singing stopped. There was a rustle behind the snow-laden branches, a foot's crunch upon hard ground.

'You...' she started, as the figure emerged from the shade of the trees.

LUCAS

All he knew was that he had run. He'd locked eyes with Sandeep for a long, loaded moment, confirmed he wasn't playing some delusional practical joke, and bolted out of the fishing hut, away from the hotel, away from everything.

For a little while, he'd been free. The fresh air had seeped into his bloodstream, his legs had pumped with hot and wild panic. The path wound away from the loch into dense forest. He was hidden. Isolated. Away from all the lies. But then – the sharp pain in his ribs.

Lucas doubled over, panting. He spat on the forest path and watched the globule of saliva run aimlessly against a patch of ice. It hurt to breathe, which obviously made sense, based on the fact he'd done no real exercise for well over a year. Well, it didn't matter. This was as good a place as any to hide until... well, until he worked out what his next moves were.

Thick, grey, leafless trees surrounded him. How was that for a pathetic metaphor? This would play out perfectly in a novel. He imagined how he'd teach it to his students: '*And what do you think those skeletal trees symbolise here then? Despair? Yes. All semblance of hope disappearing? Absolutely. The utter and final stripping of all belief in goodness and trust? Yup, that's the one!'*

He pressed forwards, dipping his head, one foot in front of the other. Stopping wasn't an option. He must keep moving. As long as he kept going, he didn't need to think about those strange and monstrous words.

It was me. I killed your sister. I killed Bebe.

How was it even possible? Lucas had found her! It clearly wasn't... murder. The thought of the word made him want to vomit. Stomach acid raced up his throat, the hot liquid burning his mouth. He spat again, trying to quicken his pace as if he could outrun the memory.

They had been at their dad's old house right by the sea in the Algarve. It was a weird place really. The views were spectacular, the villa itself was gorgeous: all white lines and cream soft furnishings. But it felt like staying in a graveyard of memories. A bright and airy mausoleum.

Sandeep and he had been having beers on the terrace, watching the sunset. Despite the blistering heat of the day, a cooler breeze drifted from the sea with the onset of night.

What had made him check in on Bebe's room on his way to get a jumper? There'd been nothing out of the ordinary, nothing that had stood out to indicate what she was planning.

The trees flanking the path seemed to bend in towards him as he passed, as if goading his mind's eye to reach the final image of the story.

The villa was chilly. The air conditioning had been on all day and hummed lazily in the background. His and Sandeep's room was upstairs, at the end of the corridor. Bebe's was on the same floor as the terrace, behind the living area. There had been no reason at all for Lucas to check on her. It was late enough for her to have fallen asleep.

Something, however, had pulled him towards her door.

Why did irrelevant details always stick out when reliving trauma? The painting on the wall was an abstract collection of blue and white squares – he remembered thinking that he could have done a better job. Bebe's lip balm was in the rose-pink bowl on the side table. The sound of a bottle breaking came from the house next door, followed by the inevitable jeers and apologies.

He'd called out her name. He remembered it vividly; he'd called her name twice.

What had never been clear was when he'd known, because he was sure it was before he'd opened the door. Something in the air – the smell? The stillness? It had alerted a sixth sense.

It was like he was there all over again. The blood. There had been so much blood that he hadn't registered what it was at first because it looked like the bedsheets were just a bright-red colour. The wrist wounds were wide and gaping. He remembered screaming. He remembered Sandeep holding him from behind, rocking him. He remembered being embarrassed. It wasn't as if he'd ever had an adult relationship with his sister, yet he was crying like a baby.

I killed your sister.

The thought was too immense for his head to contain. Had Sandeep snuck into her bedroom? Planted the knife? Had he held her down whilst he administered the cuts? Why? *Why?* Lucas's legs trembled and he collapsed on the spot. He clutched his chest, realising he was hyperventilating. Had he been sleeping with, kissing, planning his life with a killer all this time? Was he next? Is that why he'd confessed?

'Lucas!' Sandeep's voice rang out through the trees. 'Lucas! We need to talk! I... I'm sorry!'

Sorry! He was *sorry?* Lucas rolled onto his side and counted to three. He needed to get out of here. Fear caught the back of his neck like a cold hand. He was being chased! He was running for his life. Staggering to stand, he threw himself off the main path into the branches. The twigs scratched his face, but he didn't care. All he knew was that he had to get away.

'Lucas!'

Sandeep's voice rang through his ears. His chest burnt, his eyes stung, but he kept pushing forwards, pelting through the wilderness, until... he was falling. A sharp force hit his shoulder as he tumbled down the slope. He felt his head swing backwards before connecting with something solid. His eyes closed, snowflakes settling on his lashes, and darkness dragged him under.

'...but you're loaded.'

'I don't see how that has anything to do with you.'

'Weren't you listening? I'm not fucking about.'

Lucas blinked up at the white sky. His body felt pinned in place and his head throbbed. The voices sounded close.

'Help...' he croaked weakly. The sound barely reached his own ears.

A snarly, derogatory laugh made him pay attention. 'You think you can threaten me?'

'I just want what's mine, okay?'

'It's not yours, you little freak!'

There was a sound of a short scuffle, followed shortly by a gasp.

'Is that...?'

'Shit, quick – they might be suffocating. Quick, dig! Dig, all right?'

Two pairs of hands appeared at Lucas's sides. Through his hazy thoughts, he deciphered he was buried under an enormous snowdrift, which explained why he couldn't move. He tried to turn his head to get a look at his rescuers. 'Hey...'

'Don't move, all right? Lucas, isn't it?'

Well, that was something at least. They knew his name. That was nice.

'Lucas? Can you hear me? It's Calan, the gamekeeper.'

Lucas felt his body being lifted up into the air before he was placed gently back onto the ground. 'Lucas?'

'He's fine. Just a scrape.'

The other voice also sounded familiar. Lucas slid his eyes sideways and saw in the periphery it was Tim, the dickhead from the bar last night, dressed in even more dickheadish running gear.

'No signal here...' Calan was pacing around him, holding his phone in the air.

Tim frowned, his big face looming into Lucas's line of sight. 'Jesus, mate. Look, can you talk? Just sit up, maybe?'

The world was slowly becoming more clear. There was an undertone of derision in Tim's voice, which Lucas did not appreciate at all. Still, he took his hand and allowed himself to be pulled upright. His head throbbed violently with the movement and he groaned.

Calan knelt beside him and checked his eyes. 'You look okay.' He nodded, studying his face. 'What are you doing all the way out here?'

Lucas flinched, suddenly remembering how he'd ended up in the snowdrift. 'Oh my God!'

He looked to and from Tim and Calan, wondering how to explain. 'I need to get back—'

'Lucas!' Sandeep's voice rang out from behind them. 'For fuck's sake, there you are! What the hell happened?'

'Help!' Lucas scrambled to his feet, falling onto Calan for support. 'Help! He's dangerous! He's a killer...' He pointed aggressively at Sandeep. 'Do something!'

Unbelievably, neither Tim nor Calan made any moves to

detain Sandeep. Instead, Tim let out a low laugh and muttered something Lucas was sure wasn't useful beneath his breath, and Calan sort of dithered awkwardly on the spot.

Sandeep stepped towards him. It seemed unlikely he'd try anything here in front of two witnesses, but Lucas was taking no chances. He scrambled about his feet, clutching at a rock. 'Stay away from me. Stay where you are!'

'Lucas...' Sandeep took another step forwards.

'You killed her! You killed my sister, you psychopath!' The words burst from Lucas's mouth, the rage rattling through his chest. He shook the rock as a warning for him to keep back. 'You stay where you are!'

Sandeep placed his head in his hands. 'I'm sorry... shit. I should have phrased that differently. Of course you would think...'

'I'm not sure how many ways there are to confess to murdering people's sisters,' Lucas retorted, pretty proud about how composed he was, given the circumstances.

'Oh no...' Sandeep's eyes trailed towards Calan and then Tim apologetically. 'No, Lucas. I didn't mean... I didn't *actually* kill her. Shit! You thought—'

'Of course I thought!' Lucas forgot about the pain behind his forehead and bellowed the words as loud as he could into the space between them. 'What the bloody hell else would I think when you say – in the middle of me *proposing*, Sandeep – that you killed my sister?!'

'Bloody hell,' Tim muttered behind him.

Sandeep took a long breath and nodded, at first slowly, then quickly. 'Lucas, I owe you a huge apology. I thought, well, I thought it was obvious that I hadn't murdered—' He stopped after the word, his eyes large with disbelief. 'That I hadn't done that. I just meant that I... well, I've always thought I had the chance to stop her from going through with it... she tried to talk to me... and I... I fell short.' He gave Lucas one of the most caring and intimate looks he had in months. 'Look, can we chat about this in private?'

Lucas stared at him, not quite ready to let the rock go just yet. The police had been all over the scene with a fine-tooth comb, he remembered. They had conducted a very thorough investigation, given how out-of-the-blue it was. They would, he realised, have mentioned it had they suspected Sandeep. There were all sorts of things, like DNA and forensic science that would have incriminated him.

'How do I know you're not lying?' Lucas said, beginning to see the tinge of ridiculousness this situation had about it.

The edges of Sandeep's lips twitched. 'You can keep the rock for the walk back, just in case.'

Lucas nodded, his own lips twitching. 'Fine.'

JULES

Jules stood behind the reception desk, staring at her phone. She should call the police. Turning a blind eye to a missing rifle was one thing, but being held at gunpoint? She couldn't ignore that. Marta might be a danger to others too. Calan had been right.

For what must have been the tenth time, she began dialling 999, then deleted the numbers. Had she really believed Marta would shoot her? She bit her lip. She had always been a little odd. For all Jules knew, the gun could have been unloaded.

Marta would almost certainly follow through on her threat, and even if the police didn't care about Calan, the few friends she had in the community would be disgusted. Who was to say the rumours wouldn't reach Tim? Nobody would want to invest in a... Jules hated the words the rest of the world used for people like her. *Nymphomaniac. Predator. Groomer.*

She placed her phone on the counter just as Lucas and Sandeep returned. Smiling, she said in a shrill voice, 'Welcome back! The pic 'n' dip's starting in half an hour, do you need anything?'

Their dynamic had visibly changed since the yoga class earlier. They were holding hands and Lucas's head was resting against Sandeep's shoulder. Both were giggling. She would have very much liked whatever medicine they had been taking right now.

'We'll be out in a bit,' Sandeep called out as they sashayed up the staircase.

The phone sat as if in judgement of her on the desk. She should call them. She knew she should call them. But sometimes the right decision wasn't always the best one. She could see a future where this place thrived. She could reward Calan with more money, if he wanted. *He* wasn't keen on anyone knowing about them either, was he? In fact, by not calling the police, she was protecting him. In many ways, her inaction could be viewed as a selfless act.

She just needed to stay vigilant of Marta.

Something that sounded like a sniff from the bar opposite alerted her attention. She froze. Shoving her phone in her back pocket, she tiptoed her way across the hall and poked her head around the doorway. Letting out a breath, she realised she wasn't being spied on. Gracie sat huddled before the fire, weeping, by the sounds of it.

Jules backed away. She had no desire to be in a room alone with this woman again. A floorboard creaked beneath her foot and Gracie reacted almost robotically without even bothering to turn. 'Come in. It's fine.'

'Oh!' Jules swore under her breath. 'Oh no, I'll leave you to it—'

'Come in.'

Beneath the thickness of her tears was an iron-cold command. So, she was still using her husband's investment as leverage against her. Jules moved into the room reluctantly. For a few moments neither of them said anything. On Gracie's knees was the laptop, on which she was flicking through the endless photographs of Tim and his mistress. Her tears fell carelessly onto the keyboard. The logs on the fire hissed and spat as if they were mirroring Gracie's mood.

'There are so many of them,' Gracie said, finally. She cocked her head to one side at a selfie taken on what looked like Waterloo Bridge. The woman was laughing with glee at Tim's face burying into her neck.

Jules shifted on the spot before involuntarily sitting down. Watching the screen, she nodded. Despite her very, very strong reservations about Gracie, it seemed right to comfort her. A strange tug of responsibility rolled somewhere deep in Jules's stomach. It was as if, having inflicted this precise pain on another person previously, she must right the wrong... or at least offer a response.

'It's probably nothing to do with you,' she said. She watched the flames, thinking about how she had tried to explain this to Rob. 'Cheats don't think about things like that. It's separate from you.'

'But what if he loves her?' Gracie continued to click through the smiling faces. 'It looks like they're living in a fairy tale.'

Jules ran her fingers through her hair, trying to decide whether to say what she was thinking. 'If that's true, then he'll tell you. He'll leave. There's no reason for him not to, is there? He's brought you here, on this weekend, hasn't he? You don't know – he might have ended it with her. This might be his way of making it up to you.'

Gracie let out a bitter cry. She placed the laptop on the floor, her hands shaking. 'So I should just... pretend I don't know? Pretend I didn't see these? Is that what you think?'

'I don't think anything, not really.' Jules pushed herself up and placed her hands on her hips. 'Come on, people are starting to gather by the loch. It's looking pretty cosy. Why don't you try and get through the next few hours and reassess? I'm going to round the guests up.'

She left before Gracie could reply. Silently recounting the guests' names, she tried to account for everyone's whereabouts. Sandeep and Lucas were in their room; Gracie was in the bar; Tim... he'd be back from his run by now and was probably showering; Zach...

She wavered on the spot. Should she knock on his door? She hadn't seen him since dinner last night and didn't want to come on too strong. However, he had prepaid for his hamper and it was her job to make sure all guests didn't miss out on their experiences.

She jogged up the stairs, arranging her face into something she hoped resembled nonchalance, and gave his door a little tap. There was no answer. After a few seconds, she knocked again, and called, 'Mr Williams? I'm just checking to see if you're still planning on the cold swim?'

Still, only silence followed. Her stomach tied in an embarrassed knot, she retrieved her bundle of spare keys from her pocket. If he was showering or, worse, ignoring her, she could pretend she was checking the fireguard. She opened the door carefully. 'Zach... Mr Williams?'

It smelt of him inside. She entered the space with her mouth slightly parted, remembering his lips on hers. The bed was neatly made. A gown that didn't belong to the hotel – made of what she thought was silk – was folded neatly on the bedspread. His blue Aspinal bag was on the luggage stand, where it had been before.

There were no sounds from the bathroom: Zach wasn't here. But she couldn't quite bring herself to leave his room yet. Maybe she'd been wrong, maybe he hadn't left her in the lurch... perhaps something had happened to him? He'd said he was interested in filming wildlife. Maybe he'd gone out before coming to see her and got himself into trouble?

She studied his bag. Obviously, going through guests'

luggage was completely unethical. However, if Zach was in danger, then she might find a clue as to where he was. Perhaps he kept a diary or some sort of location plan? Her mind spun with images of his body sprawled in the snow, or him huddled beneath a tree for warmth. She pressed her lips together, recognising the familiar sensation of her mind slipping away from her. As she unzipped the bag, a trepidatious thrill danced low in her body. What was right and wrong seemed so fixed for most people, but not her. At times, she could convince herself of anything.

She peered inside. It had been mostly unpacked apart from an oblong-shaped box. She lifted it out and placed it on the floor. It clicked open with ease, its contents rattling slightly. She wasn't entirely sure what she was looking at. It looked like a trinket collection: rings, necklaces... a dark-blue lacy thong, all organised in sealable, transparent plastic bags. On each bag was a name written in careful, black script on a white label. Worse, behind the objects were small, polaroid photographs. Some were asleep. Others posed, their eyes bright and excited. Some were clothed, some in underwear, others naked.

Alex.
Juno.
Clare.
Finlay.

She frowned; the urge to snap the box tight and run away was strong. Then, at the side of the pile, she saw it. An empty bag with *Julia* written on it. She groaned in disgust. People like this were the stuff of urban legends, weren't they? There weren't really men who collected secret trophies from their romantic conquests like this? She picked up the bag with her name on it between her thumb and forefinger and held it up to the light. What had he planned on putting in here?

She imagined him in her room upstairs – her home, her private space – rummaging through her drawers whilst she was in the loo, swiping an earring from her dressing table. What did he do with all this stuff? It didn't bear thinking about. Whatever his reasons for standing her up, she'd had a very, very lucky escape. Gracie, it turned out, had been right. Zach was a creep. That much was certain.

The smell of the firepits from outside refocused her mind. Zach wouldn't be happy at all if he found her here, rummaging through his things. She had no idea what he was capable of, really. In a hurry, she closed the lid with too much force and the bags spilt onto the floor.

She clawed at them, panic beginning to rise, until she saw a photo of a dark-haired woman, half-asleep, smiling lazily into the camera.

It couldn't be… it couldn't be.

She brought the image closer to her face. This bag had no object in it, just a photograph. It was undeniably her. She recognised the longish nose, the dark, almost-black eyes.

Rebekah.

The name on the label was *Rebekah*. It was the woman with whom Tim was having an affair. It was the woman from the photos on his laptop.

LUCAS

Sandeep pulled an armchair onto the mahogany platform as Lucas bathed in front of the windows. He had just about stopped shivering and the pins and needles in his legs were beginning to abate. Still, he felt a little chilly.

'Are you sure it can't be any hotter?'

Sandeep shook his head stubbornly, giving him a smile. 'The doctor on the phone was very clear, Lucas. She said to start with tepid, then warm, then hot. From what we told her, she doesn't think you're hypothermic, but just in case, I hope the weather clears up tomorrow. I'd like you to see someone anyway.'

'Trapped!' Lucas laughed, submerging himself to his chin beneath the water. 'It'd be romantic if it wasn't a medical emergency...'

'I wouldn't say emergency.' Sandeep's voice wobbled and he sank deeper into the chair. 'But I'm really glad you're okay. If you hadn't been found...'

They sat with the unsaid thought for a couple of minutes. Lucas gently drummed the tap with his toe. 'Still, I don't think a bit of heat will hurt.'

Sandeep rolled his eyes, but dutifully administered the hot

water. It was wonderful, like a warming hug around his tired body. Lucas closed his eyes and let out a long sigh. 'So...'

'So,' Sandeep repeated.

'Did you want to—?' In truth, Lucas had no idea where to begin. His proposal still hung in the balance and Sandeep had yet to fully explain himself. This wasn't the way he'd envisaged the day going at all. He'd thought they'd be sipping champagne by the loch right now, bragging to the other guests. Yet, here he was, defrosting as Sandeep and he talked about Bebe, of all people.

Sandeep cleared his throat once, then again. 'I owe you an explanation, I know. It's... I've been holding this back for so long. I...'

'Sandeep, please just get on with it.'

Lucas was surprised by his own flat tone. He let his body float in the centre of the water, weightless. He was so tired. Tired of trying to impress Sandeep. Tired of pretending to be something he wasn't. The truth suddenly seemed so very important. It felt like they were on the cusp of the first real conversation they'd had... well, since that holiday.

Sandeep inhaled and began. 'Portugal was nerve-racking, Lucas. We'd not met too long ago...'

'Three months,' Lucas interjected.

'That's right, and you'd told me all about your childhood. How awful your dad was, how Bebe had never helped you...'

'You were the one who wanted to go!' Lucas opened his eyes to the vaulted ceiling. The steam rose above his head as if eliciting accurate memories. He gritted his teeth. 'If it sounded like such a hardship, then why badger me into replying to her? Why push it? I didn't want to go in the first place.'

There was no way he was going to let Sandeep play Mr Sensible Victim with this point. He remembered so very clearly telling him how bad an idea the holiday would be. Obviously, he hadn't known quite how bad at the time.

'Lucas...'

He sat up in the bath, displacing a healthy slosh of water onto the wood. Sandeep looked like he was about to admonish him, but Lucas held him by the eye. 'Sandeep...'

He imitated Sandeep's hint of condescension. 'Don't use that voice with me. You're not right about everything, you know. I made it very clear – I always have – that I wanted nothing to do with my family. It was you, *you* who was obsessed—'

'I wouldn't say obsessed.'

'Oh you wouldn't? What word would you use then? I apologise if my vocabulary choice doesn't quite reflect the minutiae of the situation, but, from where I'm sitting, I'm still waiting to hear what you had to do with my sister's death and all you can harp on about is how it was my fault you were on that holiday at all!'

He took a great breath, feeling a little dizzy and sunk back into the water. This was so bloody typical that he almost wanted to descend into hysterics. He prodded the tap again. 'More please.'

Sandeep silently did as he was asked and settled back into his position. 'Sorry,' he murmured.

'Continue,' Lucas said, flicking his hand in the air. This was all very traumatic, of course, but it was also quite nice being the one with the moral high ground. He'd make the most of it if he liked.

'All right.' Sandeep, for once, took Lucas's lead. 'I think it was, what, three, four days into the holiday? I'd noticed her watching you. She looked, I don't know, confused. It makes sense, doesn't it? I didn't know how to behave either. Here's this sister who you've had nothing to do with for the best part of twenty years, and now we're having beers, sharing stories, going out to dinner. There's no blueprint for that kind of thing...'

'I know,' said Lucas quietly. 'You think I didn't find it weird too?'

'Of course I did. I'd assumed Bebe pushed so hard for the holiday because she had some big news. If I'm honest, I thought she might be ill. Why else would she want to go away with you?'

Lucas had actually thought the same himself. It was the only reason he'd agreed to it. He'd suggested coffee, then lunch, then dinner, but she'd been adamant. She'd wanted to go back to Portugal with him, where they'd holidayed as children. *It's where we were happy,* she'd said. *Do you remember that? When we were happy?* He'd convinced himself she was terminally ill, and, as selfish as it sounded, he didn't want his sister's death on his conscience. He'd viewed the holiday as his penance for an easy life and heart. He laughed bitterly at the thought and held his arm out for Sandeep to give him his towel.

He stood and the water dripped down his body in tiny, hurried currents. Wrapping the towel around him, he clambered from the bath. 'So, how did you end up killing her?'

He'd meant it to sound light-hearted – they'd laughed about the misunderstanding on the way back to their room. But the words came out barbed. He turned away from Sandeep towards the dresser to moisturise.

'You were on the balcony reading,' Sandeep continued. 'I was about to join you when I heard her crying in the bathroom. I knocked on the door, she opened it, and, well, she was rambling to be honest...'

Lucas gazed at himself in the mirror. In his face, he saw his sister staring back at him. Her eyes wide and fiery, her mouth moving silently like she needed to tell him something but couldn't.

'...she was talking about what an awful person she was. How

she'd let everyone down, starting with you. She said something about having an affair... and then another thing about not even being able to stay faithful to that... look, it was difficult to understand. Her thoughts were jumping about and I just wanted to calm her down.'

He took a breath. Lucas suspected the next bit was significant. 'She said she just wanted to make everything right. That's what she said: she'd invited us to Portugal to make everything better. It was the least she could do. And if she could do that, then maybe she could see some hope in the world.'

Sandeep's voice took on a mechanical quality, like he was reciting words he'd committed to memory. Lucas nodded and turned to face him. 'What did you say?'

Sandeep's eyes were glassy. 'I told her you can't always make everything better, that sometimes things are just as they are. Broken. And that you can learn to live with the cuts, the bruises, but you can't fix them.'

Lucas couldn't help it – he flinched. Retrospect was an awful thing. Sandeep's words could have swung either way. They could have healed, helped his and Bebe's relationship. Instead, they drove her to despair.

He edged closer and crouched next to the armchair. 'Sorry. It wasn't your fault, you know? You couldn't have known. I just wish... why didn't you tell me?'

Sandeep's voice broke. His eyes bulged, gargoyle-like, as if he was suffocating under the weight of the revelation.

'She killed herself.'

He repeated it. 'She killed herself. She did it because of me, Lucas! I took away her hope. I as good as told her there was nothing worth living for.'

'You didn't quite put it like that...' Lucas took his hands and closed his eyes. He rested his forehead against them, sorting through his thoughts. Sandeep had kept this a secret for nearly a year. He'd distanced himself, kept Lucas away from his family. What was the point of it all? Why not just cut and run and forget all about it? And then, finally, Lucas understood. He kept a hold of Sandeep's hands and opened his eyes.

'You stayed with me out of guilt. That's why you pretended your family wouldn't accept me. You didn't want to introduce me to them because it wasn't... real? You wanted to break up with me but felt you couldn't because... because you felt guilty about Bebe? Am I right?'

He'd never seen Sandeep look so helpless. Crumpled in the armchair he looked like a smaller version of himself, deflated like an old balloon. For the first time since Lucas could remember, he wasn't attracted to him. There was a new sensation: pity.

Sandeep began to cry, nodding through the tears.

'Jesus...' Lucas stood up and walked towards the bed, then rounded back on himself. 'Well, I retract my proposal, obviously.'

It was delightful, actually. About as delightful as break-ups following conversations about dead sisters can go. Lucas cracked a smile first, then began to laugh. Tears streamed down his face as the sound rang out around him. Sandeep stared at him for a couple of seconds, until the hysteria spread to him. He wiped his cheeks, his shoulders shaking.

'Fuck's sake...' Lucas gasped between breaths. 'What a bloody day. Look, I reckon we've missed the cold swim, thank God, but let's go down, pop open the booze, and try to enjoy what's left of this shitshow of a weekend? I...'

He smiled sheepishly. 'I very much do not love you, Sandeep.'

Sandeep blew his nose and smiled back at him. 'I very much don't love you either. But let's have some fun, yes.'

CALAN

Focus on the job. Focus on the fires. Focus on serving. Focus, focus, focus.

The nausea hit him in relentless waves. He always felt like this after Jules and he were together. A moment of excitement followed by intense anxiety. 'Everyone warm enough?' he asked, looking at the only guests who had shown up, the Melroses.

Jules was nervously pacing a few metres away from the fires, tapping at her phone screen in panicked intervals. If her plan was to annoy Tim, then she was doing a stellar job.

The awnings stretched and flexed against the wind. This picnic was further proof that rich people had no brains at all. Why would you opt to sit in the freezing cold for hours when you had a whole castle a few yards behind you, full of roaring fires? It wasn't outdoorsy, it was stupid.

Gracie nodded blankly, looking straight through him at the mountains on the other side of the water. Tim was reading the label on a bottle of whisky, a deep frown etched across his forehead. He ignored the question and simply exclaimed, 'Never too early, eh?' before pouring a few long glugs into his glass.

As he knocked back the golden liquid in one go, he locked eyes with Calan. It was one of the most furious, sneering looks he had ever been confronted with. His heart hammering, he shrugged, attempting to look nonplussed, and inched closer to his own fire. The smoke made his eyes water, which was useful, because he felt like he was about to cry. Was Tim going to say anything about this morning? In front of Jules? He stared studiously into the flames, trying to ignore his mounting sense of dread.

He hadn't meant to approach Tim like that earlier. It wasn't a part of his plan. He was just so desperate. He needed to get away from here, and quickly. And Tim was the most obvious person to ask. He had all that money. He was rolling in it. He just needed a little bit of it, just a small portion. Tim would hardly even notice it was gone.

Calan ground his back teeth as he realised he'd risked everything. He felt his lower lip tremble when he remembered how he'd blurted the question out, how he'd demanded this guy's handout like a little child. Obviously, it had been a beyond stupid idea, and now Mr Melrose felt like he had something over him. Thank God Lucas had almost got himself killed: Calan was sure he'd have received a punch otherwise.

'Top-up.' Tim barked the words, making him jump. The whisky bottle was on the tree-stump table right next to him – there was no need to ask anyone to pour it. Tim held the glass towards Calan expectantly, a dark gleam in his eye.

As another wave of nausea undulated through his body, Calan stood. 'Of course, Mr Melrose.'

Where the hell was Marta? Jules had done three hot toddy runs already. The pic 'n' dip was shaping up to be a flop. So far, the only guests to arrive were Gracie and Tim. They'd settled into a bitter rhythm of snide comments, shooting back and forth at each other like spitting snakes.

'Sure you're not keen?'

Tim stripped to his swimming trunks in the middle of the deck and placed his hands on his hips. It was obvious he was holding in his stomach. 'Bit of ice water might suit you quite well, Gracie?'

Gracie, who was wrapped in a blanket, took a deep swig of her whisky and fired back, 'Careful. Wouldn't want you to drown.'

Jules checked her phone again. There was still no reply.

Marta, we need to talk.

Marta... the picnic is starting.

The guests are arriving, are you working today?

Marta, can you let me know if you're planning on doing your job?

None of the messages had been read. She'd knocked on her

cabin twice now to no reply. She'd also checked the gun room: the rifle was still missing. Jules stared at the fire and tried not to think about how Marta could be watching her right now, gun in hand.

A loud splash drew her attention to the cold plunge, where Tim momentarily disappeared from sight. A moment later, he emerged at the surface, roaring and shaking his head.

'Amazing!' he bellowed, pulling himself up the steps. He held his arms out for Calan to wrap the dry robe around him. 'Bloody fantastic! I can feel it... the endorphin rush.'

He jumped on the spot and did a couple of knee-ups. 'I feel alive!'

This was good. Jules's spirits rose just a little. The rustic wellness element of her business proposal had been a major factor. The fact Tim was enjoying this so much was an encouraging sign. She jumped up to grab some more champagne.

'Fizz while you dry off?'

He grabbed the glass and sat by the firepit, making a theatrical "blurrrrr" sound to indicate how cold the water had been. Nodding to Calan, he asked, 'What do you reckon the temperature is in there? Got to be at least minus ten?'

Calan stoked the fire and shook his head. 'I don't think so. Obviously, the top's freezing, but the density of the ice insulates the water below it. I'd say it's about four degrees, or something?'

'No, impossible. It felt far colder than that...'

'In your expert opinion?' Gracie asked, rolling her eyes.

Tim held out his glass for a top-up and Jules reached for the bottle again. He stared at Gracie, his expression one of pure exasperation. 'What do you think then, *dear*? By all means, please do share your thoughts. I know how much you like spurting crap.'

An awkward silence followed. Calan was holding himself

uncomfortably, fastidiously staring in the opposite direction out into the water. Tim downed his champagne. Gracie sniffed and buried herself deep in the blanket. The fires crackled and hissed and smoked.

Jules was relieved when she saw Lucas and Sandeep approaching. 'Ah! Brilliant!'

She motioned to their hamper, laid out between two beanbags in front of their fire. 'Please, take a seat. Champagne's still cold!'

She laughed and swiftly looked at Tim, hoping he'd be impressed. He was grimacing, his fingers moving in small circular motions along the top of his glass.

'Would you two gentlemen like a dip? It's a real rush!'

'God, no. Looks horrendous.' Lucas settled down into his beanbag and began opening the champagne. 'Anyway, we're celebrating...'

Sandeep followed suit, sighing as he languished backwards, stretching his legs. 'We certainly are...'

The cork popped, making Jules jump. She instinctively looked over her shoulder, expecting Marta to be wielding the rifle. She turned back, her heart hammering. 'Oh! Fantastic! Well, there's more champers from where that came.'

'We'll definitely be having another,' Sandeep replied. He seemed completely changed, much more relaxed than yesterday. In fact, his entire stance was transformed. His shoulders were no longer slumped, his eyes looked brighter and more alert.

Calan brought some blankets over for the new arrivals. He nodded at Lucas and, she was sure, his cheeks looked flushed like he was embarrassed. 'Glad it all worked out. Er...' He looked from side to side then added, 'Is there a ring then?'

Lucas took the blankets and snuggled himself in. He sipped his champagne merrily, his head tilted backwards and his mouth set in a continuous smile. 'No, no. And, Calan, thank you so much for your help this morning. No... we're actually not celebrating our engagement...'

He held his glass up to the sky and trailed his eyes around the group, waiting for them to follow suit. 'We're decoupling! No... no, it's brilliant. You see, we're terribly matched and Sandeep here, well, does he even like me?'

'I like you!' Sandeep laughed, although Jules was sure she noticed a small grimace of annoyance. 'We just...'

'We're not in love!' Lucas finished, his champagne sloshing around. 'So here's to it...' He raised his glass again. 'To incompatibility, to lies, to death... to The Tornivan weekend!'

A confused and unenthusiastic round of cheers went around the group. Jules cringed; it was hardly a ringing endorsement for the place. She could practically feel Tim analysing the situation, turning it into spreadsheets, working out that it wasn't profitable after all. She was suddenly filled with a deep anger towards Gracie. Why did she have to choose this weekend to uncover her husband's affair? He would forever associate this hotel with this dark cloud of arguments and bickering. Could she not have waited?

'Are we waiting for someone?' Calan came to her side and nodded at the empty beanbag. 'Zach, isn't it?'

'Probably out filming some deer thinking he's stumbled upon some new species.'

This was from Lucas, who looked particularly pleased with his remark. Gracie chuckled and threw Tim a meaningful look. 'He might not know his animals, but he was pretty astute when it came to humans yesterday. He made some very accurate observations.'

Tim looked like he might stand up and hit her right there and then. Jules sighed and stepped out of earshot from the guests. 'There's been no sign of him this morning—'

'Looking for him, were you?'

She gritted her teeth and frowned. 'Not now, Calan, all right? I've thought about reporting him missing but...'

Calan nodded grimly at the path that wound through the mountains away from the hotel. 'The snow's deep. No one's going to be searching for him in this.'

She folded her arms, trying to dispel the image of Zach half-alive and buried beneath the snow. Yes, he was an absolute creep, but it must be a slow and painful way to go. Plus, if one of her guests died, she may as well kiss goodbye to the hotel immediately. 'And he's not been gone long enough to count as missing. He told us all he was here to capture footage, claimed he was a decent hiker... I can't see anyone taking it seriously.'

'I'll keep an eye out on my rounds later,' Calan said, dutifully.

She hugged herself, a rare rush of affection surging in her belly. 'Thanks,' she whispered. 'Look, we need to liven this up a bit. Feels like a funeral.'

As if she could read Jules's mind, Gracie jumped up and began stripping in front of everyone. She was very slender, beautiful really, with a tiny pinched waist and long, pale legs. Beneath her clothes, she wore one of those fashionable swimming costumes with long arms and a high neck. It looked more like a leotard than a swimsuit, but somehow she made it work.

'I'm doing it!'

She shot her husband a triumphant pout, crossed her arms over her chest like she was in a coffin, and dropped over the edge, letting out a tiny squeal. 'It's... c-cold!' she shrieked, half-laughing.

She kicked her arms and legs around her, smashing the thin ice into tiny pieces. 'Oh my God!' she shouted.

'I wouldn't spend too long in there if you're not used to it.'

Calan was by now at the decking, watching her carefully. 'It's not really safe...'

'Oh, I'm fine!' she squealed.

For a moment, she lost her breath and bobbed under the water. Jules noted how everyone watched with a strange, silent sense of interest. Nobody jumped into action to help. For a split-second, she saw them all for what they really were: tamed animals just waiting for the next thing to suppress their boredom.

Gracie's head pushed up from the water. She was laughing, screeching. 'Oooh my God...'

Her voice was breathless and erratic. She kicked away from the decking and swam towards the centre of the loch. The ice parted as she moved, making soft cracking sounds as it impacted her skin. She'd lose the function in her limbs within minutes.

'Mrs Melrose! It's not safe out there! It's too deep!' Calan was fumbling with the storage box, pre-emptively preparing the life jacket and ring. Gracie continued to swim away from them, her delighted cries carrying behind her.

'For fuck's sake, Gracie!' Tim ran to the edge of the decking and hollered at her. 'What do you think you're doing? You're embarrassing yourself!'

'I'm being adventurous, *hubby*!' Gracie disappeared below the black gleaming water, her last syllable swallowed by the loch. Jules held her breath, but Gracie smashed through the surface again.

'Gracie! You're behaving like a lunatic!'

'Isn't that what you want?' Her voice sounded less strong now, her breathing was quick and ragged. 'Don't you wish I was more interesting, Tim? Carefree?'

Jules didn't understand what was happening at first. The timbre of Gracie's shrieks took a different turn. She still sounded frantic, but there was something deeper, darker beneath it. Fear.

'Fuck – Calan!' Jules gesticulated at him to help her. He threw the life ring in Gracie's direction and it landed only a few inches away from her.

'Grab it, Gracie!' Tim shouted at her. He snatched a life jacket from Calan, disrobed and pulled it over his torso. 'I'm coming... just hold on!'

'No, no, no, no!' Gracie's screams were high-pitched and terrified.

'What's happening?' Calan squinted, confused at what the problem was. 'She's not that far out. We can easily drag her in.'

Her screams continued ceaselessly. Tim splashed towards her, struggling to move quickly enough.

'Wait...' Lucas and Sandeep huddled at Jules's side. 'What's that next to her? That white thing?'

It was difficult to see through the snow, but there was something bobbing in the water next to Gracie's thrashing limbs. Tim finally reached her and took her in his arms.

'Is that...?'

Calan's voice broke off in horror. Jules couldn't speak. She nodded in dumb shock as Tim dragged Gracie and the thing back towards the deck. The water rippled in black and oily vibrations.

Gracie scrambled out of the loch. She slipped with a painful crack on her knee and dragged her way towards the fire. Her eyes were distant and wide.

'No, no, no...' she whispered over and over again.

Tim hoisted the limp mass onto the deck. A horrible groan vibrated from Jules's lips. Someone was weeping, but she couldn't tell who. All she could stare at was the bloated face. Her discoloured eyes. Her dark lips. Marta had drowned.

LUCAS

'We need to leave.'

Lucas rubbed his hands together in the car and frowned at the frosted windscreen. The heaters blew out stale hot air but didn't seem to be making any difference. He wiped it with his sleeve but all he could see was white.

'You have to scrape it...'

Sandeep sat next to him in the passenger seat, his arms folded. How could he possibly be so calm? This trip had been enough of a nightmare, but the last straw was that poor woman floating towards them in the loch. Lucas shuddered at the thought of it. Her mouth had been open... like a fish. That's what he'd thought: *someone close her mouth, she's breathing water like a fish.* There was no way he could stay another minute.

Lucas blew into his hands once more and steeled himself for the outside. As soon as he opened the door, he grimaced, but persevered around to the front of the car. The snow was falling even more thickly now, making it impossible to clear the windscreen. He scratched at the glass with his fingernails, and hissed as the cold burnt the tips of his fingers.

'Use the edge of a credit card, seriously...' Sandeep joined him and began scraping on the other side to much more effect. 'I really don't think we're going anywhere, especially not in this car. Look at the road, Lucas. It's not safe. They're not even sure if they can fly the helicopter tomorrow for...'

Lucas blinked through the snowflakes. He knew what Sandeep was about to say. *For the body.* A helicopter was needed to collect the body. The afternoon was already darkening and the clouds had taken on a greenish tinge. Deep down, he knew they weren't going anywhere. The road was long and remote. If they skidded and crashed, which was likely, they'd be stranded in the middle of nowhere. Being stranded in the Hotel of Horrors with his ex was bad enough.

'Okay. Okay. Look, we've got one more dinner to get through, then we can get out of this place.' Somewhere not far off, the cows mooed, deep and low. It sounded mournful, almost like they were trying to warn him about something. It was all right for them – with their big hairy coats, they were free to roam as far away from here as they liked. If he were a Highland cow, he thought, he'd be on the other side of those mountains in no time.

Reluctantly, he and Sandeep crunched back over the drive towards the main entrance. The big oak doors looked like an open mouth against the white of the snow, just about ready to swallow them whole.

***

Obviously, it was awkward in the hotel room. How was it that they were perfectly comfortable with each other's bodies yesterday, getting changed like it was nothing and walking around naked? Now, Lucas found himself scurrying into the bathroom to change for dinner.

The sleeping arrangements hadn't yet been addressed. There didn't seem to be any spare rooms, even if he could afford one. That was the downside of going to a *boutique* hotel. In hindsight, it had been a terrible idea. Lucas goaded himself as he pulled on his trousers. This whole trip had been an epic waste of money, and he hadn't noticed Sandeep offering to cough up, which, come to think of it, would be the least he could do given this morning's revelation.

They had decided, for reasons that Lucas was now questioning with intense scrutiny, that they'd eat dinner together. Their last supper, or something like it. It was probably better than eating alone and, anyway, the plan was to get blind drunk to block as much of this night out as possible.

He took another long sip of whisky and stared at himself in the mirror. Despite everything, he looked pretty good, handsome actually.

'Ready?' Sandeep opened the door without knocking. He'd bounced back from their break-up remarkably well, a little too well, to be honest.

Lucas walked past him and did a quick spin on the spot. 'Sure you're not having any regrets?'

The break-up banter was quite cathartic, in an odd way. It was somewhere to channel the humiliation which had been gurgling in the pit of his belly since he realised what the last year and a half had really been about. He'd been the object of the world's longest pity party. A burden. He flashed his best suggestive grin.

In a motion that was more affectionate and natural than he'd ever been when they were together, Sandeep slipped an arm around his waist and leant close, whispering, 'Ravishing, but still, no.'

Lucas forced a chuckle. *He thinks you're completely fine,* he told himself. *You're giving every indication you're fine. Just keep smiling and you can collapse in a heap when you get back to London.*

He gave an involuntary shiver, his limbs twitching, which had been happening since plummeting into the snow that morning.

'Sure you're okay?' Sandeep was suddenly the most attentive person on the planet, it seemed.

Lucas moved closer to the fire. The raw heat radiating against the back of his legs was amazing. 'All good, just got the chills, that's all.'

Sandeep watched him for a second then said quietly, 'I just can't get my head around how differently it could have gone. How easily you could have...'

'Died?' Lucas gave a small laugh but wasn't sure why. His mind had returned to the words he'd awoken to in the snowdrift, the exchange between Calan and Tim.

I just want what's mine.

What had they been talking about? He'd been so distracted with everything else going on that he'd forgotten all about it. It wasn't so much the words that stuck out to him, but the desperation in Calan's voice.

'What do you think about Calan?' he asked.

Sandeep looked momentarily confused, before frowning. 'The gamekeeper?' He shrugged. 'Average teen, I guess. Why?'

It was difficult to explain the odd draw Lucas had felt towards him since arriving. He knew it was stupid. Calan hadn't wanted his help when he'd offered it that morning. He'd seemed okay. But then... Bebe had seemed okay too.

'It just can't be easy for him, can it? A dead body when you're only young? I might... would it be weird if we checked on him?'

Sandeep baulked. 'I'm sure the hotel is looking after its staff—'

'No, but that's just it. When we arrived, I saw that Jules woman shouting at him, right in his face, just there.' He pointed vaguely to the spot outside the window. 'He works night and day, doesn't he? And he was scared of someone following him. I reckon it was Marta, the dead woman.'

'Scared?' Sandeep looked deeply concerned. 'What do you mean scared? How do you know?'

'I overheard some stuff...'

Lucas moved to the window and squinted into the night. In the middle distance, halfway up the foothills, a flickering light danced from the bothy. He pictured Calan, a little lonely stooped figure, regurgitating the dead woman's face over and over, staring, alone, at the bare wall. Perhaps this was the good that was supposed to come out of this weekend. Perhaps, in the face of all that had happened, he was supposed to help another young and vulnerable boy.

He turned to Sandeep. 'We should check on him. We're teachers, aren't we? Anyway, if he tells us to fuck off, then we fuck off.'

He must have come across as insistent, because Sandeep simply replied, 'Okay, okay. Let me get my coat.'

The table looked as good as possible, given the circumstances. The only thing Jules could think to do was to carry on as if everything was normal. Tonight was the black tie dinner. That's what the guests were expecting. That's what Tim was expecting. She straightened a knife and sniffed.

It was good to be alone; just herself and the roar of the dining room's grand fireplace. The conversations she'd been forced to have over the past few hours still seemed too alien to believe. The police had told her to store the body somewhere cold and away from the hotel. They would send help as soon as they could reach them.

Jules had stuttered down the phone, 'Store the body? Store her body? Is that... what you said?'

Apparently, the rocks shoved into Marta's underwear pointed to a likely suicide. She was assured there was no need to panic and that the police did not deem anyone's lives to be in further danger. They would send a helicopter as soon as the weather calmed down. For now, she and the guests were marooned.

Tim had helped her carry Marta to a wood storage hut. It was, thankfully, tucked away behind the trees and out of sight. They'd done the whole thing in silence. Even the bullish Tim had worn a stunned, emotionless expression. She would never be able to forget covering Marta's face with a bedsheet, turning her back, and leaving her on the cold, stone slabs.

As she'd expected, the police also told her not to worry about Zach. There were ample bothies in the area and, "since he was a self-proclaimed adventurer", he had likely decided to take shelter in one, rather than brave the heavy snow. She was assured a rescue team would look for him as soon as it was safe to do so.

She set a place for him on the off-chance he would return. For a few minutes, she sat on what should have been his chair. She pictured herself pushed against the wall, his hands massaging her skin, the smell of him. It was such an odd mixture of feelings. Yes, she was disgusted by him, and even afraid. But he had *wanted* her. She knew it. She groaned aloud, her mind swimming with confusion.

Dark thoughts were beginning to occur to her, surfacing when she least expected them. It was surely just hangxiety. She'd had so much booze last night. Even in anticipation of Zach arriving, before she'd suspected he wasn't coming, she'd got through at least half a bottle of gin, on top of the bottle of wine she'd been working her way through during the dinner service. And the pills. How many had she taken in the end?

The memories blurred into blackouts and fantasies and other inky, loud and sweat-inducing images. She'd read through her erratic, scribbled notes over and over again that afternoon, flattening them out on the floor. Most of them were grotesque. Had she imagined she might slip them under his door? Had she thought they were sexy? Alluring? She'd begged him to take her outside; suggested all the covert places she knew on the grounds; told him she wanted to feel the snow on her skin, have him press against her.

Meet me by the loch at 11pm. There's a fishing hut down the path, she'd written. Why there? Jules had never really cared for the old wooden shack. It was nice enough inside, but she couldn't imagine why she would want to hook up with Zach there. Such was the nature of her blackouts, though. She was never in control. Her thoughts span and fell, frenzied and random.

There were the sounds in her head too. They came to her at random intervals. Screams. All wrapped in a tight, black gauze of inebriated oblivion. *It's not real.*

'It's not real,' she repeated aloud, immediately embarrassed by her solitary voice echoing around the room. The fact she'd reported Zach to the police proved it wasn't real. If she'd done anything wrong – if she had anything to do with him disappearing – then she wouldn't have said anything, would she? She was behaving like a normal, concerned party. She was behaving exactly as any hotelier would. These were just random notes written in a state of drunken rejection. There was absolutely no reason to take any stock in them, and even less reason to think Zach was anything but fine.

She realised she was gripping the steak knife in her right hand. A slow, tiny stream of blood trickled down her forearm. The bright red against her pale skin refocused her. None of this mattered now. What mattered was getting through tonight with a smile. She had to keep it together. This hotel was all she had left. It was the last drop of life in her tired and dried-up heart. She would make it work.

She swore quietly as the blood dripped onto her sleeve. Now, she needed to change and dinner was supposed to be served soon. Thankfully, Calan had stepped in to help with what Marta had mostly prepared the day before. The *jus*, the garnishes and all the trimmings had been reduced, prepped and chopped. The main challenge would be getting the steaks right, not that she imagined anyone would be thinking much about their food tonight.

As she hurried along the guests' corridor, shouts didn't so much as waft, but vibrate, from the Melroses' room. Jules applied pressure on her cut and put her head down; she didn't want anything to do with whatever weirdness was going on there. She'd already acted with due diligence and checked in on Gracie to see how she was coping – that's where she'd leave it.

'It's the lying, Tim! The fucking lying! That's what's so humiliating, so hurtful. It actually hurts me! It hurts!'

Jules rushed past their door, her mouth pulled into a concerted grimace.

'Hurts you? You're good enough at that on your own! And of course I didn't tell you! Why would I tell you about her? Especially...'

Jules had her hand on the staircase door.

'What? Especially me?'

Tim's voice was booming with rage. *'I wouldn't tell you about any woman I love because you're fucking dangerous, Gracie! You're manipulative... you're evil. If I could count the number of times you've... or I've suspected... look, just leave it, okay? Just leave me alone.'*

Jules didn't look behind her but she heard what followed. Gracie began cackling, a dirty, gritty sound. *'Evil? Evil? I'm protective, Tim. That's what you've never understood. I protect what's mine... don't you forget it, not ever. I'll protect what's mine by whatever means I need to.'*

'You didn't... not her...' His voice didn't hit with the same

strong, confident flex Jules was used to. There was a softer quality to his words, almost like a whimper.

There was a muffled struggle and what sounded like someone being thrown against the floor. Gracie's faint, insidious laugh followed.

'*Tim, Tim, Tim...*'

Jules ran up the stairs to her flat two steps at a time.

LUCAS

'I think he's just left the fire on...' Sandeep huffed impatiently. Lucas could almost feel his eyes rolling from behind him, but he wasn't ready to leave just yet. Through the bothy's small window, he could see one of the beds was unmade. There were scattered papers strewn across the duvet – it looked like someone had been reading them, then left in a hurry. The wood-burner cast orange flames onto the wall opposite.

'We've come all this way,' Lucas whispered. 'I think we should go in.'

'What? How?' Sandeep hissed. 'Why? He's not in and this kid has nothing to do with us. Let's get back, I'm starving.'

Lucas could absolutely see where he was coming from. On the surface, this must look a little unhinged. But he couldn't shake the fear he'd seen in Calan's eyes, the vulnerability. This was his chance to make a difference.

The papers on the duvet seemed to wriggle uncomfortably as the flames reflected off them. Anyway, he didn't *need* Sandeep's permission to do anything anymore. If he wanted to break into the bothy, then he bloody well could. Ignoring Sandeep's increasingly frantic protests, he opened the door.

'See?' He turned to Sandeep. 'It's not even locked. We're not doing anything wrong!'

The warmth of the bothy hugged him like a long-lost friend. Sandeep hovered in the doorway. 'I'm closing the door either way, with you in or out,' Lucas said. Sighing, Sandeep opted for in.

'Won't be long, I just have a really strange feeling...' Lucas peered down at the papers. They weren't the sort of thing you'd expect a teenager to be reading at all. He picked one of the sheets off the bed.

'Lucas...'

'It's some letters from... no, seriously. That's odd...'

'It's not for you!' Sandeep was half-shouting, his eyes glued to the door.

Lucas ignored him. He closed his eyes. Some trick of the fire was making him see things. Perhaps he needed a nap. He sank onto the mattress, his knees giving way. His hands shook as he picked up another piece of paper.

'Lucas? What's the matter?'

It was so strange. So amazingly strange how the mind could play dirty tricks on you like this! He looked at the ceiling and then down at the sheet again. But his brain still refused to cooperate. The second piece of paper said the same thing; another letter from the same adoption agency:

```
Dear Calan,

    Thank  you  for  your  recent  inquiry
about    your    birth   parent,   Rebekah
Desouza...
```

It couldn't be right. It couldn't be right at all. With both hands, he picked up another letter, then another, then another.

We can confirm your birth parent
received your most recent photographs…
     She is happy to hear about your
apprenticeship success at the hotel…
     We regret to inform you that Rebekah
Desouza passed away on…

And then, it was in his hands. A photo of her, from years ago, but unmistakable. Bebe. It was weird seeing her full name, as well as his old surname – he'd barely ever used it. Yet, here she was on Calan's bed. Over eighteen years' worth of correspondence and updates. His eyes swam with confusion. He tried to take a breath but couldn't.

'Lucas?'

He shook his head over and over. It was too huge of a thing to take in. 'Sandeep…'

He couldn't get the words out. His chest was so tight. He had to get out of here. He needed the cold air on his face, in his lungs. He gasped. It was important that Sandeep knew. It was important, for some reason, to explain it clearly.

'I… I… think Bebe was Calan's mother.'

CALAN

The kitchen was meticulous. Calan had only ever helped with washing up and serving, so he'd never properly noticed the multiple jars of fermenting vegetables, the pantry lined with countless spices and dried fruits, the suction-packed meats in their little bags. Each foodstuff was marked with a dated sticker, which looked colour-coded according to when they'd been put away.

Although he was glad to be tucked back here away from Tim's furious stares, it was an odd sensation to be stepping into the shoes of Marta so soon after what had happened. He widened his eyes, concentrating on seasoning the slab of meat, trying to dissuade the bloated image from reappearing.

The soft hum of the creepy freezer room behind him was also disconcerting. It wasn't so much a white noise, more of an insidious green one, matching the odd light shining through the curtains. It seeped into his brain and made him shiver. Thankfully, Marta had already laid the ingredients out for tonight's dinner, so he had no need to go in there.

'Wine?' Jules popped her head around the door. 'Guests need it pouring.'

He hated the way she spoke in a hushed tone when ordering him about, so breathy and husky. It was like she was trying to pretend she was run off her feet. 'They're all here?'

She leant against the door frame, frowning. 'Both couples. Mr Williams is still... out.'

He gave a soft, exasperated sigh and untied his apron. 'Cheese soufflés are in the oven. I googled how to do them. Pretty easy, actually. Marta...' He took a sharp breath as he said her name. 'She'd already put them in the ramekins, so just don't open it.'

She nodded, apparently impressed. Then she smirked, her eyes glinting. 'Who do you think will be the first to make a Minger joke?'

He felt the edge of his lips curl up too. There was always one guest who couldn't get enough of the name of the cheese. 'My money's on Mr Melrose. Or Mr Croft.'

She winked at him and his smirk immediately evaporated. 'Let's see.'

***

The couples had opted to sit together, convening at a table of four in the centre of the room in front of the fire. They cut an odd, stooped silhouette as he entered, like a darkened human archway. As he walked towards them, Lucas stared at him as if he was expecting an answer to a question.

'White burgundy?' Calan stood behind Mrs Melrose's right shoulder. 'It's vintage is 2014 and the citrusy and oaky notes will add a layer of complexity to your starters this evening, the cheese soufflé.'

'Sounds fantastic,' she said in a much cheerier manner than she'd displayed at the picnic. 'Minger's my favourite. Hard to get it in London.'

'Why don't you move back then?' Tim slurred his words. He'd clearly not taken a break from drinking. 'Plenty of mingers to go around up here, I'm sure.'

Calan cleared his throat, disguising a small laugh. That might well have been a record; three seconds until the Minger joke. He'd never met such a walking London stereotype before.

'Oh? You'd know.' Gracie took a sip of the wine, slurped loudly, and nodded for Calan to fill her glass. 'They're your speciality, aren't they? Mingers on the side?'

Calan avoided catching Tim's eye as best he could. He felt his cheeks begin to burn.

'Sir?'

'Just get on with it.' Tim flapped his hand vaguely over the glass and turned to face his wife. Lucas was still staring at him with that strange face. Calan tried to avoid his eye.

'Speak for yourself, Gracie.'

Tim slurred his words. The emphasis fell on all the wrong syllables. He was definitely hammered.

'I saw you talking to that weird photographer guy yesterday morning. What was it? Harmless flirtation? A little smile here and a smile there?' He smacked the table, making the glasses quiver. 'You're not perfect, Gracie! Far from it. Oh, and now he's missing? I wonder, where did he go?'

He sang the last question like a demented nursery rhyme.

'Where did he go, Gracie? Do our good friends here know all about you? Maybe if they did, they'd get ideas. Do they know you steal knives and hide them in our bedroom? Do they know how you reel people in just to threaten and manipulate and play your little games?'

He swiped the full glass, downed the wine and placed it back on the table . The flames from the fire reflected on his face and he wiped his mouth with the back of his sleeve.

'If I were a betting man, oh!' He banged the table again. The cutlery rattled. 'Oh, I am! *Since* I'm a betting man, I'd wager that you did something to our young filmmaker. Something very much not good...'

It looked like he was going to point at her but he rested his finger on her forehead and traced the line of her nose down to her chin and neck. 'She's dangerous, boys and girls. She's a danger, don't let the exterior fool you.'

There was a momentary silence. Eventually, Gracie filled it with a laugh. 'Sorry, everyone. Tim's apparently had enough to drink for today!'

'Don't say I didn't warn you...' Tim sang, tapping his glass for a refill.

Gracie didn't look at all bothered. Her face remained perfectly calm, her rosebud lips pressed into a gentle smile. 'I think seeing a dead body has got to him, it, um, she, probably got to all of us. It's weird to be here, enjoying a dinner, when... after...'

'A woman died.' This was from Lucas, who finally dragged his eyes off Calan and faced Gracie. 'How do we know he's not telling the truth? We don't know you! We don't know anyone here. You could be sitting on all sorts of lies, all sorts of crazy little—'

Sandeep placed a hand on his arm and Lucas took a ragged breath in the middle of his sentence. He was still intent on Gracie.

'Is that true? About the knives?' He stood up suddenly, his eyes a little bloodshot. Calan looked at Jules, who'd just arrived from the kitchen. 'Has anyone seen her stealing knives? You!'

Lucas pointed at Jules with an accusing finger. 'You're supposed to be running this place, aren't you? You must have procedures in place! I'm a teacher, I know all about health and safety. Do you keep track of your potential murder weapons?'

The word "murder" hit the room like an invisible slap.

Jules's face fell, her eyes momentarily terrified, before she drew herself up again.

'Fuck's sake, Lucas...' Sandeep muttered.

Jules moved around the table, positioning the plates before each of the four guests. Afterwards, she stepped back and clasped her hands. 'I... I know it's not been the best...'

'It's been the worst,' Lucas said flatly.

Jules nodded, her eyes shifting to Tim who was already tucking into his starter noisily. 'Okay, yes, it's been exceptionally unfortunate, but I don't think it's a good idea to start using alarmist language. The police are convinced what happened to Marta was her own doing and they assured me they would start the search for Zach as soon as the weather made it possible. They might even be looking for him as we speak but they don't think it's anything to worry about.'

'The knives?' Lucas was still standing. It seemed like he wasn't going to sit down until he got an answer to his question. 'Bullshit aside, we deserve to know. This no longer feels normal. None of this, none of *you* feel right.'

'Errrm...' Jules folded her arms and started backing towards the doors. 'Like I say, I don't think it's useful to...'

'For Christ's sake!' Lucas slumped down and ran his fingers through his hair. 'It's true, isn't it?' He stared at Gracie, who was cutting a small portion of soufflé with a knife and fork. She delicately dipped it into the balsamic vinaigrette and nibbled at it.

Eventually, when she'd finished her portion, she set her cutlery on the table and sat back in her chair. 'Jules is just being kind, but I suppose Tim has backed me into a corner. Thank you, my love.'

Tim grunted in a dismissive laugh.

Slowly, Gracie began fiddling at her wrists. She was wearing a long green gown, with long, billowy silk sleeves. She carefully undid the tiny buttons and rolled up the fabric. Her pale arms were covered in a complex web of incisions. Some of the scars were raised from her skin, some were clearly fresh, the wounds still red and shiny.

'Thank you, Jules, for not saying anything. I stole the knives, but not to murder anyone.' She sniffed like the idea tickled her, before stretching her arms over the table towards Lucas, her fingers splayed. 'Although, I won't deny it didn't cross my mind. Tim's right. I spoke to Zach and he's an egotistical scumbag. He's just probably a scumbag sheltering in the wilderness, like the police say.'

'Shit. Shit, I'm sorry. Today's just been a lot,' Lucas said.

'Good of you to keep my wife's secret, Jules. Took her less than a day to get her claws into you, did it?' Tim didn't look up as he spoke. He split his soufflé with a knife in one smooth movement.

Jules opened her mouth and closed it again. Even in the dim lighting, Calan could tell she was growing flustered. A thin film of sweat was forming on her forehead.

'I didn't realise... Gracie said that it was for...' She suddenly changed tact, a clownish smile snapping across her face. Whatever she'd been about to say disappeared into the hiss of the fire. 'Look, let's just focus on dinner, shall we? Don't want your starters to go cold!'

Jules clapped her hands together and motioned for Calan to fill up the glasses again. Dead bodies made people drink like fish, apparently.

He moved slowly around the table, nodding reverentially as he topped everyone up. Again, Lucas gave him a funny look. For God's sake, he had enough to worry about with Tim... what did Mr Suede Shoes want? Another weird chat about how much he liked teenagers?

He was right though, Calan thought, walking back to the

kitchen: none of this felt normal. A dark tension had descended on The Tornivan like a sticky treacle and was clinging to everyone here, holding them down.

He thought about the various winding roads away from here, the ones the tourists didn't know about. It would take him a whole day to walk to the village if he left first thing, but he knew the way. A treacherous hike was preferable to staying here another second longer with this lot. But he'd have to come back to work eventually, he reminded himself. Jules would still be here, waiting for him. He'd have the same salary and the same dead-end opportunities. He would never escape her.

He found her in the corner of the kitchen, glugging on wine like always. Her breath would stink of it all night. He headed to the wine fridge to get another bottle and imagined, yet again, leaving this place for the last time ever. The picture was so vivid that it made him dizzy with excitement. Maybe it wasn't so impossible.

Jules rested her back against the kitchen cupboard and took a long gulp of wine.

She would talk to Tim tomorrow. He would have the sense to see that none of this was her fault. A staff suicide wasn't reflective of the usual Tornivan experience. Anyone with a modicum of sense would realise that. She just needed to make sure they were still on the same page. Surely, he would understand why she hadn't told him about Gracie's knife? It was none of her business really. It was all easily explainable.

Tim's outburst aside, dinner had thankfully gone smoothly. The food hadn't been up to usual standards, but it had been good enough. She watched the door between sips, expecting Calan to return any second with the dirty dessert plates. Why was he taking so long?

Popping her head into the hall, she caught Gracie heading for the bar. Tim followed her, a bottle of red wine dangling precariously from one hand. Jules smiled as Sandeep caught her eye on the way to his room.

'Heading to bed,' he said. He stretched, yawning. 'Big day.'

'Let me know if you need anything.'

'A teleport out of here,' he mumbled as he ascended the stairs, supposedly thinking he was out of earshot.

Jules ignored him and opened the doors to the dining room. The dessert plates were stacked on a side table, but it was otherwise empty. A kernel of panic began to dance in her belly. Calan was obedient. He would never leave dirty plates out for guests to see. Lucas's words echoed through her mind as she checked the kitchen again. *Murder.*

That was ridiculous. There was no suggestion of any foul play in regard to Marta, just as the police had said. But there was something else. *We're trapped here.* A snake-like anxiety curled around her spine. He was right. All the roads were blocked and helicopters were grounded. For tonight, it was only the six of them in this big old castle, surrounded by nothing but inhospitable, unforgiving terrain.

The kitchen was as she left it. There was still no sign of Calan.

She cleared her throat, turning on her heel to check the bar. There was nothing to worry about. Nothing at all. The events of the day had them all acting out of turn. He'd probably just forgotten about the plates and was doing some other chores.

Gracie was curled up on a corner chaise, her shoes discarded and her knees drawn up to her chest. She stared blankly at a glass of whisky on the table in front of her. Tim was propped against the bar, helping himself to a large measure.

'Can't get the staff these days, can you?' he said, his teeth bared like a wolf's. 'No wonder you jumped at the chance of my money. This place is a comedy show...'

Jules froze. He was too far gone to have a sensible conversation, but she didn't want to say anything that might jeopardise their deal. 'Obviously your investment would allow me to employ more—'

A shriek of laughter from the other side of the room

interrupted her. Gracie's head lolled back, and she exposed her long bare legs. 'I wouldn't push him. He's a master of his own destiny, don't you know? Likes to be in control.'

She rolled onto her stomach and inclined her head to one side, a quizzical look on her face. 'It's odd he came here, you know. This isn't his sort of thing at all. An old, crumbling castle? Chain hotels are where the money is... he's always saying it... not passion projects like this...'

'Stop it, Gracie.' Tim's voice was gruff but deliberate. He sipped his whisky, taking his time, then waved his hand dismissively towards Jules. 'It's too late for depressing conversations anyway. I'd rather deliver the blow in the morning. Run along, will you? It's too late.'

It was like he'd hit her round the face with a bag of rocks. She felt blood rushing through her brain, the shame of failure beating against her skull. He was so cold, and it sounded like he was out. He wasn't going to invest. She had no money, no hope of staying afloat.

She left the bar to the sound of his derisive chuckle. She was a failure. She was a laughing stock. What had he been doing? Humouring her? Getting a free stay at her hotel whilst all the time thinking how stupid she was? That was what she was: something to be ridiculed. She was abnormal. Useless. Nobody understood her, much less supported her. She was entirely and utterly alone.

'Will you just listen to me?!' Calan's voice rang out from the library.

Her face burning with shame, she remembered she'd been searching for him. She rushed to the door and pushed it open. At first, it looked like nobody was there. The lights weren't on and only the dull grey beam from the moon lit up the bookshelves. Then, she spotted a movement on the far side in the corner. Lucas stood over Calan, his arm raised, his face leering.

'Stop! Stop it!' She ran towards them. 'Mr Croft, please! What are you doing?'

'It's okay...' Calan stepped out from behind him. 'It's okay, Jules. We were just... chatting.'

It was difficult to think. She was so tired, so anxious. It was as if the weekend had beaten her, numbed her brain into confused submission. Eventually, she realised all attention was focused on a small photograph Lucas was holding in front of Calan's face.

'What's... what's going on?' she asked. The fatigue in her voice was palpable even to her. She nodded to the photograph. 'What's that?'

'Nothing.'

Calan slipped past Lucas and jogged to the door without even glancing at her. He seemed charged with a new energy, his limbs moving with a purposeful vigour. 'I've got stuff to do.'

The hinges creaked as the door closed behind him.

Lucas stood in silence, still staring at the picture like he was struggling to understand something. Then, as if he'd only just realised she was there, he lifted his head.

'Something's not right,' he said. His eyes were wide and his face was grave. 'There's something really off here.'

'What...?' She squinted at the photo. At first, she thought she was looking at an image of an old friend, until she realised who it was.

Her. The girl. Tim's mistress. Zach's victim. Rebekah.

She frowned, that snake coiling even more tightly around the small of her back. She felt a band of sweat wetten her hairline. 'Who's that? That woman, who is she, please?'

He took a couple of seconds to register that she'd asked him a question. As if he was disoriented, he put the photo back into his wallet.

'My sister,' he replied in a quiet voice. He shook his head. 'She's dead. Not long ago. I... I'd better be getting to bed.'

'Wait. Wait a second, will you?'

She was sure she should ask more questions, she just didn't know which ones. A strange feeling took over. She felt like she was teetering on the precipice of a huge, dark, bubbling pit, unable to step backwards.

The door closed after Lucas and she was left standing in the shadows.

LUCAS

Lucas checked their door was locked for what must have been the hundredth time and rounded on Sandeep.

'Of course I'm nervous,' he hissed at him. 'How the *fuck* have we ended up here? Where Bebe's secret child just *happens* to live? I have no idea what's going on, but it's not normal, is it?'

Sandeep stretched out his legs on the bed and raised his eyebrows in the way he did when he was thinking carefully about what to say next. His habit of taking an inordinate amount of time to reply used to annoy Lucas when they were together, but now it was, frankly, intolerable.

'Will you *say something?!*'

Sandeep crossed his legs and stared across the room. Finally, he bit his lip and exhaled. 'I agree it's a weird coincidence.'

Lucas waited for an elaboration, but it turned out that was it. 'A coincidence? A coincidence? Yes, yes... I know it's a coincidence! That's why I'm freaking out!'

He sagged onto the armchair by the fire, his fingers drumming at a distraught pace. 'Nothing makes any sense. The missing guest. The suicide.'

'Wait.' Sandeep poured himself more whisky from the

decanter on his bedside table. 'What have they got to do with anything?'

'Nothing!' Lucas blew through his lips irritably. Nothing. They had nothing to do with Bebe being Calan's mum. Nothing at all. It was just that too many things had happened. Too many awful and strange events. Too many twists and turns. It was like this hotel was cursed. 'I just want to get out of here,' he mumbled, very aware how much of a stroppy teenager he sounded.

'Yeah, me too,' Sandeep said with a sigh. Lucas sank lower into the chair, choosing to ignore how Sandeep sounded like he was speaking to a child. 'Hopefully the weather clears tomorrow.'

Lucas stared into the fire. The thought tumbled from his mouth, prompted by nothing. 'That weirdo Zach was staring at her.'

'What?' Sandeep sounded like he was about to fall asleep.

'Yesterday morning, when I dropped my wallet. I told you. When I found Zach holding it, he was staring at Bebe's photo. I thought he was just an idiot, but, well, first Calan and now...'

'I'm not following.' Sandeep gave a yawn and padded to the bathroom. Truthfully, Lucas wasn't really following his own train of thought either. Something just told him that the look in Zach's eyes had been more than mere nosiness. Had he seen a glint of recognition? A smile reserved for someone he knew?

He followed Sandeep into the bathroom. 'Babes...'

He stopped himself, but it was too late. The term of endearment was a thing of habit. Sandeep rolled his eyes as he brushed his teeth and said something like 'Don't worry' from behind the foam.

'I'm going to grab some more whisky from the bar. It'll help me sleep, what with everything.' He flapped his arm around to intimate the mess of the weekend. 'Back in a sec.'

Without waiting for Sandeep's reply, he slipped from their room and tiptoed straight down the stairs for reception. The hall was dark apart from the emergency exit lights above the main doors. Gracie's voice drifted from the bar; she was singing a song he didn't recognise in a low, drunken voice. Tim's voice also sounded: 'I still can't get through, might be the signal. I'll see if the jet answers...'

Checking over his shoulder, he slipped behind the counter to where the keys were hanging. Benroman. Zach's room. He took it off the hook and scurried back up the stairs, taking two steps at a time. He was breathless by the time he reached the corridor. In the quiet of the night, it felt like every tiny creak of a floorboard, every soft crack of his tendons was amplified. He opened the door quickly, his breath shallow, and slipped in.

For an awful moment, he thought Zach was standing by the window. He stumbled backwards against the wall, groping for the light switch. It was all right: just an old-fashioned free-standing coat hanger. He gulped down a nerve-drenched laugh. Almost instantly, he felt very stupid. He had no idea what he was searching for, nor, really, how to conduct a proper search.

A boring-looking blue leather bag was perched on the luggage stand. Honestly, if he had as much money as this Zach fella seemed to, he'd invest in something a little more luxe. He unzipped it, wrinkling his nose at the musty leather smell.

That was odd.

Inside, there were hundreds of those clear plastic airport security bags. He pulled one out: a lock of hair was pinned to a photograph of a woman sleeping. A hot panic rose from the pit of his belly. He'd seen enough true crime stories to know what this was. He pulled out another bag and winced. A scrunchie was tied around another candid photograph. This was a trophy collection. Zach *was* a psychopath. His hands began to shake as he sifted through the bags. He needed to get out of here. What if Zach returned and found him? That was precisely how people ended up killed… in the most sick and twisted ways.

Then, he saw it. Bebe wasn't asleep, but she was in her underwear on a bed, posing. An angry acid reflux burnt at the back of his throat. So, he *had* recognised her from his wallet. They'd *slept* together, along with all these other poor women. Lucas shook his head, trying to make sense of this. How could this be another coincidence? First Calan and now Zach? He gripped the bag, wondering what to do.

The police. He had to call the police. Clearly, Zach was dangerous. For all they knew, he was out there in the darkness, waiting for them to turn in for the night before he struck! He zipped up the bag and tucked it up his arm, hurrying towards the door. As he ran, something sticking out from under the bed caught his foot and sent him flying.

He cried out, ready to scream the place down for help. But it wasn't Zach. Sticking out from beneath the bed was a hunting rifle.

JULES

Jules slumped against the bookcase and stretched her legs out in front of her. She'd always liked the dark. The ghost stories that treated it as a danger had always confused her as a child. Darkness was a place to be herself. She saw it as a comfort, a thing that wrapped around her, hid her from sight.

Tim's mistress. Zach's victim. Lucas's sister. Who had this Rebekah woman been? It couldn't be a coincidence that most of the guests knew her in some way, but it wasn't necessarily ominous, was it?

She shifted uncomfortably. A book stuck out at an odd angle, pushing against her back. Reaching behind her, she pulled it into the muted moonlight and recognised it as the one she and Gracie had looked at that morning. Flicking through the pages, she landed on *The Changeling*. The illustration was sinister. A mother rocked an old-fashioned cot, her head turned away towards the hearth. Her baby smiled eerily at the back of her head, its teeth pointed, its eyes bulbous.

The faerie supplanter spies on the humans, exhibiting uncanny and often disturbing behaviours.

Jules traced the page with her forefinger, feeling her eyes close for a few moments. *A supplanter.* She had often wondered whether she was swapped at birth. The rest of her family was so perfect and easy-going. They had a natural kindness about them, no hint of selfishness. But she'd always stuck out. Throughout her childhood, she'd made a habit of saying the wrong thing; she always managed to reveal the wrong secret, make the wrong joke. Her mother had told her to be more honest, so she had been. Then, she was accused of being rude. As she got older, "rude" turned into "problematic", which turned into "personality disorder".

How did people learn to behave? The question had plagued her all her life. Where did they learn what was right and wrong? Who decided upon these things? Who disseminated the information? She tried. She really tried.

A crash came from what sounded like the bar. Jules considered staying put. She could barricade the door by pushing over one of the bookcases. She could hide out here until morning. Since the hotel was doomed to close, there was no need to attend to any of these guests' demands at all.

Another crash rang out, which sounded like a few crystal glasses smashing. They were expensive. She heaved herself up, clapping the book closed.

As she made her way down the short corridor towards the hall, she was aware of a presence at the top of the stairs but another whacking sound made her hurry into the bar.

Broken bottles lay on the ground, the shards of glass swimming in the liquid. Gracie stood over a cowering Tim, raising the fire stoker above her head. She brought the thing down with tremendous force. Tim rolled out of the way, and a deafening crack sounded as the stone hearth split.

'Help...' Tim crawled away, blood streaming from a wound on his head. 'Help...'

Gracie turned towards them, her face completely calm.

Then, her eyes flashed. It was like watching slow motion: Jules saw Gracie's mouth open, heard the curdling scream as she catapulted forwards, saw the weapon swing through the air towards Tim's skull.

She didn't think – there wasn't time for that. She felt her body collide into Gracie's, arms wrapped around the other woman's waist, wrestling her to the ground. She was aware of someone tugging at her hair, of spit in her eyes. Jules screamed as she pinned Gracie's slender arms down. There was a vague notion of someone else seizing the fire stoker. Still, Gracie continued to writhe underneath her.

'Fuck's sake,' muttered Tim. 'She's lost it.'

'A little help?' Jules twisted her head to see him glaring down at them. 'Gracie! Mrs Melrose! Please! Please...'

Gracie's eyes suddenly lost their spark. Her expression faded to a dull smile and her limbs sagged like a rag doll's.

'Got me,' she whispered, giving a gentle giggle as she looked up at Jules.

'You can let her go,' Tim said in an astonishing change of heart. 'It's over for now.'

Jules shook her head, continuing to hold her down, although Gracie wasn't struggling at all. In fact, it looked like she was enjoying herself. 'I need to keep the other guests safe. I can't just ignore this, Tim. She was trying to...'

He smiled, like she was making some sort of a joke. 'Kill me?'

'That's what it looked like,' she protested.

He laughed, a full-bellied sound. When he finished, he took a deep breath. 'She was, wasn't she? She really was.'

Then, he stopped laughing abruptly and his cheeks slackened. Jules's eyes widened in confusion.

'Look, I don't know what's going on here between you two,

but I can't have someone running riot like this. She could have killed you and anyone else. I need you to call—'

He shook his head like he was bored and tutted. 'Call who? The police?'

'Yes,' she replied, beginning to feel ridiculous in how she was straddling Gracie. 'Call them now,' she demanded.

He trailed the fire stoker along the rug until he got to the floorboards. Then, he turned it on its sharp edge and dragged the iron against the wood, denting it with a long, excruciating scratch.

'Stop it! What are you doing?'

He dabbed his forehead, bringing away a bloody hand.

'Keep up, Jules. Keep up. The Wi-Fi's down, the snow's killed the signal. I can't even get through to my company to order the jet. Details about which a hotelier should be aware, I would have thought...'

'We're all alone here...' Gracie whispered dramatically. Jules looked down at her perfect face. She wished she had something useful to say, but the words echoed her thoughts accurately.

Jules nodded towards the door. 'Can you ask her to stay here while we check the router?' The signal had a habit of going down, but the Wi-Fi was usually reliable. She was sure it was fixable but she wanted to keep Gracie contained.

'Ask me yourself,' cooed Gracie.

Jules reluctantly rolled off her and stood up. Her legs were unsteady and her head was spinning. She backed towards the door, beckoning for Tim to come with her. 'Stay there until I come back, okay?'

'Fine...' Gracie laughed, rolling onto one side and bringing her knees to her chest. 'Fine, fine, fine by me.'

Jules locked the door behind them, catching her breath. Without waiting, she jogged through the library into the drawing room, where she locked the second exit from the bar.

Tim followed her in silence. The main router was in reception, hidden behind about six months' worth of paperwork. She disappeared behind the desk to take a look at it.

'Please,' she mumbled. 'By all means save your thanks for another time.'

He laughed at that. 'What, you think I should be grateful?'

She nodded, fumbling behind the build-up of files and bills. She might as well say what she thought – no point trying to impress him now. 'I just saved your life, remember? She was attacking you.'

She grasped the small white oblong and brought it up onto the desk. The source of the problem was immediately clear: someone had taken something like a hammer and destroyed the box. Her breath caught at the back of her throat. 'Gracie?'

He didn't reply, and instead frowned, picking the box up to further inspect it. 'Do you have a backup somewhere? Big place like this is bound to? My phone might not have picked up its range.'

She nodded, trying not to panic. 'In my flat, upstairs. And one in the library.'

He looked grimly at the door behind which Gracie was locked. 'Check the one in your flat then. I'll check the library. This way?'

She nodded as she ran up the stairs, her heart fluttering between her ears. Gracie's cold stare burnt behind her eyes. *It's fine*, she told herself. *Gracie is contained. She's locked in. She can't do anything to you. You're safe. You just need to wait until morning when the police will arrive.*

She flew into the flat and sank to her knees next to her sofa, praying the router would be intact. No. The same was true of this one. It had been sabotaged, completely smashed in. Gracie had entered her space, her home. She berated herself for not locking the door.

She met Tim back in the foyer, her face ashen. 'Same there,' she managed.

He nodded, confirming her fears. The blood from his head was trickling less steadily than before, but it was still pooling on his collar at an alarming rate.

'I'll get you a bandage,' she said.

He followed her back to the reception desk, where she opened the first aid kit. She sighed, realising she might as well come clean. 'I... I know about Rebekah by the way.'

His lips trembled, very subtly, before returning to their steely straight line. She cut a length of bandage off the roll and approached him. He didn't even wince when she placed the gauze on the cut. 'I understand she was your... um, girlfriend, and, well... I know she died. I'm sorry.'

She wrapped the bandage around his head, trying to control her unsteady fingers. She was so nervous about what she should and shouldn't say.

'Gracie knows about her,' Jules continued. 'I might as well let you know, since, well, since I'm not bending over backwards for you anymore. I helped her log on to your recipient server, where you stored the pictures. And she knows. Is that why she attacked you? Is that why she's cut us off? Is she...'

She pulled tight on the knot and stepped back. The blood was already seeping through; she'd need to go to Marta's cabin for more supplies to last the night. Tim finished the sentence for her. 'A monster?'

Jules folded her arms, the muscles in between her shoulders were twitching with stress. 'Well, is she? I'm sure the police would understand if we kept her in the bar until morning. I can ask Calan to keep watch, just as a precaution.'

Tim eyed her with an expression she couldn't place.

'Gracie is a lot of things,' he said, finally. 'I know that.'

For a brief moment, a vulnerability passed across his face. 'I know what it looks like, what *I* look like to outsiders, but it isn't what it seems.' His lips twitched. 'Yes, she's dangerous. If Rebekah wasn't dead, then I'd be worried—'

His voice broke off in a small choke. He gritted his teeth and looked her dead in the eye. 'I cheat. I'm an adulterer, yes, however you want to put it, but there's a reason for it. I used to love Gracie. She wasn't like other girls. She was fierce and passionate about us... about me. It turned into something else though. Fuck. Why am I telling you this?'

Jules almost laughed at the change in tone. She shrugged. 'Um, because she tried to kill you, which would bring today's body count up to two, by the way, as well as cutting off our only communication source. And, also, because you made your way through half of Scotland's whiskies just before losing a lot of blood.'

He laughed at that. 'Fair.'

He took a deep breath. 'Things started to happen, over a decade ago. Weird things. I had female friends who began avoiding me. One actually disappeared, without a trace, a missing person. Gracie became more and more possessive. She idolised me, like she always had, but now it was controlling. She didn't want me speaking to anyone else. She was terrified I'd cheat...'

'So... you did.' Jules could relate. The more Rob had asked about her infidelity, the more she had wanted to stray.

He nodded grimly. 'Most of them didn't mean anything. Some of them did. But Rebekah...'

The look on his face said everything she needed to know. 'You loved her.'

'Yes.'

He hung his head like the pain of the memory was too much. 'She was special. Gracie never knew about her. I don't know. Maybe I was more careful, maybe I guarded her more meticulously because of how I felt. Or maybe I was well-practised. Anyway, like you say, she found out this weekend. Thanks to you.'

He laughed again at the look on her face. 'Oh, don't. She's a master manipulator, I know that better than most. She wouldn't have been able to resist the leverage she had on you. And now...'

Jules eyed the bar door nervously. 'And now.' She exhaled. 'Stay here. I need to fetch you more bandages.'

CALAN

Calan punched the mattress repeatedly, his anger manifesting in an anguished shout. He wouldn't cry. That suede-shoe teenager-obsessed weirdo had poked around his private things without asking, but he wouldn't cry. He'd thought he was so clever, so careful, but he was nothing but a child. An amateur. First, he'd mucked things up with Tim and now he'd left all his dirty laundry on the bed for everyone to see.

Thank God Lucas hadn't seen the will. At least he'd been more careful about that. He would never have left that out on the bed. He slid his hand underneath the mattress and pulled out the cardboard envelope. Good. It looked undisturbed, untampered with. Lucas definitely didn't know who his sister had left most of her money to. It was a huge amount, more than Calan had ever really conceived of. Her PR and marketing company had clearly been doing very well. *One million and four hundred thousand pounds.* All reserved for Timothy Melrose. Her "good friend and companion" as she put it (it didn't take a genius to work out what that meant). As if he even needed more money!

It had been a blow for Calan, of course. When the adoption

241

agency had let him know Rebekah had died, he'd requested her will. Apparently, only the executor – who was Rebekah's PA – was allowed to read the will until everything was settled. Calan had waited patiently, assuming he'd receive something in due course. But no. He hadn't quite believed that his mother would be so cold, so cruel, to leave him nothing. But it turned out to be true.

It had taken him a few days to get over the disappointment. Then, he'd begun to formulate a plan.

After all the legalities had been completed, he was able to request the will himself.

Calan remembered the excitement from when he'd first googled Timothy Melrose. *Melrose Investments: Specialists in Hospitality and Hotels*. It had been too perfect an opportunity not to take. If he could just talk to the guy, plan what to say and how to say it, he was his ticket out of here. He must have loved Rebekah, right? Nobody leaves that amount of money to someone who doesn't love them. And if he loved her, then wouldn't he want to take care of her son? The baby she'd given up for adoption?

Calan had practised his speech over and over in the mirror, in his head whilst working, aloud on hikes. The plan had been to introduce himself, to explain how even though his mother hadn't explicitly left him the money, he believed she'd want him to be happy. She would want him to follow in her footsteps, surely? To get away from this place and start a life for himself in London. He wouldn't expect Tim to hand over all of it, but perhaps they could come to a sensible, mutually agreeable sum.

The next step was getting to London to speak with him. Train tickets were extortionate, and, anyway, he couldn't afford to take that much time off. He started saving up. The spare pound, here and there, a tenner's tip from a guest, all stuffed into a tin box with the idea it would be used to get to Timothy Melrose.

He had not believed it when he'd seen the name on the booking system about a month ago. The company name had confirmed it: there was no need to travel down and grovel. Timothy would be on *his* turf, amongst his habitat, and at the behest of his expertise! He would have all weekend to find a quiet spot in his schedule and propose his idea carefully. It was too good to be true, yet the man seemed to have fallen into his lap.

Calan let out another frustrated cry and buried his face in the mattress. He'd completely failed. He'd tried to bully him, for God's sake! Of course Tim hadn't wanted anything to do with him.

It was useless. He wiped his eyes and folded up the will, studying it one last time. He needed to get away from here, money or not. He stuffed the will inside his coat pocket and grabbed his rucksack. There was nothing for him here. There was no hope. Perhaps, there never had been. He needed to run.

Lucas paced back and forth in their room, the rifle resting menacingly on the dresser. 'Why? Why would he have a gun in his room?'

He was sweating through his shirt. He ripped his jacket off and fiddled with the cufflinks to roll up his sleeves. 'Sandeep? Sandeep! Have you been listening?'

In vain, he tried calling 999 again, but the line beeped dead. It seemed a reliable signal was too much to ask for in these parts.

Sandeep, to be fair, looked concerned. He was in his pyjamas in bed, a book resting on his lap. He removed his glasses and pinched the bridge of his nose. 'Forget the gun, Lucas. I'm still focused on why Zach has a photograph of Bebe in his room. I think you're right. He sounds unhinged.'

'Unhinged and out there!' Lucas flung his arm towards the window. 'We're sitting ducks. He could be watching our every move. He could have... he could have *rounded us up* here!'

'Rounded us? What do you mean?'

Lucas was nodding and speaking very quickly. 'It makes sense, in a messy, terrifying way.'

He counted on his fingers. 'Calan knows my sister. Zach

knows her. Who's to say the others don't? The owner – that Jules woman – she basically accosted me in the library when she saw Bebe's photograph. What if she connects us all, Sandeep? What if this is some psychopathic game of Zach's? What if he's really...' he lowered his voice, 'here? In the building? Waiting for us all to fall asleep until he takes us down one by one.' He mimed shooting a rifle, then stopped because the thought sent his stomach into convulsions.

Sandeep glanced at the door. 'You locked it?'

Ah ha! So, he wasn't being so paranoid after all. Sandeep the Great Calm was also nervous. 'Of course I locked it. I'm not an idiot.'

Sandeep shook his head. 'It sounds a little bit too much like those true crime shows you like.'

Lucas hit the bed with his fist in utter disbelief. 'Do you know what *everyone* – and I mean *everyone* – always says on those programmes? I'll tell you! *I never thought it would happen to us. Just such a normal town, a normal day, a normal holiday...*'

He raised his eyebrows significantly. 'Nobody, Sandeep, thinks it's happening to them until it *actually* is happening to them and, judging by the gun I found in his room, I'd say it's happening! It's happening to us right now! And if we don't get clever very soon we might end up as skin wall hangings—'

'Jesus, Lucas, please.'

'Sorry...' His heart was hammering against his ribs. 'Sorry, I didn't mean to say that. I don't think you'll be made into a wall hanging...'

His voice trailed off to the sound of a distant banging. They were silent for a few moments until it happened again. Somebody was thumping or hitting something downstairs.

'Can you hear...?'

Lucas nodded. It also sounded like a woman was shouting.

Lucas backed away and grabbed the rifle. He aimed it at their door. 'We should stay here. It's too dangerous—'

'Don't be an idiot.' Sandeep was already pulling on his dressing gown. 'We're going to see if she needs help. We've got a gun, we'll be fine. I learnt to shoot yesterday, didn't I?'

Lucas was well aware that he was required to do nothing Sandeep asked of him anymore, but also he had no desire to stay in the room alone. He handed Sandeep the rifle.

'Right, of course, you're right.'

As they descended the staircase, the banging got louder and more frantic. 'Help me! Please! Somebody help!'

'It's the bar.' Lucas ran forwards and knocked on the door. 'Er, is everything okay in there?'

'Oh thank you!'

He mouthed to Sandeep, 'I think it's Gracie.' Sandeep nodded.

'She's locked me in! That bitch! She's locked me in here and... oh my God... there's blood everywhere. Please! Help me!'

It was Sandeep's turn to mouth to him, 'What the fuck?'

Lucas shook his head. He could not believe they had willingly walked right into the middle of more drama.

'Jules locked you in here?' Lucas asked, doing a quick turn on the spot to check nobody else was about.

'Yes! Her! Please! The key's behind the reception...'

Really, thought Lucas, *this place needs to re-evaluate its security measures.* He raised his eyes at Sandeep who whispered, 'We should let her out. You saw how flirty Zach was with Jules. They might be in something together.'

Well, he'd changed his tune. Who sounded too "true crime" now? Either way, locking someone inside a room for the night was most definitely not normal. 'Hang on...'

He grabbed an unmarked cluster of keys and, after a couple of tries, opened the door. Gracie was an absolute sight. Her hair was matted and somehow mounded on top of her head in a messy knot. Her left cheek was puffy and red, the first sign of a bruise pushing from underneath. There was blood smattered over the front of her gown which was dried and crusty.

She smiled, sweet and calm, like nothing was out of the ordinary at all. 'Thanks.'

Lucas peered over her shoulder into the room. 'Why is there blood all over the floor?'

'Why are you carrying a gun?'

It was a reasonable response, he supposed. Resigning himself to the fact he was unlikely to get a wink of sleep until the police arrived tomorrow, he sighed and marched straight into the bar. He skirted around about a dozen broken bottles, climbed up the ladder, and grabbed an unopened one from the top shelf. Swiping three glasses, he returned to the foyer. 'You tell us and we'll tell you.'

CALAN

Calan hoisted his rucksack over his shoulders and squinted into the thick flurry of snow. He knew these paths. They were dangerous in bad weather, especially at night. But he had no choice. Things were closing in on him. It felt as if the walls of this place were crumbling around him, squashing him, stopping him from breathing. He couldn't stand another night with Jules. He was afraid of what he'd do, what he'd say if she came knocking. He was afraid of himself, of his own confused, diseased mind and messed-up thoughts. *Messed up.* That was a good way of summarising his life. Messed up.

He turned to close the bothy door behind him for one last time, when he saw the figures in front of the hotel. The semicircular driveway was lit up; from up here in the hills, he was hidden. He shook his head, reminding himself that none of those idiots were his problem anymore, but something struck him as odd. The figure at the front was a good way ahead of the person behind. The person behind moved like they didn't want to be seen, flitting behind a pillar and keeping to the shadows of the bushes.

He rounded into the bothy and grabbed his binoculars. It

was difficult in the dim moonlight, but he found his focus. Jules was in front. It looked like she was heading around the side of the building, which was the quickest way to Marta's cabin. Tim followed her. Calan had been right: he was moving in quick bursts, crouching down, and then running to conceal himself behind something else. However, this wasn't the most alarming detail: it was the expression on his face. It was worse than the look he'd given Calan on the decking that morning. An expression of pure and unadulterated hatred.

Jules was nothing to him. *She was nothing to him.*

Calan swore into the darkness. He had to follow them. Yes, he wanted nothing more than to be rid of her, but he wouldn't ever forgive himself if anything happened and he could have stopped it. Especially after the events of this weekend. There was only so much one person could take.

He swore again and chucked his rucksack back into the bothy. Switching on his head torch, he ran down the familiar path, skidding as he hit a patch of ice, but skilfully keeping his balance. He skirted around the loch and slowed as he approached the outbuildings, turning his torch off. He kept low, against the wall, his ears straining for any sound of human voices.

A shadowy movement caught his eye a few metres ahead of him. He pushed himself closer against the wall and edged a little further into the courtyard. Craning his neck from this position, he could see he'd been right: Jules was inside Marta's cabin. The lone lightbulb was on, illuminating her clearly against the darkness outside. By the looks of it, she was staring at some pictures stuck on the wall. Tim leant against a stack of barrels, his arms folded, his eyes completely set on the small window. The pure hatred on his face was evident even in the dark. His eyes seemed like two black seething pits.

Calan thought about his packed rucksack up at the bothy. If

he left now, he'd be on the paths within fifteen minutes, escaping from this place. The urge to leave was so, so tempting.

Tim moved towards the cabin in fluid steps. Calan held his breath and watched him open the door.

'Oh, Tim – sorry, you startled me. I'm just fetching your bandages—'

Jules sounded completely calm. Calan sighed, itching his forehead beneath his head torch. Was he going mad? With everything going on, had he imagined Tim's menacing face? A hot flush of embarrassment made his cheeks grow hot.

Jules took a picture from the wall and pointed at it, frowning. 'Is this her? This is her, isn't it? Your Rebekah?'

Rebekah? Calan kept low and took three more steps closer to the cabin. He could see the picture from here and it didn't make any sense. Jules held a photograph of his biological mother. It was definitely her – much younger, not much older than Calan was now – but her eyes, her smile, her thick hair. It was undeniable. The heat of embarrassment turned into a sharp confusion. Why had Marta had a photo of his mum in her cabin? The question seemed so unlikely, so ridiculous that he didn't believe he was thinking it. Marta? Crazy old Marta? Marta, who watched him when she thought he didn't know. Marta, who whispered what he assumed were Italian prayers. *How* had she known his mum?

Tim stood very still for almost a minute. It was so silent that Calan could clearly hear the snowflakes hitting the gravel in gentle, wet drops. Gently, Tim took the photograph from Jules and bent his head over it, the sound of his sobs carried through the courtyard.

Jules placed a hand on his shoulder to comfort him. 'I'm so sorry.'

The reaction was explosive. It was as if her touch galvanised the hate Calan had seen in Tim's eyes and whipped it through his limbs. He pushed her away, his scream deep and primal. 'Don't touch me! Don't touch me!'

Jules hit the wall, her neck snapping back like elastic. She seemed dazed for a moment or so, before lifting her gaze to Tim. 'I don't understand...' she slurred.

'You don't understand?' Tim was bellowing now, his hands shaking as he clutched the picture of Rebekah. 'You don't understand? Of course you don't, you stupid, spineless bitch.'

The final word seemed to hit Jules like another physical blow. She shook her head and made her way to the cabin door, but Tim blocked her. Calan tensed. What would he say if he intervened now? *Oh sorry, I was just spying on you and saw you were in a spot of bother?* Jules didn't look like she was in any real danger yet, not properly.

'Let me out,' she said. Calan could hear the fear in her voice.

Tim shook his head, slowly at first, and then more violently. 'She was happy, you know?' His voice fell in short, sharp shards. 'Rebekah was happy. She had everything going for her. Her business was thriving, she was getting back in touch with her brother. She had me. We were serious!'

His shout came out of nowhere. Jules winced under the volume of it.

'We were going to get married. I was going to leave Gracie. And then...'

Jules took a step towards him. 'Tim? Tim, I'm so sorry she died, but I...'

'You what?!'

He took her by the shoulders and shook her. 'You what, Jules? You what...?'

Her mouth hung open in confusion. Calan kept very still, watching the scene unfold. The way Tim was talking, it sounded like he knew something Jules didn't. Something about Rebekah? If he interrupted now, he might not finish.

'Tim, I don't know what you're talking about.' Jules batted him away and tried to sidestep him towards the door. He pushed her back into the centre of the cabin.

'You'll listen. That's the whole point.'

His voice had changed. He was no longer shouting; a chilling calm had set in. He inhaled and placed the photograph on the coffee table beside him. The tenderness in the gesture was evident even from where Calan was watching.

'She was happy,' Tim repeated. 'So, so happy. And then, she was stressed. She'd never been stressed by work before, there'd been no need. She was good at what she did, took it seriously, did her best job for everyone. You don't build a company unless you're like that.' He turned to Jules. 'But then a bitch of a client starts sending messages. It's her fault, apparently, that her shithole of a hotel is failing. It's her fault the owner's too stupid to understand how to run a business. It's her fault nobody's booking. It's her fault staff have been let go left, right and centre!'

Jules's eyes were wide. Calan's mind was racing: it sounded like The Tornivan had been using Rebekah's PR company. Jules had done business with her.

'You didn't have to send threats, did you? You didn't have to say you'd write appalling reviews everywhere, send emails to the hotelier alliance about how awful a PR person she was? Stuff like that ruins businesses. Rebekah knew that. I told her to ignore you, to block you but you kept coming back, didn't you? Different email addresses, threats once, twice, three times a day?'

He exhaled and it sounded like a thousand pent-up emotions finally escaping his lips. 'You didn't seriously think an investor would be interested, did you? This place is nothing more than an embarrassing, middle-aged hobby. You're not a serious person, Jules. You're an old washed-up bag with bad breath who wears clothes too tight for her. Do you see how unfair it is that someone like you—'

His voice wobbled. 'Someone like *you* drove her – Rebekah – to... to do what she did? It was your fault! It was your fault, I know it! The stress, the pressure you put on her... threatening to ruin everything she'd built from the ground up.'

Jules was trembling; Calan could see it from where he was hidden.

'I came here to see you in person. I came here to find out as much as I could about this place, to shut you down. You're breaking, what, about twenty health and safety laws? Probably more. I'll have you ruined within a week. Just like you did to Rebekah, I'll tear everything you've worked for to meaningless, dirty little shreds. That's what you are...'

He swung open the door and re-emerged in the courtyard. Calan flung himself deeper into the shadows, concealing his breathing by placing a hand over his mouth.

'You're a meaningless, dirty rag of a woman, Jules. Remember that.'

JULES

Jules couldn't stop crying. She remained in a heap on the floor of Marta's cabin for about half an hour, staring at Rebekah's photograph. An image. A face attached to a name at the end of an email. She had never seen Rebekah in person. She'd only ever spoken to her on the phone once, maybe twice, and then they'd switched to email correspondence. The name was a slightly unusual spelling, but, to be honest, she'd forgotten all about her. This had been just over a year ago, when she and Rob were at the height of their shouting matches and silent treatment. She'd been drinking a lot, relying on her pills even more. At the time, she'd believed that if she could make a success of the hotel, then Rob might come around.

It had all been hopeless. And now – she gulped, a wet and strangled sound – she knew it had been more than hopeless. Her behaviour had resulted in a woman's death. Tim was right. She was meaningless, but she was also evil. All the evidence pointed to it. She was rotten at the core. She took and took and took without ever thinking about the consequences. *A bad egg.* That's what her mother used to say. *Julia, the egg factory must have been faulty on the day they packaged you...*

She swayed from side to side, turning the photograph over in her hands. Some Italian was written on the back – it must have been Marta's handwriting. She knew enough French and Latin to make out most of the words. *Vero amore* meant true love; *per sempre* was forever, or always; *lo proteggerò...* I will protect him.

She moved her lips over the next few words. *I will protect...*

That didn't seem right. *nostro figlio* meant "our son", didn't it? *I will protect him. I will protect our son, Calan.*

Calan? Jules looked at the photograph again. She could be Calan's mother. They had the same eyes, the same pinched lips. He had said, many times, that Marta was following him, watching him. She stared at the photograph, her head throbbing. Calan was Rebekah's son? It both made perfect sense and none at all.

Tim, Zach, Lucas, Marta, Calan. All connected to Rebekah Desouza. She imagined that lovely face, enlarged to phantom-like proportions, hovering over the hotel with gargantuan spider's legs. Her web held all of them together, had them stuck here... for what? And, more importantly, how? No one knew each other before coming here. At least, no one had said they did.

A tight ball of fear tightened in her belly. It was as if reality was steadily slipping away from her. She tried to think clearly. When did things start going wrong? When had everything started to feel strange? Like the colours were melting away?

Yesterday morning, when she'd woken up. Her notes. She'd tried to ignore them. She'd thrown them away. It was as if she'd been trying *not* to see something, not to remember...

Her chest tightened and she struggled to catch her breath. There were words she didn't want to read. Words she wanted to forget. Horrible, horrible words.

She ran out into the cold and back towards the hotel.

Sandeep, Lucas and Gracie were huddled together at reception, sipping whisky. They jumped when she entered, their expressions set like they'd seen a ghost.

'There she is!' cried Gracie, pointing at her accusingly. So, they'd let her out? Fantastic. She was their problem now.

Lucas and Sandeep glared at her. She kept her head down and made for the stairs.

'Off to lock more guests up?' Lucas trilled, almost gleefully.

'The blood isn't hers,' she replied.

'So much for a luxury Highland weekend!' Lucas's bitter laughter followed her up the stairs before he apparently registered what she'd said. 'What? Oh... er...'

Closing the door behind her, she fought another surge of tears. It was past one o'clock in the morning and her body ached at the sight of her bed, begging for sleep. She shook herself, panting through the rising panic, as she eyed the bin next to her desk.

Emptying out the balls of paper, she opened them again. It was mostly nonsense, scrawled in erratic, almost unrecognisable letters. She squinted at her writing, trying to make out something at least.

Loud sound... bang! Too much blood.

Acid climbed up the back of her throat as she raked at the words. She shook her head, willing herself to stop, but she had to know.

No, no, no. Limp. Dead.

She gasped, biting down on her fist. This couldn't be. She couldn't have done something like this. She wouldn't have! *Evil. A bad egg. Take and take and take.* The words circulated through her mind. Her bottom lip quivered as she remembered the searing anger at having been rejected by Zach. She could have done anything in that state.

She turned the page over.

I want him dead. I hate him. I want him dead.

It was too much. A high-pitched whine rang out from her lips. She found herself on all fours, retching into empty space. She rocked backwards and forwards, allowing the motion to calm her mind. They were just words. These were just words. That's all. Zach was sheltering in a bothy somewhere. Marta had killed herself. Just as the police had said. Everyone was accounted for. These words were fantasies. They weren't real.

But there was the phrase that stood out at the bottom of the page. One that didn't make any sense at all.

Big freezer kitchen.

The image of Rebekah clasping the hotel with her spider legs resurfaced as Jules felt herself pulled back downstairs. It was like the sticky, webby thread knew exactly where to lead her, where to take her. The three guests had disappeared from the main hall. She walked straight-backed, tight-lipped. It was like she knew what she was going to find.

Closing the kitchen door behind her, she made towards the greenish light behind the PVC curtains. The air was cool here. Her shoes squeaked against the white tiled floor.

Big freezer kitchen.

She opened the lid. The rush of freezing air hit her face. Her mouth fell open into a silent scream.

'You knew she was your mum? You kept this all to yourself?' Jules ogled at Calan as he tugged on the straps of his rucksack, readying to leave the bothy.

Her hair was crispy with fresh snow and she was still panting from running up the hill. The thing from the freezer loomed large behind her eyes. She blinked, undecided about whether to tell him.

'I've said everything I need to say.'

He gestured impatiently to the pile of adoption agency letters. 'I was as blindsided as the next person when Lucas told me Rebekah was his sister, *and* that she knew Marta, but...' He shrugged, not nearly as perturbed as he should have been. 'Like I said, I'm out of here.'

His eyes darkened. 'And before you ask, no, I'm not interested.'

She stared at him, genuinely not understanding, before realising what he meant. 'Jesus, Calan. I'm not even close to being turned on right now.'

His lips trembled with something that resembled anger and he turned towards the door. 'Right. Well, thanks for everything, I guess.'

A sharp gust of snow blew through the door as he opened it. She rubbed her hands together, squeezing her eyes closed as she thought through her options. Two distinct possibilities had occurred to her as she'd slumped against the kitchen wall, her head buried in her hands at the sight of Zach's cold corpse.

The first was too horrifying to comprehend fully: that she had, indeed, killed Zach and forgotten about it.

The second was more of a collection of thoughts that were beginning to solidify. What if she hadn't killed Zach? It was a coincidence that both he and Marta had turned up dead on the same weekend, wasn't it? That, coupled with the fact that everyone in the hotel had some connection to this Rebekah woman.

Someone had gathered them here. And perhaps someone had framed her.

Someone wanted them all, all eight of them, at The Tornivan Hotel this weekend. She already suspected Gracie had broken into her room to smash the Wi-Fi router. What's to say she hadn't fabricated those notes?

She couldn't trust anyone, not even herself, but she needed help. She bit her lip, still not certain she was doing the right thing. Just before Calan disappeared through the door, she whispered, 'Zach's dead. The missing guest. He's in the freezer in the kitchen.'

She stopped herself there. He didn't need to know about the notes. Then she added, 'I think whoever gathered everyone here is the killer. I think they killed Marta too. I don't know how, it looked like a drowning, but...'

He stopped with his back to her, silhouetted against the white night. It seemed like the news hit him like a punch to the stomach, then, he turned to face her. His eyebrows were drawn close together, deep stress lines running along his forehead. 'What did you say?'

'I know.' She walked towards him and brought him back into the warmth, shutting the door. 'I know, it's a lot. I found the body. It looks like he was shot in the chest, but I'm not sure. I came straight to you. I haven't spoken to the guests.'

He remained impassive.

'Look, did you hear what I said? It's not safe out there. The killer's here at the hotel!'

His eyes darted around the bothy and then to the darkened windows. He nodded very quickly. 'Right, then that's even more reason for me to leave.'

She caught him by the arm. 'I need your help.'

'You can fuck off.'

'Please.' She affected her voice, making sure it wobbled at the end. 'Please don't leave me on my own, Calan. You're my only friend here after Marta...'

'I'm not your friend, Jules. Neither was Marta.'

He spoke with force but she was relieved when he removed his rucksack and sagged onto the bed.

'I should have known. You never come here unless you want something. If it's not sex...' He sounded almost as exhausted as she was. 'What do you need?'

She couldn't help but feel triumph at the resignation in his voice. Persuading people to do things against their will always gave her a little buzz. As soon as she thought it, a deep shame reverberated through her insides. Who had she become?

She clasped his hands, rubbing them for comfort. 'The booking system... someone must have hacked it... or, I don't know... done something technological I don't understand. It's all I can think of that explains how all of us are here at the same time.'

He blew through his lips. 'That's unlikely. And, anyway, the guests booked their own rooms, didn't they? Nobody could have put that idea into their heads. No one forced them to book for this particular weekend. That's impossible.'

He seemed older than yesterday; his eyes were clearer, laced with a new flint-like rigour. He raised his eyebrows and added, 'Are you sure you're okay, Jules? Maybe just get a good night's sleep? Lay off the booze... and the pills. Stay here if you don't want to go back to the hotel. You'll have it to yourself.'

He'd never spoken to her like that before, like he was in control. Like he found her mildly amusing, annoying.

'I'm not making it up!'

She hadn't meant to shout but she *needed* her theory to be true; she *needed* Zach's death not to be on her hands. She took a deep breath as an idea came into focus. 'Sorry... wait... what did you say?'

He shrugged. 'It's impossible. Nobody could have—'

'*Put that idea into their heads*! Oh my God.' Her entire body started to tingle. 'The bookings. I couldn't find the promotion, nor any trace of the email they had, so I checked them in manually. Lucas kept referring to some deal... I thought something was off. I thought I was losing it. It was the same for Zach.'

'What about Tim?'

'He got in touch with us, chose the dates... it's complimentary, so...'

Now she said it aloud, it was obvious. Tim was the only person who could have set this up. She gaped at Calan, realising how she'd been alone with Tim only an hour ago. 'It's him. He did this. He killed Zach! And Marta...! Why would he do that? What had Marta done to him?'

Calan shook his head in deep thought, his brows still furrowed. 'He had a reason to hate Zach, if he found out about his weird little photography hobby, especially if Rebekah was sleeping with both of them at the same time. I've no idea about Marta, can't see why he'd bother with her. He seems pretty techy though, I bet he'd find it easy to build a convincing email and re-route it to our internal booking system.' He grimaced. 'I don't know, Jules. It's all a bit far-fetched, isn't it?'

She nodded along before responding with as much sarcasm as possible, 'Yes, yes, far-fetched, I agree. Apart from the *body in my freezer*.'

He tutted and stood, looking like he was preparing to leave again. 'Is there anything else?'

'No.' She folded her arms as he made for the door. 'You're not really going? It's awful out there.'

'Thanks for caring,' he said, before slamming the door behind him. She listened to his footsteps crunch through the snow until there was just silence.

LUCAS

Lucas stared at the gun, which he'd propped up against a bookcase in the library. He and Sandeep sat upright on the floor, legs covered by their duvet, facing the door. A sinister atmosphere of lawlessness had descended upon the hotel. This gun would be glued to them right up until the second the police came to the rescue.

Going to sleep was impossible. They'd both tried after their conversation with Gracie. First, Sandeep had returned to their room while Lucas had patrolled downstairs, then they'd swapped. In the end, they'd admitted defeat and occupied a random corner of the building. If Zach was really out to get them, he'd try their room first. Or, at least, that's what Lucas hoped.

'I'm sorry,' Lucas murmured.

'For what?' Sandeep threw another log on the fire. It spat and sizzled.

'For bringing you here,' Lucas said. 'It's been a nightmare from start to finish. I just wanted to impress you and now we're surrounded by crazy people in a nightmare horror show.'

Sandeep chuckled. 'Oh, don't be too harsh on yourself,' he

joked gently. 'Hardly the stuff of nightmares. Just a drowning, your sister's stalker, her secret son, a madwoman.'

Lucas sniffed. 'Do you reckon Gracie went to bed?'

'No idea.' Sandeep yawned and spoke with closed eyes. 'I couldn't work out what she was talking about by the end. That fight with her husband sounded mental.'

'Maybe we should have left her locked up,' Lucas said. She'd seemed so fragile when they'd found her, but, as they'd swapped stories, her voice had grown darker, more insistent. Sandeep was right: by the end, she'd been ranting about all sorts of disconnected stories about affairs and random women, her eyes glassy and detached.

'Jealousy can send people over the brink.'

'"O, beware, my lord, of jealousy! It is the green-eyed monster which doth mock the meat it feeds on".' Sandeep's eyes remained closed as he recited the line.

'Omigod!' Lucas laughed, resting his head against the books. 'You wait until we've broken up to tell me you like Shakespeare?'

Sandeep opened his eyes in mock disbelief. 'You mean you thought I couldn't do *Othello*? Shame on you!'

'Yeah...'

Lucas laughed softly. Sandeep was only playing about, but the truth was there was a lot about him Lucas had failed to notice over the past year. He'd been so swept up in his own life, so obsessed with how others saw them. He'd wanted to be a part of *that* couple, the couple people envied. The stylish couple whose social media was littered with idyllic images of Mediterranean hotels, infinity pools, classy cocktails. It hadn't ever mattered, he realised, who the other half of the couple was. He'd been so invested in the fantasy, he'd forgotten about his partner.

'I'm not surprised you said no, by the way.'

Sandeep's eyebrows jerked upwards at the change in tone. 'Lucas, we've talked about this...'

'No. No, I know you felt you had to stay with me because of Bebe, which I still think is bloody ridiculous. But if I'd given you the time of day, if I'd paid you any type of proper attention, things might have been different. You might have felt able to talk to me. You might... you might have actually loved me. But how do you love someone who's so obsessed with themselves? Who's so shallow?'

This struck Sandeep harder than he thought it would. Dewy moisture swelled in his eyes. Sandeep turned away, suddenly very interested in the books next to him.

'Sorry, I didn't mean to upset you.'

'No, it's fine.' Sandeep's voice was thick. 'I appreciate that, Lucas. Really. It's, um... it's all got so messy, hasn't it?' He grasped Lucas's hand. 'It'll all be over soon.'

A single set of footsteps sounded from outside the door, moving closer down the corridor towards the library. Lucas slid his hand towards the gun. Whoever it was dithered outside the door, before moving away.

'Who was that?' Lucas whispered.

Sandeep pouted and checked his watch. 'It's gone 2.30am. I guess nobody can sleep.'

A prickly sensation moved at the back of Lucas's neck like a premonition. Then came the sound. The scream was more than loud. It was deafening. It carried down the corridor with shocking momentum. It was a siren, a terrifying mixture of fear and sorrow.

Lucas pulled the duvet to his chin, wishing he was anywhere else but here. 'We should, er...' he began.

Sandeep nodded, equally as reluctant.

'We should,' he agreed, pushing himself up.

JULES

Jules heard it as she walked across the driveway. It was an animalistic sound. It was so desperate that it sprang her into action immediately. She ran towards its source without thinking about anything else. As she flung herself through the doors, Lucas and Sandeep approached from the opposite direction. They met in the middle, stopping momentarily, then ran through the bar and into the drawing room.

Jules had never really understood what people meant when they described how it took a while for the brain to make sense of traumatic scenes. But now, as she stood in a daze at what was before her, she got it. Nothing looked real. Blood was smeared over the floorboards. It seemed like a grotesque, multi-limbed monster, drenched in liquid and writhing in the centre of the room.

'No!' a voice screamed. 'No! No! No! No!'

Blood rushed to Jules's head. She heard a thumping sound growing louder and realised it was her pulse. Finally, her brain caught up with her eyes. It was the Melroses. Tim's crisp white shirt was covered in blood. It pooled darker at the centre of his stomach, where it looked almost black. Gracie knelt over him, screaming into his chest. She tried to sit him up, but lacked the strength and fell down again, her bare feet skidding in the blood.

'Is...' Jules couldn't get out the words. 'Is he...?'

'He's dead! He's dead!'

Gracie spat the words out. Her face was covered in the dark-red liquid. Jules's stomach flipped. She had no idea what to say. She'd been right. Someone very dangerous had gathered them all here and they were being picked off, one by one.

She pointed at Gracie. 'You. You cut us off. You killed Zach. And Marta! And now this! You.'

She seized the gun Lucas was holding, prising it from his hands, and pointed it at her. 'Get up.'

Her voice shook, but she held the gun steady. Calan had shown her how to shoot before. She didn't want to, but she would pull the trigger if she needed. 'Up!'

Gracie inclined her head at an odd angle. It was like she was listening to a voice no one else could hear. She was clearly completely insane.

'I said get up!'

Gracie stroked a long strand of hair with a bloody finger. Silent tears spilt down her cheeks, making thin canals through the dark blood. Her mouth twisted into something that looked like a smile, but reminded Jules of the Changeling's sneer. 'You think I did this?'

The question caught Jules off guard. It was obvious she had. She'd been chasing Tim around with a fire stoker less than two hours ago. 'Just stand up.'

'Errrm, maybe you should put the gun down...' Lucas shifted behind her. Jules was fairly sure he would change his tune once he heard about Zach.

'You called Zach a creep,' Jules said, taking a careful step towards Gracie. 'Remember? You told me he'd upset you just before you forced me to hack into Tim's computer. Now Zach's body is in my freezer and you're covered in your husband's blood.'

Lucas and Sandeep reacted simultaneously. Lucas swore loudly and Sandeep exhaled. Jules kept her eyes on Gracie. 'Just do as I say. It's over. I know what you've done.'

Gracie started to giggle. It would have been a beautiful sound if not for the grim setting. She threw her head back, exposing her blood-flecked neck and laughed and laughed. She stood, holding her sodden dress off the floor. 'He said you were an idiot. I can see what he meant.'

She tiptoed through the blood towards the gun. Her bare feet made a soft, squelchy sound as she moved. Then, she took the barrel into her hand and leant forwards, resting her forehead against the muzzle. She looked Jules straight in the eye. 'So shoot me then.' Her lips curved into a grotesque smile. 'I dare you.'

Jules's hands began to shake. She held her gaze for a moment, and lowered the weapon.

Lucas came to her side. 'Look, are you saying you didn't kill him? Let's be clear here.'

Gracie shook her head. 'Not me. There are times when I'd have loved to, believe me, but I didn't do this.'

With her last word, her voice cracked into a sob. It was impossible to know what to believe. Every time Jules tried to think the events of this weekend through, she was led off-track with question after unanswered question.

'Then who did?' Jules rounded on the three of them. She tried to stop her lips from trembling as the reality of the situation hit her. 'Someone here did it! Someone here... someone here...'

The scrawled notes resurfaced behind her eyes. *In the freezer. Loud bang. Hate him. I want him dead.* It couldn't be her. It couldn't.

'Christ, put the gun down,' Lucas said, holding his hands up.

'No!' She nodded towards the door. 'In the bar, now.' The smell of Tim's blood and whatever else was pouring out of him was making her sick. 'Now!'

She could barely believe what was happening. Her three guests traipsed through the door into the bar, a gun to their backs. Once they were inside, she gestured to the armchairs. 'Just... just sit down.'

They all settled on the chairs before the fire which was a mass of glowing embers by now. She had no plans of going anywhere else tonight. 'Okay...' she breathed. 'Okay.'

'It is very much not okay,' replied Lucas. He was sitting straight-backed, his eyes wide and unblinking. 'Can you just put that thing down? It's making me nervous.'

She raised her eyebrows at his hypocrisy, but conceded, leaning against the wall facing them and lowering the gun at her side.

Very quietly, Sandeep said, 'Is it true what you said about Zach?'

She inhaled deeply. She wanted to get all the facts straight in her head before she started talking. 'Yes. Yes, he's dead. I found his body in the kitchen a couple of hours ago. It looked like he'd been shot in the chest.'

Silence followed. Gracie gave nothing away; she was back to weeping again. Jules continued. 'There's something else. All of us here seem to have some connection to a woman called Rebekah Desouza—'

Lucas moaned impatiently. 'You've already bothered me about this, she was my sister.'

Jules held a hand up to silence him. There wasn't time for his dramatics. 'Right. And Calan's mother. Zach was involved with her too, and she was, er...' It seemed indelicate to bring this up now, but she didn't have much choice. 'She was having an affair with Tim. I was just in Marta's cabin and she had a photograph of Rebekah on the wall. She looks a lot younger. I think they might have been girlfriends a long time ago. From what I could read, I think Marta had an obsession or... some sort of protective feelings towards Calan. I think it's why she applied to work here.'

'And you?' Sandeep asked the question very gently. She wished he hadn't.

'I harassed her about a year ago. I was using her company to promote the hotel. Tim told me that my messages might have pushed her over the edge.'

Her words sounded blunt even to her. A hot rush of shame crawled up her face as Lucas glared silently at her. 'I'm sorry,' she added.

Lucas bit his lip, his eyes were bloodshot. 'So what are you saying? You invited us all here because we knew Rebekah? Why?'

'No.' Gracie raised her head. 'No. We weren't invited. Tim got in touch himself.'

'That's right.' Jules moved to the centre of the chairs. 'No, I'm saying that *someone* invited you here. Whoever sent the original email to you about the special price for this weekend is my best guess. I'd never heard about the promotion you mentioned when you arrived. I think it was fake.'

Lucas immediately took out his phone. 'Still no internet, but I can look at my inbox...' He scrolled down his screen. 'Okay, here. Just looks like a generic email: *admin at Tornivan dot com,*' he read out.

Jules walked back towards the fire, still clutching the rifle. Whoever it was – and she was sure it was someone in this room – would be feeling very nervous now. 'We're *co dot uk*, not *dot com*. And there's no "admin" address.'

'You can trace it with the IP address,' Sandeep interjected. He took Lucas's phone and nodded. 'Right, give me a moment or two. It's in the email's header, I don't even need Wi-Fi. Most email providers include it...' He shrugged. 'We're here for the night anyway, though, aren't we? Even if I found out where it was sent from, we're still stuck here.'

'But we'd know who to lock up,' Lucas said, his eyes moving between Gracie and Jules.

'Good point.' Sandeep tapped on the screen, squinting as he worked. It took all of about ten seconds. He frowned, as if he'd made a mistake. 'That's odd...'

'What?' Jules's hand tightened around the rifle.

Sandeep got out his own phone and started typing what looked like digits, shaking his head.

'I teach Computer Science and there's this data protection module.' He held up his phone. 'This is an IP look-up tool app I use in class to demonstrate how easy it is to find someone's very specific location, and even their internet provider, through IPs. It's basically just an offline database.'

He typed in a series of numbers again, his frown deepening.

'So, you know who sent the email?' Jules readied herself to spring into action. It was strange: none of them seemed to be acting suspiciously at all.

'It says the location's Tornivan, which is here.' Sandeep studied the screen. 'And the internet provider is listed as FreeNet, under the name of *Calan's iPhone*.'

The lights went out before Jules had a chance to respond or aim the gun. Her eyes hadn't adjusted to the darkness before she heard Calan's cool voice ring out.

'I'm armed, so you'd better do exactly as I say.'

CALAN

Calan gritted his teeth as he advanced into the bar. The four figures were stunned at first, before a sense of panic erupted. Lucas made a frenzied dash to the drawing room and Jules lifted her gun.

She really was beyond useless. She hadn't even checked to see if it was loaded. As usual, she displayed utter ineptitude. And in this case, it played in his favour.

'I wouldn't bother.'

He aimed his own gun at the ceiling and shot. Plaster crumbled in a soft cloud around them. The noise put Lucas off his course.

'Get back to your seats!' Calan shouted.

Jules pulled the trigger of her rifle in vain. She was such a bad shot that she would never have hit him anyway. She actually whimpered as he walked towards her. 'Give it here.'

She let it slide from her fingers. He waited for everyone to be seated. Lucas crawled back towards his chair and snatched Sandeep's hand to hold on to. It sounded like he was praying beneath his breath but it was difficult to tell.

'It's not loaded,' he explained, kicking Jules's rifle to the other side of the room. 'You should have listened to me about Marta.'

He'd never seen Jules look so pale. She tried to speak and her voice croaked into submission, before she tried again. 'What do you mean? Calan, what—?'

'You should have listened!' he shouted, without further explanation. Lucas screeched in response and he rolled his eyes. 'Will you shut up, please?'

The lot of them made a pathetic picture, apart from Mrs Melrose. She sat quietly, covered in blood, yet perfectly serene. It was like she was somewhere else behind those green eyes. Calan had watched her throw herself across Tim's body through the drawing-room window earlier. He'd seen how she had wailed, her red lips bent wide out of shape. The change in her mood was unbelievable.

This was going to be a difficult tightrope to tread. He hadn't wanted to come back, but Jules had left him no choice. Why did she have to bother him? Why had she jumped to conclusions about the emails? Once he knew she suspected the guests had arrived under false pretences, it was only a matter of time before his name was associated with the invite. Nobody would ever have suspected anything otherwise. She'd as good as forced him into this.

'I just need everyone to listen,' he said slowly. 'I...' He stumbled over his words, but took a deep breath. 'You're right, I sent the emails. I made sure you were all here for the weekend. But it's not...'

'Please!' Jules was shaking. 'Please, Calan, whatever this is, please don't do it!'

He pointed the gun at her head. 'I said listen!'

Sandeep and Lucas flinched. Gracie let out a soft gasp, her hands fluttering to her face. Calan counted to ten. He had to get this right. He knew that much. It was still salvageable. He just needed to explain everything as clearly and as concisely as possible. 'Just let me speak.'

Jules piped down. He nodded, blinking back the hot onset of tears. 'Okay. Okay, nice. I just needed you all to be here, okay? You don't know what it's like.'

He took Rebekah's will from his pocket.

'She didn't either. She didn't care, not even a bit. Not about me.' He looked at the will, and his tears dropped onto the paper in bulbous splats. 'She had more money than I ever could imagine. And she left it to you lot.'

He displayed the will to the room. Sandeep was wearing a deep frown, studiously avoiding making eye contact. Lucas was sobbing gently. Jules had as good as collapsed against the wall, her breathing shallow and quick. Gracie watched him with an intense interest.

He continued. 'Everyone's here! The most "important" people in her life. Boyfriend number one, Tim, he gets an enormous share. And look, even boyfriend number two, Zach. All that money to a guy she knew so, so well... she just missed the fact he was a complete sociopath. And Lucas, the estranged brother, who she's barely seen! Again, a pretty tidy sum for you. Not a penny for the son she gave away!'

He was panting with adrenaline. It felt good to get it out. The lead-up to this weekend had been excruciating.

As well as the amount she'd reserved for Tim in her will, Rebekah had also left Zach one hundred thousand. He'd been more tricky than Tim to track down. Luckily, Rebekah had been very active on social media. A guy whom Calan presumed people in London would find attractive, with his baggy trousers worn with creased suit jackets, popped up on more than one occasion. There was a photo from a photography exhibition at a gallery named Muse in Mayfair. It didn't prove anything explicitly, but the way he draped an arm around her shoulders was enough to convince Calan that he was *something*. Sure enough, when he searched up the exhibition online, he discovered the photographer's name matched the name in the will: Zach Williams.

One more name had appeared: Lucas Croft. As soon as he'd googled the guy, Calan had known it must be her brother. They didn't have the same surname, but Lucas's many, many Instagram posts about "moving on" and "not letting your family define you" suggested he might have changed it. His and Rebekah's features were so similar that they could have been twins.

Once he'd known Tim Melrose was going to be here, he'd decided to invite them too. Rebekah's legacy all in one place. All that money. All that power. All that potential freedom.

He tried to speak, but his voice broke at the back of his throat. 'I didn't mean to...'

He drew himself up. He couldn't afford to look weak. His cheeks burnt with the truth of it all. He had never meant to end up here. He'd only wanted to talk to them. He'd only wanted to ask them for help. For money. Tim had clearly been such an arse; anyone could see that. Zach had seemed quieter. Yes, a weirdo, but more pliable. So he'd started with him.

'Calan,' Jules whispered. 'Please, whatever's going on here, we can work through it. You don't need to do this.'

'I do!' He shouted so loudly that his legs trembled. She didn't understand, how could she? He did need to do this. He had no other choice.

'I told you...' As he spoke, last night's events flashed painfully behind his eyes. 'You should have listened about Marta. If you'd listened, then... then I wouldn't be here!'

'Calan, Marta's dead. It's okay. Whatever you've done, or think you've done, I'm sure we can work through it.'

'Shut up!' A burning tear rolled down his cheek. He'd spied

Jules all over Zach, heard about their plan to meet, and left a fake note in Zach's room to lure him to the fishing hut.

The plan had been to frighten him a bit with a gun. He'd only brought it as a prop. He'd been about to put it down but then everything had gone so, so wrong.

'She followed me! She followed me with the gun she stole! I heard a rustle behind me.'

His breathing grew quicker. 'I saw a thing moving towards me in the dark. I jumped, my finger flinched, and... I shot him. I shot him.'

He repeated the words over and over. His hands trembled as he remembered how calm Marta had been about the whole thing. How she'd told him she would protect him, help him clean up. How she'd hissed at him to help her move the body to the kitchen while she worked out what to do. *Accidents happen,* she'd said. *You are a good boy, Calan. You're my good boy.*

Jules's eyes widened in realisation. 'You wrote the notes. In my room. You tried to make me think I'd killed him. I... I almost fell for it.'

He nodded, forcing the next words out. 'You were out cold after all your booze. It seemed like a good idea in the moment, I reckoned you'd believe anything. You black out all the time anyway.' He took a deep breath. 'But she was crazy. You know that, Jules? Marta was insane. I couldn't sleep last night, thinking about how she'd always have this thing over me. She saw me shoot him. She *saw* it. She was stalking me again this morning, gun in her hand. I...'

This didn't feel real. Saying it aloud solidified everything, turned the nightmare into lurid fact.

'I had to do it. I had to come up with another plan. You see that, don't you? I had to... shut her up. There was no reasoning with her. I had to do it. What if she told someone? I had to do it!'

His breathing filled the silence. He saw it all in flashes. How he'd picked up her discarded rifle and pointed it at her. How he'd forced her further into the water. How he'd sung the tune he'd heard her sing so many times to soothe her before he... The violent splashes reverberated around his skull. Marta's awful, final gurgling breaths. Her lungs filling with icy water. The rocks he'd placed inside her clothing.

How he'd wiped the gun clean, emptied it of bullets. How he'd lifted Marta's freezing hand out of the water and wrapped it around the gun's grip stock, before putting it in Zach's room in the hope it would confuse things enough to keep suspicion away from him. It might have worked. If only Jules hadn't gotten so hung up on the bookings.

Nobody said a thing. They were scared. He didn't blame them. So was he.

He adjusted the aim of his gun to point it at Sandeep. He held up his hands in protest as Lucas cowered next to him.

'I'm not going to hurt you!' Calan shouted.

He steadied himself, gulping a hot acidic taste down.

'You're good with computer stuff? It's what you said. You're a teacher or something? I need you to make the emails untraceable. I'm leaving. Disappearing. I had to come back to make sure nobody knew it was me who sent the message. I just wanted the money... I just wanted some money...'

Sandeep nodded slowly, keeping eye contact. 'It's all right. We can all agree to stay quiet about the emails, can't we?'

A murmur of agreement rippled through the others.

'We'll just delete them off the server. We can do that. We need to wait for the internet to be back up and running, but we can do that.'

Calan wanted to believe him so much. His chest rose and fell in panic. He felt so useless, so childlike. He had no idea what to do. He needed to be certain the emails would be deleted before he left.

'Do it now!'

Sandeep twitched at the volume of his shout but kept calm. 'Calan, I can't. But I promise I will as soon as possible.'

Gracie's head jerked upwards. 'Why Tim?'

Her eyes were glazed over and glassy. It was as if she hadn't been listening to anything.

'What?' Calan took a step back. Should he just run now? Trust that Sandeep would do as he said? He let out a ragged yelp.

'My husband, Tim. Why did you kill him?'

She was terrifying. Her voice was laced with a mixture of intrigue and anger. Her eyes locked onto him and his skin crawled.

'What are you talking about?'

'Tim!' She held up her bloodstained arms and waved them in the air. 'Why? I'm asking you why you did it!'

Calan stared at her in utter confusion. 'I don't understand. I didn't do anything to him.'

CALAN

'Liar!'

Gracie launched from the sofa and crashed into him, knocking the gun from his hands. 'Why did you do it? Why did you kill him! Why?'

Her blows came hard and fast against his face. She clawed at him with her fingernails. She was a wild animal, her arms moving in quick and deliberate swipes. 'Just tell me!'

Her weight was pulled off him but he remained on the floor, panting at the ceiling. His head was a mess. He was still holding on to the vague notion of running, getting away from all this, but a heavy fatigue had descended upon him. This was the end, wasn't it? He couldn't outrun what he'd done. He'd never outrun the writhing monster inside of him. He was a murderer. *A murderer.* He had killed someone in cold blood.

A manic laugh rang out and he realised it was his own. Of course these people wouldn't keep a secret for him! His cheeks streamed with tears. He continued to laugh, his whole body shaking. What had he been thinking? They were strangers. Dickheads. Out for themselves, always. Why would they lie for him? Why would they ever cover this up for him?

He rolled onto his side and a heavy calm placated his limbs. This was it. He saw himself in prison. He saw his mum and dad's faces as they found out what he'd done. This was it. He relented to his future. The disappointment. The failure. The disgust.

'Hang on...' Lucas sounded very far away. It didn't matter what he was saying anyway. 'Yeah, that's what I thought...'

Calan rolled his eyes up to see Lucas studying the will. 'How did you get hold of this?'

Calan found he was rendered senseless. The madness, the horror of the weekend had caught up with him. His brain refused to comply. He blinked at Lucas, unable to respond.

'Wills become public after the grant of probate is issued.' Sandeep read over Lucas's shoulder. 'He must have applied for a copy. You would have been notified you were a beneficiary?'

'Obviously.' Lucas nodded. 'But Rebekah's assistant said there was something like a delay. Some sort of clause that meant the money wouldn't come through for at least a year?'

'Yeah, that's right.' Sandeep pointed at the will and read aloud, '"For all beneficiaries, Rebekah Desouza mandates a survivorship clause of twelve months. Assets will remain within her estate, including business shares, until this time has passed. In the event of any beneficiaries (named as Timothy Melrose, Zach Williams, and Lucas Croft, in no particular order) dying before this time period has passed, their inheritance will be divided between the remaining beneficiaries equally. Only in the event of all three beneficiaries being deceased will the next of kin of the last remaining beneficiary inherit the full estate".'

Calan remembered scanning through this paragraph, but he'd largely ignored it. As far as he was concerned, it was irrelevant information. All three of them had been alive when he'd hatched his plan.

'So, nobody has actually inherited any money yet?' Jules

stepped forwards to read the piece of paper. 'By the looks of that date, Lucas, you're due to become very wealthy in a few weeks' time. Zach and Tim are both dead. That means everything goes to you.'

Lucas didn't reply. He walked to the centre of the room, shaking his head. Eventually, he said to nobody in particular, 'Why the hell would you put that in a will? It's not normal, is it? This survivorship clause thing?'

Gracie chuckled. Calan rolled his head towards the sound; she was also on the floor, leaning against the leg of an armchair. 'It's Tim, or sounds like it. He did the same with his will. If a portion of your assets are shares in a business, it gives time to get the finances in order.'

She stopped for a moment to think, then smiled. 'She killed herself, didn't she? Which means she probably knew when she was going to die. I reckon the clause was a shrewd move to maximise the inheritance. Her company was due large investments over the next year, courtesy of my dear husband. Your share value is worth more now than it was then.' She slumped further down, eyes closed, talking to herself. 'See, Tim? I paid attention...'

'Bebe...' Lucas began to weep. It was a broken, haunting sound. Sandeep moved to console him.

Jules cleared her throat and knelt next to Calan. He flinched as she touched his shoulder. 'Calan... about Tim... you said you didn't hurt him...?'

All Calan could manage was a shake of the head. He wanted to go home. He wanted to hide away and never come back. He hadn't touched Tim! The first he'd seen of what had happened to him was through the window when he'd followed Jules back to the hotel.

Jules patted him on the shoulder and stood very slowly. Calan watched her eyes fall upon the loaded gun, which had slid half under the sofa close to where Lucas and Sandeep were standing. She stood in front of it, blocking it, before she addressed Gracie. 'It's an unusual clause to have in a will, like you say. The money would normally go to the beneficiary's next of kin.'

'What are you suggesting?' Gracie closed her eyes like she was bored.

'I think you thought you'd inherit Rebekah's money if you killed Tim. You're nosey, you went through his stuff... who knows? You might even have known Rebekah had left him most of her money. I think you made a mistake.'

Gracie made a great show of yawning. 'So, so stupid. I don't think that stands if you commit *murder*, Jules. And I'm rich anyway. Remember, Tim's an investor?' She wavered over his name. 'I didn't need Rebekah's money, even if me being next of kin had meant anything.'

She unsteadily pushed herself to her feet and folded her arms. 'Tim loved it when I got angry. It was our thing. Whatever he said, he was addicted to the drama. He would never have left me and I would never have actually killed him.'

She sniffed and her eyes became watery again. Looking around the room, she asked in a low voice, 'So who did?'

LUCAS

The five of them formed a bizarre, tense circle. Gracie was rigid, her eyes flicking from one person to the next. Calan was a mess on the floor; thankfully, he was no longer waving a gun about. Jules looked like she was ready to run at any second. Sandeep's arm rested around Lucas's shoulder, which was a nice gesture. Time was moving both very quickly and very slowly.

Lucas read the will again. He'd had no reason to request to see it in its entirety. The executor had just told him an estimate of what he could expect to inherit and that was that. In the aftermath of Bebe's death, he'd been grateful to have as little to do with it as possible.

After a few moments, he became aware Gracie was staring at him. He raised his eyebrows at her, daring her. 'If you've got something to say...'

'Look who's got all the money now.' She enunciated each syllable so that it hit through the cooling air like needles.

'Fuck this.'

There was no way he was going to stand around and be accused of murder. It was ridiculous! He made for the door.

'Lucas, wait—'

He rounded on Sandeep. 'No. I'm getting out of here like I should have done hours ago. I'll take the snowy roads over this... *massacre*, thank you! There's room in the car for you if you're coming. I'm sure the police will be busy here for a while, so they can catch up with me in London.'

He thundered up the stairs and began packing as quickly as possible. Being alone in the room was horrible. The sight of all of Tim's blood, the knowledge of Zach's body in the freezer downstairs, the confession from Calan about killing Marta... it all smacked him at once like an iron fist. He doubled over, tears clouding his eyes.

'Come on,' he whispered to himself. 'Time to leave. Get your stuff and go.'

He checked his phone yet again for a signal, but still, there was nothing. It didn't matter. Soon, he'd be at Inverness Airport – he'd sleep in the car if he needed to – where he could alert the police about everything.

He double-checked he had his passport and zipped up his bag. There was a soft knock at the door.

'Mr Croft?'

Oh, please not her. 'I think we're on first-name terms, by now, Jules.'

She swung open the door and peeked her head in. 'Can I come in?'

'Sure...' She could stay as long as she liked – he was out of here. 'I'm about to get the car started.'

Her eyes filled with pity. 'You know the road's completely blocked. There's no way you'll make it even to the end of the driveway. I just came up to warn you. Sandeep's worried about you crashing.'

He brought his hands down hard onto his bag in frustration. 'I'm going to try, okay? I can't stay another moment here. Need I remind you that one of your employees just confessed to a double murder? That you have another dead body which is so far unaccounted for? How are you so calm?'

She looked like he'd slapped her.

'I'm not calm,' she whispered. 'I'm... I'm just trying to work out...'

'There's nothing to work out! This place is a living nightmare! It's dangerous to be here.' He eyed the door. 'Where is Sandeep?'

'He's fine.' She wiped her cheek. 'He said he'd watch Calan.'

Something about the way she said it gave him shivers. He'd been fine leaving Sandeep alone when Jules was still in the bar; as annoying as she was, he was mostly suspicious of Gracie and Calan. Didn't she have a duty of care to guests or something? Shouldn't *she* be watching Calan?

'Sandeep?' he called down the stairs as he jogged two steps at a time, panic tingling at the base of his spine. 'Sandeep?'

Calan had moved into the corner of the bar, his knees drawn to his chest. He was staring into thin air. There was no sign of Gracie, nor Sandeep. He should never have left him with these people.

'Hey.' Lucas approached Calan with caution and scanned the room. The loaded gun was gone. 'Calan?'

'Hmmm...' Continuous tears were running down his cheeks.

'Did you see where Sandeep went? Did he go somewhere with Gracie?'

Calan nodded. He was clearly in shock, his eyes were wide like he was in a trance. Lucas knelt and shook him gently. His heart had begun to race. Something felt very wrong.

'Please tell me where they went. It's really important...'

He shook his head, his eyes glazing over. Jules re-entered the bar at a run. 'Did you find him?'

'No!' Lucas's hands formed into fists. 'Calan! Will you just tell me what you saw?!'

Finally, Calan turned his face to him. The boy's skin was sallow and creased from the salt in his tears. 'Mrs Melrose was waving the will about. Shouting all sorts of things. I covered my ears. I can't listen to it anymore. They went that way…'

Lucas felt sick. 'Where? Where did they go?'

'I *knew* it,' whispered Jules. 'She's a barefaced liar. Of course she killed Tim. She's a lunatic.'

Lucas's chest tightened. 'Which way did they go?'

Calan pointed to the hall. 'Outside. Outside.'

Lucas hurled himself out of the room, through the hall and into the drive. The cold stung his face, but he didn't stop. 'Sandeep!'

The darkness was thick but the snow reflected the moon to cast a silvery light. Lucas spun on the spot. Whichever way he decided to turn could be critical. If Gracie was planning on hurting Sandeep, she wouldn't hang about.

'There!' Jules followed at his heels. She pointed at the decking, where two figures were locked into a brutal-looking wrestle. 'Quick!'

Lucas hurled himself towards them, screaming Sandeep's name. His legs pumped as fast as he could make them. 'Sandeep!'

He slid on a patch of ice when he reached the decking, a sharp pain shooting up his knee. He wrenched himself back up and launched forwards. Gracie was straddling Sandeep; she pressed the gun over his neck and his eyes bulged.

'Stronger than I look,' she said, straining as she pushed with even more force.

'Stop!'

She was startled when she saw Lucas. He held out his hands, begging. Jules shouted something from behind him but he didn't want to take his eyes off Sandeep. His face was becoming slack. Gracie smirked, her face hardened. Lucas launched forwards. He crashed into her and they both seemed to be suspended in the grey air until what felt like jagged knives speared his body. He opened his mouth to breathe but icy water rushed into his throat.

Gracie was pushing down on his shoulders. He kicked his legs, struggling to break through the surface of the loch. She held on to him, pressing him further down. He convulsed either out of panic or cold; his mouth opened in a watery scream.

Suddenly, she let go. He reached his hands upwards, his face twisted in pain. His lungs felt as though they were on fire. Hands dragged him onto the deck. He was shivering violently. His chattering teeth sent excruciating shoots up his face.

'It's okay. It's okay. You're okay.'

Lucas realised he was on all fours. He vomited water onto the deck and curled up into Sandeep's arms.

'You're all right.'

Across from him, her pale skin already covered in snowflakes, was Gracie's still and limp body.

JULES

They were huddled on the sofa in her flat. The early push of orange fingers began to reach beneath the heavy clouds. Soon, help would be on its way.

Calan had said nothing since his announcement. He was obviously in complete shock. She, Lucas and Sandeep had made an agreement to keep a close eye on him, but, to be honest, Jules was fairly confident he was no longer dangerous. He seemed a hollowed-out version of himself. And, anyway, he'd confessed to everything. Short of killing all three of them with his bare hands, all he could do was wait for the police to arrive.

Lucas emerged from the bathroom, having borrowed her fluffiest dressing gown which was pulled tight around his waist.

'Hypothermia's starting to grow on me...' he muttered, pouting his blue-tinged lips in the mirror. She appreciated his attempt at humour; it was better than what was whirring around in her own head.

How long had she really needed to hold Gracie under for? Long enough for her to stop drowning Lucas? She had not wanted to kill anyone. That hadn't been her intent. Yet, she had pushed down on her head until the thrashing stopped. Had she held her under for a few seconds too long? Could she have avoided it? She shivered, bringing her blanket close to her chin. The image of Gracie and Tim lying beside each other in the drawing room slipped into her mind's eye again. It seemed right to put her there while they waited.

'So, she was just angry... or mad? Is that it?' She wasn't directing the question to anyone in particular. It made some sense that Gracie had killed Tim, but Jules couldn't see why she'd want to hurt Sandeep.

'She just said she was sick of pretending,' Sandeep said, massaging his temples.

'You don't have to go through it all again,' Lucas said. He plopped himself next to Sandeep and put an arm around his shoulders. 'Must be traumatic.'

Jules watched the two of them nestle close to one another. From where she was sitting, it looked like they were in the throes of getting back together.

'Yes, but pretending to be what?' Jules traced her finger along the edge of her whisky glass, trying to decide whether it would be acceptable to pour another one.

Lucas sighed. 'Probably spent her whole life acting normal, fighting the urge to kill people. Finding out that her husband loved Bebe probably tipped her over the edge. We've had a lucky escape, I reckon.'

Calan removed himself from the rug and walked into the bedroom, slamming the door behind him. Presumably, he didn't want to talk about fighting "urges to kill" just yet. Jules thought that was understandable. She sat back and gazed at the curved top of the sun shimmering through the clouds.

'The snow's stopped,' she said. 'They'll at least be able to send a helicopter now.'

'Hopefully,' murmured Lucas. His eyelids were beginning to close. He shivered and sat up straight again.

'Babes, you need a hot drink.' Sandeep placed Lucas's hands in his and rubbed. 'Do you have coffee up here?'

Embarrassingly, Jules had been saving money by using the hotel supplies. 'It's in the kitchen,' she said.

Sandeep's eyes widened and she realised that Zach's body was also there. Lucas pulled his blanket tighter.

'It's okay. I'll go...' Jules offered, half-heartedly.

'No.' Sandeep smiled. 'No, it's fine. I'll just grab it and come straight back. Put my big-boy pants on.'

She settled back down, grateful to be able to stay put. Lucas shuffled to a foetal position on the sofa and stared blankly at the wall. 'I guess that's it for this place then?' he said, without looking at her.

It took her a couple of seconds to realise what he meant. 'Oh.'

She let out a bitter croak. 'For The Tornivan? To tell you the truth, it was over a while ago. Without a hefty investment, there's no way I could have run this place alone. But now... well, obviously...'

He nodded. 'It was supposed to be this big, extravagant, perfect weekend.'

The way he said it made her feel like he wanted her to apologise. She sank lower into her chair. 'It looks like all's not lost.' She nodded her head in the direction of where Sandeep had just disappeared.

His head jerked up at that. 'You've noticed too? He's being more affectionate than he's ever been before. I don't know, maybe all this has... changed how he feels.'

She shrugged. 'Shared trauma is an aphrodisiac. Also, you saved his life. That's not nothing.'

'Yeah...' He looked suddenly thoughtful. 'It's something, isn't it?'

Calan emerged from the bedroom and stood in the door fram. 'What will happen?' he asked.

Jules watched him very carefully. His face looked younger than it ever had previously. He seemed so small, so lost. A sour grain somewhere in the pit of her belly gnawed at her. She was partly, no, near fully responsible for what he'd done. There was blood on her hands, even if not in the legal sense. He had been so desperate to get away from this place – from her – that he'd tricked people into coming here to beg them for money. Her chest felt unbearably hot and she was filled with the urge to crawl out from her own skin. Anywhere else would be better. Who the hell would want to be her? She owed him honesty, at least.

'When the police arrive you just tell them everything, like you told us. Explain how you didn't mean to hurt Zach, how Marta was following you, how...' She didn't have the stomach to go on. 'They'll probably arrest you. Just do as they say.'

A heavy silence filled the space between them. He nodded, sliding onto the floor, and placed his head in his hands. Lucas looked as if he was about to add something, but thought better of it.

'Here we go...' Sandeep called up the stairs, and kicked open the door as he carried in a tray laden with a cafetière and mugs. He set it on the coffee table and poured out the steaming liquid, handing the mugs around.

Lucas accepted his gratefully, holding it close to his chest. 'Hmmm. Oh my God, heaven,' he said, letting the steam emanate around his face. 'Fresh coffee in the morning makes everything better.'

'Well, you've got a lot of those to look forward to.'

Sandeep planted a lingering kiss on Lucas's lips. Lucas looked momentarily surprised, before being unable to suppress a grin.

'So... does that mean you want to...?'

'I say let's give it another try... only if you want...' Sandeep settled next to him, sporting a shy smile. 'After everything, I mean... it's been a lot. It's made me see what really matters.'

Jules slurped on her coffee noisily, trying to give them a hint. She really wasn't in the mood for this public reconciliation scene. All she wanted was everyone to be out of here as soon as possible so she could start planning her next moves. Most likely, she'd go back down to London. Rent somewhere abysmal. Hide away for as long as she could. Metamorphose into something – somebody – less repulsive.

Lucas chuckled. 'Sorry, we'll stop.'

She pursed her lips. 'It's okay.'

Lucas's smile widened and he nudged Sandeep. 'Sure you're not just after my money?'

Sandeep laughed and settled back down, his eyes closing with relaxation. 'It'll be over soon.'

As she mused upon what a strange response that was, a soft sound came from the doorway. Jules's gaze slid to Calan, who had slumped onto the floor, the remainder of his coffee spilling from his hands. Jules frowned. The room had begun to slip and spin, she blinked, trying to find her focus.

She turned towards Lucas and Sandeep. Lucas was also bent over. Sandeep placed his coffee mug on the table and his eyes met hers. A jolt of fear clutched her heart.

Sure you're not just after my money?

She tried to speak, but her words were slurred.

'Shhhh...'

Sandeep crouched in front of her. 'Don't fight it. It's just the pills I found in your loo. Strong stuff. You've not had as much as these two... just enough to incapacitate you.'

She tried to stand but he pushed her down. The room was spinning, her eyelids were heavy. He pressed something cold into her hand and her head slumped forwards. Her vision was fuzzy but she made out the handle of a rifle. He was whispering into her ear from behind. His breath was warm and gentle.

'We'll do it together. All you need to do is pull the trigger. I'll help you. We just need your fingerprints. The police will determine the obvious: you tried to shoot me, after Calan and Lucas, but failed. Then, at the end of your drug-induced tirade, you shot yourself. I'll get your prints on the knife you used to kill Tim too. Obviously, people will assume you killed Marta. You sorted Gracie out all on your own... thank you for that. I'll be the sole survivor, the only witness to this bloodbath. I'll drink a sip of the coffee to make it look like you also tried to drug me.'

I'm stronger than you thought. That's what Gracie had shouted before. She hadn't attacked Sandeep. Sandeep had attacked her. She'd been retaliating, fighting for her life. And she had killed her. She had killed an innocent woman. Her insides felt like they had turned to ice.

'Why?' The word didn't come out as she'd hoped – it was a wordless moan. Her head hung forwards. She was dribbling.

'You know,' he breathed over her shoulder. 'I was worried someone might spot it when we read the will downstairs. Nobody picked up on it: *I'm the remaining beneficiary's next of kin.* Lucas has nobody else. He made me his next of kin about two months into our relationship – keen, isn't he?'

She felt tears dripping onto her lap. She tried to fight his hand, but it was useless. Her muscles wouldn't do as she told them to. 'Please—'

He breathed into her neck and her hairs prickled. 'It's already happened,' he said. 'It wasn't my plan, Jules, it's important you know that. If it wasn't for stupid Lucas freaking out about his wallet in Calan's bothy, I wouldn't have stumbled upon Rebekah's will. Of course, I recognised her name and Lucas's immediately, but I couldn't understand why it would be here, at Tornivan. I kept it quiet from him... he panics, doesn't he? Always frantic about something. I couldn't stomach his mania. It wasn't until the next morning that I overheard Calan begging Tim for his fair share of cash. I realised that Tim and Zach from the will were also here. I suspected what Calan was up to. I'm grateful to him for killing Zach for me, of course. I didn't see that coming.'

Her plea was cut short by the first shot to Calan's head. She screamed, but her neck muscles were sluggish. The sound was more of a pathetic gurgle.

'It was too good of an opportunity to miss. I'm a good person, Jules. Remember that, I'm a good person.'

His voice caught, shook slightly. 'I need to help my family. This money will pay for Dad's care. It will give my mum a rest. Sometimes we need to do extraordinary things to help ordinary people. That's what Lucas never appreciated: the ordinary. And that's me. I'm ordinary. Overlooked. No one would ever think I'm capable of this.'

She felt her body reverberate at the second shot, which hit Lucas on the side of the face. Her shoulder rotated, her elbow being forced into her thigh, as the gun turned to press against her chin. She closed her eyes. The last sound she heard was the mechanical click and the impossibly loud crack before the world went blank forever.

Sandeep spent just over an hour with the bodies in Jules's flat. He practised his speech constantly:

'I think she and Calan planned the whole thing from the beginning. It's remote here, barely any staff... I think they got weird ideas in their heads, became, what do you call it... co-dependent? She was clearly upset about her divorce – behaving oddly all weekend. They made the cook's death look like a suicide and we believed it... it was horrible. I believe her body was put in an outhouse. I wouldn't be surprised if another guest is dead: Zach Williams, I think? He went missing yesterday. Oh my God... this is all so... so...'

This would be his cue for tears. 'My fiancé... Lucas. I'm not precisely sure what happened, but she made us coffee... I think she drugged it. My love! My love!'

He would take a breath. Make it seem like he was steadying himself. He needed to be brave so justice could be properly served.

'I remember her saying something about the Melroses – those were other guests – leaving early. It didn't make sense to me because the roads were blocked... then I noticed I was feeling fuzzy. She just walked up behind us and just started shooting. First Lucas, then Calan – clearly she'd used him for what she needed. I was on the floor. I heard a gunshot... she thought she'd hit me... because the next thing that happened was she turned the gun on herself.'

Sandeep nodded. The story made sense. Jules was already a drug user, already unhinged. The hotel was failing: it was the perfect cover. There was even the email proof that Calan had tricked them all here.

He took Jules's lighter and held the will in front of his face. It burnt quickly. There would be no reason for the police to suspect Lucas had ever seen it. He hadn't even requested to see the other beneficiaries. The money would quietly make its way to his account in a few weeks' time, no problem, no questions.

His phone beeped to life. The service was restored. He picked up his phone and dialled 999. 'Hello, hello, yes, police, please. I need help! Please hurry! I need help! There's been a shooting. Oh God... please... help me.'

THE END

AUTHOR'S NOTE

It would be remiss not to mention the novel without which this book would likely not exist; that is, of course, Agatha Christie's *And Then There Were None*. As far as I'm aware, she was the first to subvert the murder mystery genre in this way, augmenting the whodunit victim count without verging into the ridiculous. Much as I would never dare to compare myself to the great Queen of Mystery Herself, I strive in her wake and hope I too steer clear of anything too farcical (though, I admit I am partial to a pinch of farce).

This is my second novel set in Scotland (and for good reason: it is, in my opinion, the very best place to set a mystery thriller). I won't give away which hotel The Tornivan is loosely based on, however, if you see some similarities and think you have an inkling, then I would safely suggest you have guessed correctly!

Some stories arrive without much delay at all, and others take a longer time to percolate. Falling into the latter category, *Seven Bodies* has been brewing since 2022. The cast has remained the same from the beginning, but I was like a child in a chocolate shop trying to decide whose backstories would be given the limelight. There are plenty of histories that didn't make the final draft. I hope you can sense them slithering beneath the surface.

The last year has been exceptionally difficult following the loss of my brilliant Dad. It is bittersweet to be releasing a book without his being the first pair of eyes on it. As I say in the foreword, I do believe he's somehow with me while I'm writing, which is probably why I have managed to be so productive through my grief. How nice it is to have something which keeps me close to him!

Lastly, it seems prudent to say something about Artificial Intelligence and the publishing industry. I would like readers to be vehemently assured that no part of this work (and this applies to ideas, characters, plots, line craft, *everything*) has been created using A.I. These are human words (mine) which have come from a human heart (also mine). Please do keep in touch by signing up to my newsletter at victoriarandleauthor.com.

ALSO BY V.J. RANDLE

The Athenian Murders

The Saturn House Killings

Cold Secrets

ACKNOWLEDGEMENTS

Firstly, many thanks to my editor Ian Skewis. I very much appreciated your steady hand through the layers of twists and turns, as well as your encouragement.

To the team at Bloodhound, as always, thank you. You've made so many of my dreams come true by getting my stories out there into the world! I am forever grateful and humbled. In particular, thank you to Tara for always being on the end of an email with calming answers to my many convoluted questions!

Over the last couple of years, I have been lucky enough to have made some lovely connections in the Bookstagram/Booktok community. I would like to name a few here who have supported, inspired, and generally encouraged me with their posts and enthusiasm for books:

Thank you so much to Manon Wogahn (a.k.a. Mystery Manon) for her support and her unwavering dedication to the mystery genre. Her "cluesletter" (www.manonwogahn.-com/cluesletter) is one of the best out there and I strongly suggest that everyone follows her insightful and expert opinions on BookTok (@mysterymanon). Whenever I watch one of her videos, I add at least two books to my to-be-read list!

Many thanks to Noelle Holten, who is a completely fantastic crime author, as well as running the brilliant blog crimebookjunkie.co.uk, and posting daily on her BookTok (@author_noelleholten). Thank you, Noelle, for always lifting fellow authors up!

Thank you to BookTok's @bookspluschocolate, for her

wonderful, cosy posts about the mystery and crime books she is reading, as well as her support of my work. You are brilliant!

Many thanks to Nicola Winter (Instagram: @nothing.beats.a.good.book) for featuring authors like me and championing little-known books to get the word out there!

Lastly, thank you so much to Kobe (BookTok: @frostgalaxy) for her support of a previous title of mine, *Cold Secrets*, and her excellent, intelligent reviews of books: always a go-to for reading recommendations!

ABOUT THE AUTHOR

Victoria read Classics at King's College, University of Cambridge before teaching Latin and Greek for over a decade. She has given many a tour of Hellenic sites over the years, both in the capacity of educator and holiday-maker. If you spot an excitable woman in a maxi skirt waving her arms about on top of The Acropolis, chances are it's her. Do say hello!

She now lives and writes in the North-East of Scotland with her husband, Will, and cat, Athena (who is every bit the goddess of stratagem as her namesake). Sign up to her newsletter at victoriarandleauthor.com to be the first to hear about all her writing news and the occasional bookish treat.

She is the author (under the name V. J. Randle) of *The Athenian Murders*, *The Saturn House Killings*, *Cold Secrets*, and *Seven Bodies*.

A NOTE FROM THE PUBLISHER

Thank you for reading this book. If you enjoyed it please do consider leaving a review on Amazon to help others find it too.

We hate typos. All of our books have been rigorously edited and proofread, but sometimes mistakes do slip through. If you have spotted a typo, please do let us know and we can get it amended within hours.

info@bloodhoundbooks.com